Praise for

The Agency

"Flirting With Danger" had a great set up and the action was quick to begin, making it a real page turner from the start...As is always the case with Ms Lapthorne there is plenty of mystery and intrigue in the story, James Bond style plotting and action and a hot dose of the seriously steamy stuff to boot!
~ *Miz Love Loves Books*

Total-E-Bound Publishing books by Elizabeth Lapthorne:

Wicked Teacher

THE AGENCY
Volume One

Flirting with Danger

Courting Passion

ELIZABETH LAPTHORNE

The Agency Volume One
ISBN # 978-1-78184-509-7
©Copyright Elizabeth Lapthorne 2012
Cover Art by Posh Gosh ©Copyright 2012
Interior text design by Claire Siemaszkiewicz
Total-E-Bound Publishing

Published in 2012 by Total-E-Bound Publishing, Think Tank, Ruston Way, Lincoln, LN6 7FL, United Kingdom.

Total-E-Bound Publishing is an imprint of Total-E-Ntwined Limited.

FLIRTING WITH DANGER

Dedication

With grateful thanks to Laura, Lily and Cindy. You guys rock!

Chapter One

Skye Adams knew first-hand that life was never easy when your dad was the equivalent of James Bond. She'd known this to some level from her very youngest days—though it wasn't until her late twenties that she understood the true nature of his work. Her only knowledge while growing up was that her daddy's work was 'important'.

She couldn't count the number of missed dance recitals, parent-teacher interviews or times someone else had had to drop her off home because she was the last one waiting to be picked up, seemingly forgotten by her father.

Lucy Adams, her mother, had died of cancer before Skye turned twelve. Skye knew her parents loved her very much, but that didn't help the overwhelming loneliness that marred the ten or so years after her mum's passing.

A chill of fear always shivered down her spine when she thought back to how she had almost passed by the one time her father had reached out to her for help. When the phone had rung at a little after two a.m., a bored-sounding operator had asked if she'd take an emergency, reverse charges call from Victor Adams who was at an unpronounceable hospital in Helsinki, Finland.

Skye's first thought as she'd run a hand through her shoulder length, brown curls had been that the call was an elaborate joke being pulled over her by a friend. Laughing, still half asleep, she had assured the operator that, sure, she'd take the call. Skye had expected a howl of laughter followed by some quick commentary and identification of the friend forthwith.

Instead, a very shaky, weak, male had spoken, then stopped to clear his throat. The undeniable tone of her father had come once again over the scratchy connection.

"Skye, can you hear me? Damn this abominable hospital phone to hell," her father had growled.

"Daddy?" she'd gasped, her warm blue eyes widening in the darkness of her bedroom as she shot bolt upright in her bed. She hadn't wanted to believe that the call was from Helsinki and from her father, but his voice was unmistakable.

"I've run into a minor problem, sweetheart," Victor had continued, pain evident in his every word. The very faint slurring had made Skye wonder what kind of painkillers they had given him, or possibly just how very much suffering he must have been enduring for his voice to sound so ragged. She'd never seen him so much as flinch before in her life.

Always her father's voice and manner soothed and calmed her every fear. Victor Adams had always been the strongest, most steadfast man of her acquaintance. Fear had clutched at Skye's heart, as to what could be going on, confusion had clouded her mind.

She'd reminded herself that, whatever happened, her father could handle it. Obviously something extreme had occurred and he'd turned to her for help. She needed to keep a grip on herself.

Skye had followed her dad's clipped, precise instructions to the letter and, in what had felt like both forever and no time at all, she had made it to his hospital room, his travel suitcase packed, assisting him to discharge himself.

Victor had been shot in the leg, beaten and abused. She'd overheard the nurses gossiping that he'd nearly died from the blood loss. The transfusion and her father's foreigner status as well as lurking police suspicion surrounding his true motivations for being in the country had convinced the doctors that the most stringent requirements regarding this man needed to be in place.

They would only release him to a family member.

His protégé and sometime partner, Garth Spenser, had also been present that evening when Skye had arrived. Tall, dark-haired, olive-skinned and with a neatly clipped beard, he sat in the corner of the room on the single chair and glowered at her as she'd tried to make sense of what her eyes told her. Garth had left, muttering something to Victor about 'giving you some space'.

The moment they'd had privacy she'd demanded a full explanation. The dislocated kneecap and evident beating around his face and upper body did not point to the vague 'financial broker' career he'd always talked about.

Her dad had finally told her the truth. He worked for an agency in the espionage industry for the United Kingdom.

Initially Skye hadn't been able to help but feel the story was preposterous, a fabrication for who knew what reasons. She had pressed him, annoyed by his seemingly frivolous attitude. All too soon, random dots she'd never thought twice about had connected, until Skye's eyes were opened to the full picture.

Her father was a spy.

In the years since then, despite his frequent travel and near endless overtime, they had grown closer. One of Skye's greatest pleasures was that they'd discovered a mutual love of good food. Eating out at different, new restaurants had become a semi-regular occurrence, where they could relax, get to know each other once more and reconnect on a new level as adults, as well as father and daughter.

For her birthday the week before she had been looking forward to enjoying her first experience at a newly opened Thai restaurant they had both been curious about. Victor had called her, however, and informed her he had a quick mission he needed to take care of.

"It will be a few days' turnaround, tops, sweetheart," he had assured her. "It's personal this time, I can't entrust it to anyone else. I swear I'll shout you the full banquet and I've organised something special for your birthday as soon as I return."

True to his word, when he'd texted her the details of his return flight they had organised their lunch date at the Golden Mih Goo Wak Restaurant.

The day was sunny and clear, though the wind still held the crispness of early spring. Skye was led to the table her father had booked for them. She smiled as she realised it was along one side, midway between the front door and the back entry to the kitchen.

Perfect placement to both monitor their surroundings and beat a hasty retreat in either direction should the unthinkable happen. Her father took his planning and strategies seriously.

Knowing she was a few minutes early, Skye pulled out her e-reader and opened up her latest purchase. Engrossed, she kept half an ear out for her phone to ring in case her father was delayed — now, without fail, he'd call her — but she lost track of the time.

When Skye's stomach rumbled, she looked up with surprise. Frowning, she realised a lot of the people who had surrounded her when she'd sat down had eaten and left. Powering down her e-reader, she checked her watch.

Astonished, she discovered it was almost two o'clock. Digging in her handbag, Skye pulled out her phone and made certain it received reception inside the eatery. Scrolling through her inbox to check she hadn't missed a call or message, she tried to stem the small spurt of worry that tingled through her.

You're being silly. Your father is a seasoned agent, well versed and a tutor within the industry. There's no need for concern.

From memory, Skye punched in his private number. After the hospital incident, her dad had bought a new mobile phone, one he kept with him at all times and used in emergencies. He'd told her less than half a dozen people had the number. Even if he was in a meeting, he'd answer this call.

The phone rang and rang. After what seemed like an endless time, it turned to voicemail.

"Dad, it's me," she said. "I'm at the restaurant. It's two, where are you? Please call me back, even if it's just to cancel. Love you."

Skye reached out and took a sip of her now lukewarm tea as she thought hard. After far too much time with her father, she'd also mastered the fine art of leaving oblique messages. Victor always insisted you never knew who would listen either to a voice message left behind or on an open line. She'd teased him for his paranoia, but they both knew it was largely responsible for his longevity in an industry not known for agents who retired owing to old age.

Shaking her head, she punched the numbers for Victor's home line and waited for the call to connect. He'd texted when his plane had landed at Heathrow airport, so she knew he'd made it safely. There were always debriefing meetings, reports to file and tons of other small errands to wrap up a mission that Skye didn't fully understand. It hadn't crossed her mind to check on him after she knew he'd made it safely back into the country.

After only one ring the phone switched directly to the answering machine. Skye frowned harder. The thought that Victor hadn't turned his home line from instantly activating the answering machine to allowing him to receive calls struck her as odd.

Victor was a master of the small details. It was something he'd been trained as an agent to never let slip.

She wondered if Victor's native paranoia had sunk further into her psyche than she had realised. With barely a thought she decided to leave a vague message, a feeling of foreboding settling into her bones.

"Dad, it's me," she repeated for the machine, loath to just hang up without acknowledging it. "It's two and I'm at the restaurant. Where are you? Call me, please."

Skye hung up and took a deep breath. She was not going to lose her cool over something as simple as her father being caught up with work again. Yes, it was unusual, but old habits die hard. Obviously something 'important' had come up. That didn't mean she needed to worry.

The waitress who had been hovering nearby came forward when Skye caught her eye.

"Could I please just have a chef's salad to go?" she asked with an apologetic smile. The young woman nodded and headed back towards the kitchen.

With a sigh, Skye thought about her now-disappeared lunch hour. Lost in her e-book, the time had flown by. Five more minutes to wait for some food would not annoy her boss any more than taking a full hour for her usually forty-minute break. Besides, she was starving.

Unable to settle back to reading, Skye people-watched out on the busy city street. The end of the lunchtime rush had her spotting more than a few suit-clad men and women hurrying back to desks and cubicles, faces intent. She always enjoyed watching those around her, and some pointers from Victor on how to be aware of her surroundings had sharpened those observation skills.

Glancing back towards the kitchen, she was wondering where the waitress and her salad were when the bell above the door tinkled. Skye's head swung around, hope lifting in her chest that it would be her dad.

In her mind's eye she could picture him, his dark brown hair greying more and more as each month passed. His light brown eyes would be amused and his standard wry grin would be firmly in place. She knew he'd smile as he approached the table, with an explanation on the tip of his tongue.

Instead, a tall, handsome man in his mid-thirties entered the restaurant. His black eyes glinted and his neatly clipped beard darkened his olive complexion. Garth Spenser caught sight of her and stalked with a purposeful stride. Skye stood up, every fear for her dad that she'd suppressed returning tenfold.

"My dad?" she asked before Garth had made it to her. "Is he okay? What are you doing here?"

"Skye," Garth ground out, glancing around at the few scattered remaining patrons. "Not here, I need you to come with me."

Stubbornness was a trait she shared with Victor. More than a few times they had both rued the familial similarity that made one of them reluctant to give in to the other. Figuratively speaking, she dug her feet in.

"What's happened? I'm not going anywhere until you explain, Garth."

"I don't have time for this," he replied impatiently.

A scowl crossed his face fleetingly, though the annoyance remained in his eyes. From their previous, albeit brief, meetings she knew Garth didn't dislike her. He'd struck Skye as a very driven man, with firm goals and timelines mapped out.

However, there was a darkness that resided inside him. It was a trait she could not bring herself to overlook. In many ways, Garth idolised her dad. Her disposition was so different from her father's and Garth's. Carefree, optimistic and often seeming to be frivolous, despite her keen intelligence, she'd wondered a few times if Garth thought of her as a changeling, swapped at birth.

Skye sat back down with faked nonchalance. She refused to be bullied or rushed by her dad's protégé, despite her own earlier impatience and now her growing concern.

"Sit down, Garth, have a cup of tea. I'm waiting for my salad to arrive and then I need to get back to work," she said, waving a hand to the half-empty teapot. "Please just explain things to me. Where's Dad? What—"

"He's missing," Garth hissed as he leaned over her.

Skye blinked, recognising the tactic as one her father used to use when they argued and she wouldn't budge to his way of thinking. Garth didn't intimidate her in the least, though she understood how a lesser person might have quaked with the threatening tone and large, muscled build of the determined man.

"Victor disappeared from Heathrow last night," Garth continued. "He climbed into a taxi and hasn't checked in since. His flat is untouched, he never arrived there. We're studying the CCTV images but we lose him half a mile out from the airport. It was only as I studied the date-book from his desk I discovered he was supposed to meet you here."

Fear washed over her. She knew the kind of work Victor and Garth performed, but most of the details were still kept from her. As such, her concerns were shadowy and more from an overactive imagination rather than fact. Nevertheless, the mental images playing out in her head terrified her.

"You need to find him," she insisted. "I wouldn't even know where to start looking for his enemies, but you and your colleagues should be pros at this sort of stuff."

"Victor has more enemies than I could poke a stick at. That doesn't mean any of them knew his flight itinerary or the alias he was using, let alone his real name or where he lived. The Agency thinks you might have information we need that can help us understand what's at play here. Victor spoke of you warmly and often amongst his closest friends. None of us who work with him have a clue, which means any hints he's left behind are likely to be with you. Regardless of all that, I still need to you come with me. We'll keep you in protective custody. Victor would skin me if I didn't take such a precaution."

"I don't need protecting," Skye insisted, shaking her head. "I'll try to think over anything helpful he could have told me, but we almost never talked of his work, and certainly not in any detail. I don't see how I can help you. I'd rather you were out there, searching for him and not babysitting me or worse, asking endless, pointless questions."

She knew Garth spoke sense, but she'd never been able to shake the uneasy feeling he gave her. Victor trusted him as much as anyone he worked with, but he'd always told Skye to go with her instincts, that they were sound. Waves of pressure resonated from Garth and Skye's gut told her to not go with him, at least not yet.

Garth uttered a strangled sound of pure, masculine frustration. His hand closed around her upper arm as he tried to raise her forcefully to her feet.

"Skye," he ground out, "I'm not used to repeating myself. I need—"

It was as she leant back to try to wrench herself from his grasp that the bell on the front door tinkled again. Garth cursed as he turned to look at the new customer. Skye turned to look, curious about who'd upset him so much.

A woman with golden blonde hair tied back in a chignon had entered and was hurriedly walking towards their table. Large, warm brown eyes were set into a pretty oval face. The strict cut of her navy blue suit did little to diminish her curves. Skye began to feel rather under-dressed in her simple black trousers, cream business shirt and rusty red cardigan.

"Katherine," Garth greeted the blonde with a dry, resigned tone to his voice. "I presume Tarek is coming in from the kitchen?"

The blonde nodded. She cast a curious glance at Skye, tilted her head in silent acknowledgement, then returned her gaze to Garth.

"You were supposed to come in for questioning," Katherine chided him. "Management warned you we hadn't finished to our satisfaction. You're lucky we were able to tail you, despite your half-hearted attempt to ditch us."

"I felt it was more important to get Skye to safety than answer useless questions," Garth jeered as a beefy, muscled, sandy-haired man in a navy suit joined their table, seeming to melt out of the very walls.

"We plan to bring her in too," Katherine assured them with another quick glance at Skye. Skye felt her temper spike at being treated like an ignorant child. She might not have been trained like them, but failing to work at the Agency did not make her a moron. At the earliest opportunity she planned to give them all a sharp piece of her mind.

Garth's words, eerily similar to her own, were humorous to her ears, but it didn't cool her annoyance at their treatment of her.

"Look, you know I belong out in the field, not sitting in your damn cubicle helping you fill in a bunch of tick boxes on reams of standard forms," Garth growled, a scowl on his face.

Tarek stepped closer, his hand moving beneath his suit jacket.

"Just try it you—" Tarek taunted Garth.

Skye had had enough. She picked up her handbag, slung it over her shoulder and stepped away from the table. In the aisle, out of grabbing distance of all three agents, she glanced at each of them in turn.

"I am not some teenager with a brace and plaits needing Daddy's babysitters to hold her hand," she insisted. "I'm starting to think the lot of you are a few bricks shy of a load and I'm not going anywhere with any of you. You are welcome to stay here and bitch amongst yourselves, but I'm out of here."

Turning on her heel, Skye didn't let any of them get a further word out and made for the front door. She hadn't gone more than a few paces when the first gunshot sounded. Were it not for the cracking of the enormous floor-to-ceiling glass windowpanes at the front of the restaurant, Skye would have assumed the popping sound was a car backfiring.

Glass shattered, the sound of even more gunshots disintegrating vases and the windows echoing in the now silent restaurant.

"Skye! Get down, damn it!" Garth shouted at her.

Rough hands grabbed her shoulders and pulled her down on to the carpet. Before she could even blink, Garth had upended one of the small tables to give them cover from the continual shots. As her senses acclimatised to the unusual sound she could begin to work out where they were coming from—multiple sources across the street.

A loud boom nearly deafened her, and Skye jumped as she smelt the acrid scent of something burning. She turned her head and saw an enormous weapon in Garth's large hands, the dull black of the gun drawing her gaze. With a grim look on his face, Garth shot again.

Every piece of glass was destroyed and the cool spring air now permeated the restaurant. Nothing except the table they crouched behind protected them from whoever was shooting out in the streets. The dozen or so clients and workers either screamed hysterically in their seats or stampeded into the kitchen. More than a few were shouting into their phones, presumably having called nine-nine-nine.

Garth shot his gun yet again, the sound painfully loud. Skye clapped her hands over her ears to dull the noise. For the first time in her life she wished she'd listened to her father and invested in a gun. She'd practiced with her dad's weapon a number of times — indeed, she was a naturally good shot — but she'd scoffed at his suggestion that she would ever need a weapon for herself.

She made an oath never to so casually dismiss her dad's instincts or suggestions again.

"They're only warning shots," Garth yelled at her. Skye turned to him, incredulous.

"You have to be kidding me!" she shouted back.

Katherine yelled something at them both from where she had been pinned by a couple of tables behind them. With the sound of sirens blaring, the gunshots and all the other noises, Skye couldn't hear what the woman had tried to convey. Garth leaned closer and spoke again, his voice raised over the general din.

"If these people have your dad, whoever they are, they might try and use you as leverage against him. Your dad is tough, he can withstand almost anything, but if they get their hands on you, prove to him that you are in genuine physical danger from them, he will give them anything they want."

What Garth had said was clearly true—she knew it in her soul. Her father was the toughest, strongest, most capable man she'd ever known. His strength and bravery were near God-like to her eyes. She had no doubt where he was concerned that he could do almost anything. She was not ignorant, though—when it came to her he had a soft spot. She was one of his few weaknesses. Anyone clever enough could use her—however unwilling she might be—against her father. Skye couldn't let that happen, not under any circumstances.

Icy fear knotted in her stomach. Suddenly, much of Garth's annoyance at her made sense. Why the idiot couldn't have told her this in the first place she didn't know, but Skye knew she couldn't live with being used as a blackmail tool. Especially not against her father.

Skye's knees wobbled as she crouched behind the upturned table. Overwhelming fear for her dad, for his safety and health, nearly crippled her. Somewhere deep in her soul she found an iron-strong determination. She would not be some pawn, an innocent used and traded for knowledge or power. Skye lowered her hands to the floor as she gathered every scrap of her courage and prepared herself to bolt.

Mouth dry, she balanced herself, pretending it was one of the races she used to run against friends as a small child. She told herself this was just a friendly, quick dash. It was anything except for the reality of possibly being a literal flight for her life—for her father's life.

She would not be used against him, not while she still drew breath.

"Go!" Garth commanded. Gunshots still fired, both from outside and from behind them where Katherine and Tarek hid.

"What if you're wrong?" Skye asked, a tremble in her tone. Garth shook his head.

"Then we're both dead anyway. But I'm not wrong. When they realise they have us all pinned they will use heavier weaponry. You have to go, right now!"

Trust your instincts, her father's voice reverberated in her mind. Every nerve and brain cell inside her insisted she run now, that her window of opportunity was closing. Knowing it could be the last decision she ever made, Skye took a deep breath. She pressed her lips together in a vain attempt to stop them trembling and pushed herself upright into the fastest sprint she had ever managed.

A hail of bullets rang out.

Skye dimly heard Katherine and Tarek both shout across the dining room, but the words were lost in the clamour of sound. Garth yelled what sounded like a war cry as he returned fire like a man possessed.

In seconds, Skye had cleared what used to be the glass windows. Ducking and weaving around the neighbouring cafe's tables and chairs, she half crouched in an attempt to make herself as difficult a target as possible. Panting hard, she tripped and stumbled.

Knees and palms scraped raw, Skye didn't feel a thing with the level of adrenaline coursing through her body. A frantic glance over the street showed a nearly empty diorama, the gunshots and alarms having cleared the road. Cars stood idling, their windscreens cracked and broken, doors left open as people had abandoned everything and scrambled away.

Crouching behind a large barrier that was meant to protect those enjoying the cafe's food from the pedestrians, Skye found her eye drawn to an alley opening. A small delivery driveway opposite the street facing the restaurant held four men. Her gaze was caught on them simply because they were the only other people visible.

Each of the men wore black camouflage trousers and black T-shirts. Two of them crouched and continued to shoot out many of the car windows and other storefronts. To her untrained eye it looked like they were not aiming for any person or thing in particular, more like just wanting to cause damage and make a lot of noise, perhaps to pin everyone in the restaurant. As she watched, a long metal cylinder was brought out of the shadows of the alley's mouth and lifted on to the shoulder of one of the men in front. In the back corner of her mind she recognised the weapon, but it took a moment to piece together what was occurring before her eyes.

"Oh no," she whispered. The very real danger didn't even cross her mind. She turned back around and tried to shout loudly enough to be heard.

"Garth!" she screamed. "Get out of there, right now!"

Skye caught a faint glimpse of Garth's head popping up from the overturned table. She pointed to the alley, but she feared it was too late. The cylindrical cannon-like object rested on one man's shoulder, braced by a second man. The third stood guard as the final man slotted a large rocket into the hold.

"It's a rocket launcher," Garth shouted, terror etched into his face. "Get the hell out of here!"

In the split second before she turned and fled, Skye saw Garth stand, screaming at the others behind him as he waved his hand and headed for the back exit. Having no real understanding of the kind of damage a rocket launcher could do to a simple city street, Skye felt as if a million hellhounds from the fiery depths of the underground were nipping at her feet.

She ran harder than she could ever recall having run in her whole life.

The loudest boom split the air behind her. The deep sound filled the street, the very stone under her feet shaking and rumbling as the world shook.

Car alarms sounded, people screamed and the sound of breaking bricks, mortar and glass filled Skye's head until a painful ringing blocked her capacity to hear more. Everything seemed to disintegrate around her, her lungs burned with the need for oxygen and still she ran faster and further down the street.

Curious despite herself, Skye looked back over her shoulder. A smoking crater remained where the shopfront had once been.

Pieces of masonry rained down over her. As the smoke began to clear she could see an enormous, gaping hole where the building had been a moment ago. The walls on either side of the restaurant appeared chipped as bricks continued to fall into a pile of rubble on the ground.

Chaos reigned.

Fearful that her world had suddenly and irreversibly turned on its head, Skye continued to run as if chased by her every nightmare.

Chapter Two

It was almost a mile later that the sting in her palms, knees and a strong burning in her lungs finally let Skye know she had to stop. Looking around, she hurried to a nearby railway station. Making a beeline for the ladies' room, she grabbed a handful of paper towels and locked herself into a cubicle to try to get a hold of her savaged emotions.

Gasping in deep breaths, tears squeezed out of her eyes as her brain tried to assimilate everything that had just occurred.

"Oh, Daddy, what the holy hell have you fallen into? What just happened?" she whispered as she caught her breath. Mopping at her face, Skye tried to still the trembling in her hands.

Realising that if any of those four men had chased after her she'd be thoroughly trapped, Skye felt panic rising in her chest. Sniffing and pulling herself together, she left the cubicle and checked each empty stall, relieved to find no one present. She ignored how paranoid she felt doing such a thing.

Walking to a basin, she ran the cold water, splashed her face and stared at her reflection for a moment. Her curls corkscrewed in every direction, her blue eyes looked wide and wild, and her face appeared pale, but otherwise she looked normal. The image in the mirror was completely at odds with the thrumming of her blood and the unsteady beating of her heart.

Skye tried to think of what she could do. She couldn't return to the smoking hole that used to be the Thai restaurant. Neither did she want to go in to the Agency. Katherine and Tarek had obviously been suspicious of something in relation to Garth, and the dark-haired man had himself always seemed a little too far on the edge of respectability for her to be completely comfortable with him.

While Skye had good friends she knew and trusted, she couldn't bring this — whatever it was — to their doors. It wouldn't be right, and any trouble she brought with her would be her responsibility.

Lost and alone, Skye trembled as she wished she could turn to her father right now. Ironically, at the most important time in her life, when she wanted to be able to rely on him, it was he who needed her, who only had her to support him.

He needed her. She was probably his only hope.

She had to stop.

To think.

Her dad placed a business card down on the table between them.

"I met the most interesting man the other day, sweetheart. Jack Berwick. He's a private investigator, but savvy and smart enough to impress me. I tried to bring him in to the Agency. Sadly, much like you, sweetheart, he refused to join. I get the feeling he likes working on his own too much.

If you should ever find yourself in a bind, and for whatever reason I'm not around to assist you, call him. He owes me a few favours and knows if you ever call he can repay them by doing anything you need and keeping you safe. I was quite clear about that with him."

Skye laughed, certain her father was teasing her in his dry manner. Victor stared calmly at her, his expression unwavering and with no twinkle in his eye or tilt of a smile on his lips.

She sobered. "You're serious?"

"Certainly," he insisted. "I'm not ignorant. I know I can't always be here for you. You know I always have a backup plan. Well, sweetheart, this is one of my contingencies for you. If ever you are in trouble and have need and I am unable to be there, call Jack. Swear it to me."

She had sworn, caught somewhere between amusement and a warm love that her father thought of such things and wanted to always protect her. Many times since then she had cleaned out her wallet, or moved her cards and money into a new purse. Jack Berwick's business card would again be unearthed amongst a fistful of others she had collected over time.

Recalling her oath to her father, she always kept the business card, replacing it in her new wallet and promptly forgetting it all over again. With shaking fingers, she dug into her bag, grateful for that natural instinct of a woman to always keep it close even when her brain was filled with other, far more terrifying things.

"Come on, come on," she chanted as she sorted through dozens of business cards. How did the things manage to breed on her like this? Surely she'd cleaned out her wallet just a few weeks ago?

Finally the dog-eared, worn card turned up near the bottom of the pile. Placing it between her teeth, she shoved all the other cards and receipts back into her wallet, replaced the leather item into her handbag and pulled her phone out again. The screen was blank. Mumbling a curse around the card, Skye tried to turn her phone off and then back on again.

'No Reception', the screen flashed at her.

"Damn it," she swore. Shouldering her bag once again, phone in one hand and the business card in the other, Skye made her way out of the ladies' and then back out on to the street.

Skye stood out of the way of the foot traffic near the corner of a shop. The trembling of her fingers had almost stopped as she pressed in the mobile phone number written on Jack's card. A dozen thoughts flashed across her mind as she tried to focus on the number and hit the right keys on the keypad.

Had her father really been kidnapped over something he'd done or found on his last mission? He'd insisted it was personal, though, something he only trusted himself to do and couldn't leave to the Agency. Was he being interrogated? Tortured? Skye wondered if her imagination was getting the better of her or whether she'd simply watched too many Bond movies and thrillers.

Feeling nauseous, Skye forced her brain to close down on that train of thought. She couldn't lose control just yet—she then wouldn't be of any use to him. The phone rang and still Skye struggled to stop thinking.

Why had Agency people come after Garth? Was he suspected of being a party to her father's problems? Were the questions they wanted to ask him routine? Skye didn't think Garth would turn traitor, but there had always been that 'stay away' sign keeping a gulf between them.

"Yes?" a deep, masculine voice answered the phone, capturing Skye's attention.

"I'm calling for Mr Berwick, please," she replied with a faint tremble in her tone. She hoped the number was correct and still active. "My name is Skye Adams and I've been given this number to reach him."

"This is Berwick," the voice answered. Despite the smoothness of his tone, Skye could sense a trace of curiosity lurking beneath the lilt of his accent. She decided to go for broke.

"We've never met, so you don't know me, but my father gave me your business card in case I ever needed some investigative assistance. I'm not sure how busy you are but I was hoping you could spare some time in the next day or so. I really don't know where else to turn—"

Her voice cut off on a hitch and Skye took a slow, deep breath to calm herself. Even to her own ears she could hear the pitch of her tone rising with anxiety. Jack didn't let the pause grow, not seeming to want or need to let her try to explain again.

"Victor spoke to me of you, at great length, actually," Jack said. "I know exactly who you are and I can make time right now if you need. We shouldn't discuss this over the phone, though. I'm not at my flat right now, but I can be there in fifteen minutes on my bike. I assume you're in London?"

The assured manner with which Jack took charge told Skye a lot about this man. Her father trusted him, which was all she needed to know—Victor was an excellent judge of character. And the similarities between the two men that she could sense from the manner in which he spoke helped calm her.

"Yes," she replied. Her tone was steady now, with only an underlying current of panic. Skye told him the street name and station she had come from. In a quick, terse style Jack told her how to reach his flat and gave her the address.

"Okay," she said, under control once more. "I'll meet you there."

"It'll be all right, Skye," Jack said with surprising warmth. For the first time since she'd arrived at the Thai restaurant she smiled, even though the man on the other end of the line couldn't see her. "Whatever has brought you to my door, I can make it right. Don't panic, I'm sure I've faced much worse."

"Thanks, Jack. I'm glad now that my father gave me your card. He always has contingency plans—after this I might have to stop teasing him about paranoia."

That got a chuckle from the other end and Skye felt some of the tension ease out of her. The world still felt like a crazy, dangerous, illogical place, but she no longer felt alone.

"I'll see you soon," Jack muttered gruffly. Skye spoke her goodbyes. Closing the phone she replaced it in her bag and returned to the station to catch the train.

Twenty minutes later, jittery once again after being alone with her thoughts circulating around in her brain, she pressed the unmarked buzzer for the flat Jack had given her directions to. A large chrome and black leather motorbike leaned against the wall to the side of the building, looking both menacing and tempting.

"Yes?" the same voice greeted her. A small section of the knot filling her belly loosened as she knew she'd found his place.

"Jack? It's Skye."

The pressurised whoosh of the door being released sounded and Skye leaned in to grab and open it. Jogging up the stairs, she glanced at the numbers until she found Jack's. Lifting her hand to knock, the door opened before she could rap. Six feet two of athletic, muscled man rested against the frame. Skye felt her heart race within the confines of her chest. Blood pounded in her ears and she had to consciously close her mouth.

Blond hair clipped close on the sides had been left slightly spiky on top. Piercing blue eyes met hers with an electric, almost neon intensity. For a moment they each stared at the another. Skye struggled to not swallow her tongue.

Sexual chemistry, thick and potent, weighed in the air between them. Jack Berwick, she discovered, was her own personal wet dream. A walking, talking sexual fantasy come to life. She wanted to feel those strong arms wrapped around her. She longed to have the heat from his body penetrate through her cold fear and wrap her utterly in the heat of his possessing embrace.

"Jack Berwick?" she spoke with astounding poise. Considering her knickers were getting damp, Skye felt she pulled off the civility rather well.

Jack nodded and stepped back, allowing her to enter the flat. Skye took a deep, calming breath as he shut the door behind her. The light, spicy scent from his aftershave filled her senses. She felt her stomach clench with lust. Trying to distract herself, she gazed around his home. Thinly furnished, the room was clean, but masculine. Without needing to enquire, she could tell no woman lived here with him.

An almost dead plant stood in the sunlight by the window, and a large plasma screen took up a lot of space along one wall with a well-worn couch and single easy chair set up clearly for Jack to relax in at the end of a day's work. A scarred coffee table held a few pieces of what appeared to be unlooked at mail he'd clearly just tossed there, probably from habit. An overflowing bookcase finished what she believed to be the main living area.

She could see the entrance to the kitchen off to one side, and a hallway led back to where she presumed the bathroom and bedroom were. Jack's flat was clean, utilitarian and an utter bachelor pad.

"I've already put the kettle on," Jack said when her gaze met his once again. "Come sit down and tell me what the problem is."

Skye moved to the couch as Jack indicated it with a wave of his hand. Dropping her bag to the floor by her feet, she perched on the edge of a cushion. Jack sat down on the other end of the couch, pressing a finger to his temple and watched her with seemingly endless patience. Skye let her gaze linger on his hot blue eyes for a moment, enjoying a tiny, hidden thrill at being the recipient of his sole attention.

Recalled with a jolt to the serious nature of 'her problem', Skye sighed and recounted what had occurred during what was supposed to have been her birthday lunch.

"My father returned from one of his missions late last night. I know that because he texted me saying he'd landed safely and confirmed our lunch date today. He'd been out of the country for my birthday earlier in the week and we were going to celebrate. Only he didn't arrive. Garth Spenser—dad's partner and protégé—turned up, saying he was missing, and then two other agents turned up to bring him back for questioning, and then — "

Skye cut herself off, hearing the rising tone as her words sped up. Getting a handle on herself, she paused for a second to try to recount everything coherently. A hysterical female would not be any use to Jack or her father.

"I can safely say neither my father nor I will ever get to try the cuisine at the Golden Mih Goo Wak Restaurant," she started again. "While Garth, Katherine and Tarek were all arguing, I started to leave, but a group of four men were on the other side of the street and started taking pot shots at us. Garth and the other agents returned fire and the restaurant was pretty shot up. Garth insisted I should make a run for it, and, after a moment, I did."

Skye paused there and swallowed. Her voice had thickened and it felt like a lump had lodged in her throat. After a moment she continued.

"That was when they pulled out a rocket launcher and… Well, you can imagine how it went from there."

"So the others are dead?" Jack replied, his voice grim.

Skye shook her head.

"I don't think so. I went back, called out a warning. I know Garth was escaping as the building was decimated, so I'd like to think they got away, though I can't be sure and I don't know how hurt they were. If they ran for it they might have got out relatively unscathed, but I was busy fleeing in the opposite direction at the time." They were both silent for a moment. "The reason I called you, that I'm coming to you like this, is I don't know who to trust. If my father has been kidnapped, if he's being held hostage for something, we need to find him."

"I'm sure the Agency —" Jack began, but Skye cut him off.

"Of course they're looking, but they're not solely focused on it, like I want to be. They're bogged down in chasing after Garth and probably covering everything up like mad. I don't care about anything except getting my dad back. Garth said... Garth said these assailants were only laying down suppressing fire. They might have been trying to flush me out before they decided a rocket launcher was a better option. Garth warned me they might try and use me as leverage against my father. If they have him, if they're...if they're trying to get information out of him, I would be used against him. I need to get him back, safely."

"Tracking someone like your father down will be bloody difficult," Jack warned her. "Though, if he's being held against his will, at least he will use any opportunity to help us — or anyone else — looking for him. Do you know anything about the mission your father just returned from?"

"No. He did say that it was something personal, something he needed to do himself. He made it clear he wasn't missing my birthday lightly." Skye leant back on the couch and searched her memory for anything that might be helpful.

"I didn't get the impression he went because he was ordered to. Dad sounded like he felt he needed to be the one to do it, whatever it was," she finished.

"Okay," Jack replied. His eyes glanced at the wall behind her as he appeared lost in thought. "We need to make a few assumptions to begin with. Let's assume it's not chance or coincidence that now is when he's missing. This isn't random or a fluke. It's possible this is in relation to a long-term plan being put into place, but it doesn't strike me as being the case."

Skye frowned and shook her head, not following his reasoning.

"If those four men, presumably acting on behalf of your father's current nemesis, had been given a cohesive plan which was the result of a long-term greater strategy, it would have been more convoluted — and likely more successful — than simply laying down suppressive gunshots, then when you seemingly escaped, using a rocket launcher to obliterate the restaurant and any witnesses. That's not a finely tuned plan, that's a by the seat of your pants reaction when things don't go your way."

A tiny smile twitched at the corner of Skye's mouth. The sexy man had a good point. When she didn't comment or question him further, he continued.

"There's certainly also a reason they took your father and didn't kill him outright," he mused almost as if to himself.

Skye's stomach lurched and she felt grateful she was sitting as a tremor ran though her legs. She pressed her lips together but nodded, not that Jack appeared conscious of her movement.

"They need something from him — they want him for some reason," Jack continued to think aloud. "It could be anything, though. Access codes, knowledge from his mission, an item in his possession. Hmm, yes, they need something from him. That fits. But would he hide it, or is it something already in his possession?"

"If it was in Dad's physical possession they'd have it already," Skye answered. Jack's eyes jolted to her and he gave her an apologetic smile.

"That's true, so he must have hidden it."

"But if he gave it to Garth, or someone at the Agency… No, that doesn't make sense," she shook her head. "They'd not be looking so hard at why this was happening, they'd be focused on retrieving my father if they knew what was going on. He can't have sent it to Garth."

"That means he sent it to you," Jack replied.

Skye shook her head in disbelief.

"Not at all. I got a text from him when he landed last night, it's true, but I haven't received any packages from him in the last few days. Why couldn't he have sent it to you? Or another acquaintance not associated with the Agency he felt he could trust?"

"If Victor didn't want this to fall into the hands of the Agency then you're the logical choice for whom he'd send it to," Jack insisted, sounding stubborn. "There isn't anyone—oh, of course!"

Skye couldn't help but smile. Jack's eyebrows rose as if a bell had sounded in his head.

"Your father once mentioned to me, if I ever had something that needed safekeeping but I didn't or couldn't trust a regular system, he knew of an alternative safety deposit box outlet." Jack sat forward on the couch, exuberance clear as his hands gesticulated.

"If you're positive Victor didn't send anything to you, maybe he sent it to Tank. But we still don't have the key," Jack lamented.

Skye glanced at her watch, surprised at how quickly the afternoon had flown by. "There still should be an hour before any banks close," she began. "If we're quick we should be able to make it to this Tank's store and—"

"No, no, I said alternative," Jack interrupted with a grin. "Tank's pub won't open until at least seven, and the man himself might not arrive until after that. We have plenty of time."

"Oh," Skye replied, a little deflated. She moved back on the couch and felt her body relax for the first time in hours. "Let me get you that tea," he insisted. "Have you eaten? If your lunch date with your father was interrupted…"

Skye's stomach rumbled at the mention of food.

"I'm ravenous. I'll eat anything you can give me, thank you, Jack."

Jack stood with a small, wry smile, not unlike the one her father often gave her when he was amused by something she'd said or done but didn't want to laugh aloud. She felt oddly comforted by Jack's presence, intelligence and willingness to take her ideas on face value and not question everything. He paused, seemed on the verge of saying or doing something as he towered over her.

He shook his head and walked around the coffee table, picking up the mail on his way past. As he entered the small nook where she'd noticed the kitchen earlier, he sifted through the letters. Skye closed her eyes with a sigh as she heard the familiar sound of cupboards opening and closing, crockery rattling and the kettle being poured. Comforted by the normality of hearing a light snack being prepared, she let the tension seep from her body.

"Huh," she heard Jack mutter from the kitchen. Instinctively she sat up straight and tilted her head in his direction.

"Is everything all right in there? Do you need some help?"

It wasn't until the words fell from her lips that she flushed at how stupid the suggestion was. This was

Jack's home and his kitchen—it wasn't likely he needed her assistance.

"This arrived in today's mail," Jack replied as he entered the living room and held out a postcard for her to look at. Skye took the small card from him and a grin crossed her face as she glanced at the large military tank stranded on a grassy green lawn. An unpronounceable German town name was printed on the bottom corner.

"Turn it over," Jack suggested.

Flipping the card over, Skye's eyes widened in shock as she recognised her father's handwriting.

'Found the quaintest Pub which I think you'd enjoy. You should see the gorgeous Sky line over the hills. You'd be amazed at the discoveries I've made. Victor'.

She reread the few sentences, only partially aware of Jack returning to the kitchen. A minute later he placed a plate and a mug of steaming hot tea on the coffee table near her knees.

"So Dad sent you the message of where to get his package?" Skye surmised. "You said the owner's name was Tank, hence this particular card. Then the capitalised mention of both the pub and the sky."

"I can think of a few possibilities. Maybe he knew something would happen—though not when or what—and he's reminding me of my promise to help if you ever called. Or perhaps you still know more than you think you do and I'll need you when we get to Tank's."

Skye reached out and grabbed one half of the sandwich he'd placed before her. A quick glance showed her it was filled with ham, cheese and tomato. She took a few bites in quick succession. Nothing had tasted this good in ages.

"I'm still not sold on the thought that I know anything the least bit useful." Skye returned to their conversation after inhaling half the sandwich. She sipped her tea before picking up the second half.

"What I wouldn't put past my father is him pointing you in my direction to make sure I'm protected while whatever he's involved in unravels. That kind of convoluted, near-paranoid level of obsessive planning sounds exactly like the Victor Adams I know and love."

"I think you underestimate yourself." Jack sat down next to her on the couch. "You know how your father thinks, how he would react in certain circumstances. That closeness could be vital to his rescue. More importantly, you have no idea how some subtle, previously believed inconsequential word, gesture or casual reference Victor spoke of weeks or even months ago might be instrumental in solving this thing. All I can guarantee is that I don't plan to let you out of my sight until I deliver you back into your father's safekeeping."

Skye wiped at her mouth to be certain no crumbs lingered on her lips. Swallowing more of the tea, she replaced the mug on the coffee table with a small sigh, her stomach sated. She turned to face Jack and once again her heart fluttered in her chest.

He was so handsome.

"I'm not a lost schoolgirl who needs returning to her parent," Skye chided him. "But I would definitely like to stick close to you. At least until the vision of that rocket launcher and those four men dims somewhat in my memory. Right now, it's far too vivid for comfort."

"Hey," Jack said softly. He leant forward and rested one large, warm hand on her thigh. Heat from his skin soaked through her leg. Skye caught her breath, her gaze lifting to catch his.

Chemistry burned between them as they stared at each other in silence.

Skye lowered her hand to lace her fingers through his, testing the waters between them. His fingers clenched hers, his grip tight but not painful. For a suspended moment she felt as if they were hovering on the brink of an enormous, sheer drop. They leaned in and their lips touched.

The world ignited, her ears rang and Skye felt as if she had just been electrocuted.

Tingles shot across her body and, without even realising it, she scooted closer to him. Jack moved forward and soon she straddled him, eating at his mouth with her lips as they strained against each other. She ran her hands over his shoulders then down his back, loving the warmth of his body even through his shirt.

He threaded his fingers through her short curls, his palm cupping the back of her skull. He wound a strand around his digit, his touch tender, as if he wanted to memorise their texture. She stared into his fiery gaze, ensnared in its depths. Need washed over her as her pussy flooded with moisture.

Rocking into him, Skye rubbed her spread centre over his jean-clad erection. Even through the thin denim she could feel his searing heat, the hard, thick length of him straining as if to reach out to her in kind. Their tongues tangled and it took a moment for her to hear their joined gasps as they both struggled for breath.

"This is just a reaction to how close to death you came earlier," Jack finally managed to pant as he pulled his mouth from hers.

Her cheeks flushed and Skye could only shake her head at him.

"Trust me, darling, I don't want to take advantage of the scare you've had. It's understandable — "

"Can't you feel the attraction between us?" Skye cut him off. "It's electric and potent. It wouldn't matter if I'd met you at the bus stop, Jack. I want you and I need this. Please don't deny me."

"I must be mad," he muttered. Regardless of his words, he cupped her jaw and dragged her closer to him. Wrapped in his warm embrace, Skye gave herself up to the soul-searing kiss they exchanged. She tasted him, his spicy scent enveloping her. Her hands fell to the waistband of his jeans and she struggled to unsnap them and drag them down his legs, realising it was impossible while they were both sitting.

"Not on the couch, damn it," he groaned as he raised his head again. "If we're doing this we're bloody well going to do it right."

Before Skye could form a coherent thought or ask him what the hell he meant, Jack stood up, his arms wrapped around her as he lifted her with him. Locking her legs around his waist, Skye held on for all she was worth. As if she weighed nothing at all, he carried her down the hall towards his bedroom, kissing her the entire way.

Chapter Three

Skye barely had time to do more than cast a quick glance around Jack's bedroom. A large wooden bed was neatly made in tones of dark blue and green. A dresser stood against one wall with a few personal items on top of it. An alarm clock was visible on the bedside table. Everything else faded as Jack lowered her onto the duvet and scrambled to remove her trousers.

Eagerly, she assisted him out of his jeans, then pulled his shirt up over his head to reveal his smooth, chiseled chest. Running her hands over the well-defined pectoral muscles, Skye once again found her breath catching in her throat. The man was built.

Cool air hit her as he bared her chest. Beneath the lacy, white bra her nipples beaded, part in arousal, part from the breeze. Jack palmed one breast in his hand, his thumb and forefinger expertly twisting the nubbin so pleasure rocked through her blood.

Her back arched and heat tingled up her spine, connecting her erect nipples and allowing the decadent lust to pool down in her pussy. Need slammed into her body and Skye lost all restraint. Her hands dipped into Jack's snug briefs and she cupped his balls, her fingers stroking over the roughly haired skin and seeking his every secret.

Jack groaned as if he were in pain, his voice barely a rasp, guttural in his throat.

"Fuck, yes. Just like that, darling," he panted. With his urging, she pushed his briefs down his legs and freed his thick cock. One hand remained, cupping and caressing his balls, while she encompassed his warm prick with her other hand and ran a smooth motion up and down his shaft.

She moved her palm over the head of his erection and slick wetness collected along her skin. His pre-cum acted as a lubricant and as she continued to stroke his length. Pumping her fist harder and faster, she built upon the rising passion between them. Jack licked and kissed a slow, wet trail down the line of her jaw, along the slender column of her neck and made his way with light, grazing nips of his teeth around the full curve of her breast.

He removed the last of her underwear and she lay spread before him on the bed. Skye continued to pump him as he gazed at her, his eyes bright with lust and need. As if he couldn't bear to tear himself away, he lowered his body onto her length and suckled her hard nipple as if it would give him the elixir of life. Her back arched again, pleasure shooting across her body, her senses overwhelmed with the heat of her arousal.

Unwilling to lose the intimacy of the moment, Skye kissed the lean line of Jack's collarbone. His skin tasted salty from his sweat, a delightful, masculine musk filling her senses as she grazed her teeth in response to his talented fingers probing between her slick pussy lips.

"I need to be inside you," he panted.

Skye groaned and spread her legs for him.

Her hands released his slick cock and she raised her glistening fingers to her lips. Capturing his gaze with hers, she slowly inserted her index finger into her mouth, licking it. Jack groaned, his gaze riveted. Pushing himself up on to his elbows, he hovered above her and watched as she lapped his juices from her hand.

"I thought you needed to be inside me?" she teased. Her voice sounded husky, unlike how it usually sounded to her ears.

"I do." Jack grinned at her, a masculine, proud, complacent smile that spoke volumes of his confidence.

Twisting around, he reached into the bedside table and she heard the faint crinkle of foil. A moment later he turned back to her and lifted her legs high.

With his hands under her thighs, supporting her, he helped her thread her legs over his shoulders, opening her pussy wide for him. Thick, warm fingers stroked her sensitive lips and he parted her to reveal her most intimate secrets. Skye moaned, arching her body to entice him to finish what they'd both so greedily started.

"Please," she pleaded with him, her eyes devouring every inch of his flesh. She reached her hands out to him, resting on his shoulders and drawing him down onto the mattress with her.

"Of course," he replied. In a slow, sensual thrust he fit his cock at her entrance and pushed himself inside her folds. Inch by agonising inch he sank into her, each sensation enticing as he penetrated her depths.

After what felt like a lifetime, he lay fully lodged within her, swallowed by her clenching cunt. Skye squeezed her inner muscles, bearing down on him. Jack groaned. She chuckled, pleased her actions added to his enjoyment.

Skye clasped his shoulders as Jack steadied himself, placing his large hands on either side of her waist. As he withdrew from her she tried to tighten herself around him, but she was no match for his strength. With the tip of his cock barely at her entrance, he pressed back inside her once again.

Setting a slow, luxurious pace as if they had all the time in the world, he possessed her body, staking a claim. In and out he rocked, the need building within her chest like a fiery ball. Panting, she canted her hips up, desperate to draw him in deeper.

Need, thick and hot, ran through her blood. Skye's orgasm built within her. She lowered one hand from his shoulder to her clit and rubbed herself. Jack's electric blue gaze turned molten at her actions. He watched her with unabashed joy and he growled low when she stopped.

"No, take your pleasure. I want to watch you."

Skye forced her eyes to remain open, though the intensity of the passion surging through her blood made them flutter. Her hand returned to her clit, the burning in her belly growing as she stroked herself. The thick hardness of Jack's cock pounded within her and all too soon she felt an incredible detonation.

Pleasure seared through her senses and her toes curled as her body arched in lascivious release. She pressed her head into the rumpled duvet and a scream tore from her lips as hot waves of pleasure crashed over her.

"Oh yeah, darling, that's how I love it," Jack groaned as he pumped her. He lifted her hips, tilting her for maximum penetration. With a muted roar he climaxed before Skye could come down from her own intense high. Her body shook, the fierceness of his possession ratcheting up her own arousal yet again. As he emptied himself into her a smaller, but this time longer, orgasm crashed over her on the heels of her first.

Gasping and shuddering at the unexpected peak, Skye found herself ultra-sensitive to the gentle caresses as Jack stroked her skin. Collapsing to one side of her, he rested his head on his hand, propped up on an elbow as he looked over her with an utterly rugged, self-satisfied and smug look.

When she had managed to catch her breath, she whistled softly at him.

"I've never felt that before," she confessed.

"An orgasm?" Jack clarified, clearly pleased with himself. Skye laughed softly and shook her head.

"Multiple orgasms. It's not as common as men seem to presume."

"I guess we're just that good together."

He sounded, if possible, even more smug.

Feeling frisky and far more playful now the initial consuming need had been assuaged, Skye used one hand to roll Jack on to his back. She moved her mouth along the edge of his jaw, enjoying the prickly stubble. She ran her fingers through the blond spikes on top of his head and gazed into his beautiful eyes.

The man was alluring in a potent manner. She found him intoxicating. Few men had captured her attention like this before, and Skye could well believe that all too soon she might be addicted to this man. Particularly to earth-shattering, back-bending sex with him. Jack Berwick had become her personal drug of choice.

Seeming content and sated, he allowed her to explore his body as her whims dictated. He didn't snap or growl at her, nor did he roll over to nap or appear to feel the need to rush off to the shower and escape her. Skye could feel her heart catch at his indulgence and open curiosity.

Straddling him once again, she explored to her heart's content. Following wherever her mouth — and tongue — led her, Skye soon found herself with a mouthful of his sac. Her tongue probed the delicate skin beneath his scrotum and she had to suppress the chuckle of delight as she felt his cock harden once again and stir back to life as if revitalised after a brief appetiser.

"Why, Miss Adams," Jack teased her with a lilt in his tone, "I do believe you're not the only one drawn into a multiple."

"I've been told I am very stubborn. And persuasive. I do have a few of my father's genes, apparently."

"You're beautiful and alluring to me, not to mention talented. I do believe that tongue of yours could raise me from the dead."

"That's the idea, surely?" she murmured and returned her mouth's attention to bringing her lover back from *la petite mort*.

This time he allowed her free reign. Only after his cock had fully hardened once again and her pussy wept with the need for him, did she reach for another foil packet. She finally lifted herself over him and sank down on to his thick shaft.

From this higher angle his penetration seemed to fill her body and block her throat. She felt as if she had never before experienced real pleasure between a man and a woman. It was as if Jack were her first. Her heart pounded so hard inside her chest she feared it might explode.

Braced against his chest, Skye lifted and sank on to his body, his cock hot and enormous within her. He let his hands fall to her hips once more, gently assisting her to manoeuvre to find the greatest pleasure.

When he scraped along her G-spot, she screamed and trembled. She paused, overwhelmed. On the verge of climax, she vibrated with need. With a gasp, she leaned a hand down, stroked the tender skin of his scrotum and found that sensitive cluster of nerves around his tightly puckered hole.

"Fuck!" he swore, rigid now with his own need for release clear.

Only then did she lift and fall again, driving them both over the edge and into screaming oblivion. Skye could feel him pumping into her like a man possessed, both their cries rising so loudly around them she thought the neighbouring flats had to hear them.

They trembled together, sweat beading along the slender line of her spine. Thrusting furiously, Jack came as her release washed over her in a near overwhelming wave. This time it was she who fell next to him on the bed, shaking and unable to catch her breath.

They lay curled together for a few minutes, each of them thinking their own private thoughts. Slowly, sensually, their heads moved together as if they'd shared the same thought in identical moments. They shared a heated, passionate kiss. As if they had all the time in the world, they tenderly explored each other's mouth.

Jack pulled his lips away.

Skye's eyes fluttered open when she realised she'd closed them in pure bliss, caught up in the perfect moment they shared. Gingerly, Jack pulled his cock out of her body with a faint plop. Reaching between her swollen, lust-bruised legs, he inserted one thick finger into her pussy.

Removing the creamy digit, he inserted it into his mouth in mimicry of her earlier motion. Hot lust unfurled deep in her belly. A part of Skye wanted to re-straddle her lover and start all over again, right from the very beginning, but faint twinges from her rarely used inner muscles informed her a break was in order.

"You'd be amazed how wonderful a joint shower could be right now," she murmured. Surprise and pleasure shone in his gaze as his eyes widened appreciatively. A wicked, knowing grin crossed her face.

"I wield an amazing detachable shower head," he boasted, following her train of thought.

Skye snickered and lowered her chin to her shoulder, gazing at him with heated longing. The pose was simultaneously innocent and naughty, perfect for how she felt right now.

"How much time do we have before we need to be at Tank's?" she teased him, tired but willing.

Jack threw his head back and laughed.

* * * *

Jack watched the show Skye put on as she dried her body off from their shower with a big, fluffy towel. Never in his life had he come three times in such a short time. Something about Skye drew him. He wondered if he truly would follow wherever the sultry woman led.

She ran a finger through her short brown curls. They spiralled in every direction and he knew now for himself just how soft they were. Her warm blue eyes shone at him as she grinned. This woman clearly knew exactly how alluring she was to him.

He wanted her on every conceivable level. Physically, emotionally, intellectually and with a fierce passion that burned deep in his soul. Now he'd finally met her, come to know her a little, he didn't think he could let her go. He should have known any daughter of Victor Adams would be a complex mixture and utterly addictive.

A part of him understood they both flirted with danger by entertaining the wicked fantasies that overwhelmed his brain. Victor was not a man to cross, and, despite his placid façade, contrary to his cool, calm demeanour, he could strike like a viper and was the epitome of protective when it came to his only child.

Skye, on the other hand, did not seem to understand how dangerous this entire situation could become without any notice. Yet still Jack found himself drawn to her. Classic moth-to-a-flame situation. Jack only hoped neither of them found themselves singed.

Skye grinned at him, her pale flesh flushed from the heat of her shower, her curls framing her face, her eyes warm and filled with amused hunger. He loved how the colour in them deepened when she found her pinnacle with him. Jack was insatiable when it came to this beautiful woman.

She was the kind of woman Jack found himself willing to die to protect.

Nothing else mattered.

"You might find this hard to believe, but I'm needing to remind myself just how important it is we make it to Tank's tonight," Skye laughed. "I'm not usually so easily distracted by a sexy man, though I know my actions haven't proven so in the last few hours."

Jack reached out a hand to stroke along the soft curve of her cheek. She grinned impishly at him, charming him and heating his blood. His exhausted cock still managed to twitch in lusty interest. For the first time since he'd met her, Jack ignored his prick's instincts and forced himself to focus. Their lives— Skye's life—relied on his attention to what went on around them now.

"I've never been so instantly attracted to anyone, darling," he assured her as he stroked her delicate skin. "Considering the circumstances, I think we've both just been overcome. This isn't your usual scenario, so we can't apply the normal rules."

Skye leaned her face into his palm, studied him with shining eyes and grinned at him. Jack felt his heart leap. He knew it was impossibly fast, but his certainty was unshakeable. He loved this woman fiercely.

"You make even the insanity of this afternoon feel natural, good. How do people like you and my father manage to do that?"

In that moment she reminded him of a pixie. Innocent, sensual and with a naughty sense of humour he couldn't resist.

"I'm insatiable when it comes to you," he chuckled. Leaning in, they kissed now with the languid comfort of two people who knew they had a long time to indulge themselves. The heated rush of their first few couplings had passed and now they were enjoying the time they'd been granted, exploring one another on every level.

Reluctantly, Jack pulled away from the woman who held his heart.

"If I don't get dressed we'll never make it. Despite your words, I know you feel the need to see whatever it is Tank is protecting for your father. Take your time getting ready, though. I know better than to rush a lady."

She was laughing, clearly amused as he forced himself to leave the bathroom and enter his bedroom. Pulling on briefs, black jeans, a dark navy blue sweater and his boots, Jack opened his closet and removed the false floor. Twisting in the combination to his gun safe, he opened the door and perused its contents.

Jack preferred sleek handguns to the bulky, unwieldy kind—he always had. Discretion was always his first choice, destruction his second. As a PI it had served him well and those professionals whom he respected and liked—Victor Adams, for example— usually held a similar outlook. Enormous, flashy guns were more the style of weapon he found amateurs, or worse—insecure—people preferred.

If your enemy didn't know you had a weapon until it was too late, success was that much easier. Waving around a hand-cannon and blustering, or attempting to intimidate, all too often resulted in you ending up six feet under. Jack never underestimated the elements of surprise and discretion.

This time, however, with the scent of Skye still in his nostrils, the taste of her on his tongue and his body sated, his eyes were drawn to the small calibre, compact lady's gun he'd purchased on a whim a few years earlier. He'd seen it at one of the stalls at a showing. The slick salesman had struck a nerve with the comment about how a man could never over-protect his lady.

It had spoken to something deep within his soul, that comment. He believed it with every fibre of his being. Skye — her father's daughter in more ways than she could see — was not some weak, defenceless damsel, despite her fear and reaction at what she had witnessed earlier in the day.

He had a feeling she didn't recognise or appreciate the strength and courage she had shown at the Thai restaurant. She had not frozen, or fallen apart. She hadn't dissolved into hysterics or wept and clung to the agents who had been present. She had stood firm against her fear and while, yes, she had been shaken, she had also turned back to protect virtual strangers. She had thought coherently enough to contact him — for which he would be eternally grateful — and she had a steely determination when she spoke of rescuing her father.

The flinty look in her beautiful eyes showed that nothing would deter her from her chosen course of action. Jack could only hope she knew how to shoot a gun. He couldn't imagine Victor not teaching her, but then Jack could also imagine the lengths the man would go to in sheltering his daughter. The thought of one day his own little girl needing a gun to defend herself turned Jack's blood to ice.

A little girl, with blonde or brown corkscrew curls like Skye's, that cheeky little-girl grin. The thought of such a precious soul being trapped in a situation like the one he now found himself in with Skye was enough to chill him to his core. He'd want his child to be able to protect herself. Oh yeah, it might have frozen Victor to think it could be required one day, but Jack would bet everything he owned that Victor would have trained his daughter in the use of a hand weapon.

Jack pulled out his favourite gun, checked it and then grabbed the small lady's pistol with his other hand.

"I've never seen a man so intent on the floor of his closet." An amused chuckle came from behind him.

"Just accessorising. I presume you can shoot?" Jack turned around and grinned at his lover, as he held up both guns.

"My father insisted." She wrinkled her nose in seeming distaste. "Until we discovered we both loved good food, it was our only father-daughter time. Mandatory ever since I learned the truth of what he does."

Jack handed her the smaller gun and she gingerly took it. He could tell from the manner in which she held the weapon that she knew about guns, but either didn't like them or didn't yet feel comfortable around them. She checked it with a staggering efficiency that showed better than words how thoroughly Victor had trained his daughter.

When she held it out to him to return it, instinct stirred within him. Jack shook his head.

"No. Keep it. It's yours now."

"But this is a good piece," she insisted, sounding surprised. "It's well weighted, light but sturdy and is the perfect backup. You can't just give it away."

"It's mine, of course I can just give it away. I want you to have it. I can't tell why, but I get the feeling it's already yours. It's perfect for you and, let's face it, right now you need one. We can argue about it another time. For now, please, it's yours."

Skye knelt on the carpet beside him, her free hand resting on his shoulder for balance. She leaned in and they shared a heated, searching kiss. When she pulled back she smiled, seeming bemused.

"You know, after the first date most guys give a girl flowers, maybe even a necklace or something. I've never been given a destructive weapon before."

Jack ginned lopsidedly.

"Think about it, your father would approve, too. Especially considering the circumstances."

Laughter gurgled from her, the sound light and cheerful in the early evening gloom.

"Very true. I've never dated to appease my father, though. I must admit it's nice to think he won't be able to run you off."

"Not a chance, darling," Jack snorted.

Jack relocked the safe and stood up. They returned to the living room. He watched as Skye checked the safety then placed the gun in her handbag. After a last series of checks he slid his own gun securely into the waistband of his jeans at the small of his back.

"I don't think there will be trouble at Tank's," he insisted, "but I've learned the hard way to always be prepared."

Skye drew her bag strap over her shoulder and ran a hand through her soft curls once again. Jack had to resist the urge to reach out and tug the silky strands. He frowned, a thought crossing his mind briefly.

"You should call your landlord, or maybe a neighbour," he suggested. "It might be wise to check you haven't received any packages from your father. We'll look stupid if he actually sent whatever needs to be kept hidden to you before he left to return to London. Since the card he sent me arrived in today's mail, it's possible a box or parcel arrived for you today, too."

"Why would he send us to Tank's if he sent me the item he wants to keep safe?" Skye asked as she crinkled her brow, appearing thoughtful.

Jack shrugged his shoulder and kept his initial thoughts to himself. Should Victor have known he was in trouble, it was possible he wanted to warn Jack of the danger to his daughter. If he had money, passports or other useful items stashed away somewhere at Tank's, Jack could use them to ferry Skye to safety and keep her hidden until this all blew over.

That plan, however, would mean Victor knew his life was in danger and would strengthen the possibility that he was dead or in grievous trouble. He disliked speaking of such a pessimistic outlook to Skye.

She raised her eyebrows at him, obviously waiting for him to answer her.

"There might be something else helpful at Tank's, not the actual item Victor is currently protecting," Jack hedged. "Or maybe over the years there's been a number of items Victor has kept hidden away out of the wrong hands and we're his backup plan to ensuring they don't fall into any terrorist's clutches. There could be countless explanations."

Skye looked soberly at him. Jack felt uneasy for the first time since their meeting.

"My dad could really be in danger, couldn't he?" she spoke softly.

Jack simply nodded.

He watched silently as she took a slow breath, held it in her lungs for a moment, then seemed to gather herself. She rummaged in her purse and pulled out her mobile phone. Scrolling through the address book, she pressed a button and waited while it rang.

"Hi, Wendy, it's Skye. Say, could you do me a favour and use the spare key I gave you? Can you check and see if a box or parcel has arrived for me? Sure, I'll wait. Thanks, sweetie."

After a second Skye looked at him and whispered, "She has a key to my flat—she's just going to check if a notice has arrived in the post."

Jack nodded. After a few minutes, Skye's attention was riveted back to her phone.

"And no notice either? No, I just thought something might have arrived today. It's all good, I promise. Thanks so much, Wendy, I owe you a drink."

Skye closed her phone and replaced it in her bag.

"No parcel, no box, no notice of something waiting for me at the post office. I'm unsettled by the thought of Dad sending you that postcard now. If he was activating one of his contingency plans, he must have known how much danger he was in. He must have thought he wouldn't come back, that he might be—"

Jack reached out and drew her into a warm embrace as her words choked off. She clung to him and despite the circumstances it felt good, right for them to find strength in each other like this. Brushing his hand over her silky curls, Jack comforted her as best he could. A minute ticked by. Skye drew in a shuddering breath, blinked her eyes hard and gave him a weak smile.

"It's okay, I know we need to get moving. The faster we work this out, the quicker we can rescue my dad. I'm good."

Jack stroked a finger down the soft plane of her cheek before he nodded. He picked up his keys and leather jacket.

"We'll find him. He's strong. Don't worry about it, Skye."

Jack opened the cupboard and pulled out his black, tinted bike helmet. Rummaging in the back of the shelf he found the second passenger helmet he kept as a spare. Handing it to Skye, he found her eyes still serious, but a smile tilting the corner of her mouth.

"That gorgeous black and chrome beast out front is yours?"

Jack merely grinned, not needing to say a word.

"After everything we've been through, you can't convince me you're afraid of a bike."

"Afraid?" Skye chuckled and took his hand in hers, their fingers twining intimately together. "I can't wait. Bring it on."

Pride and fierce satisfaction raced through Jack's blood at her words, the eagerness in her tone clear. He led them out into the hallway, locked his flat and brought her down to the bike. Without a hint of hesitation she straddled the back seat as he turned the key in the ignition.

His beautiful beast roared to life and he revved the engine. Skye's slender arms wrapped around him and he felt excitement spike his adrenaline. His cock hardened in his jeans. Oh yeah, this would be one hell of a ride.

Kicking the stand back, he revved the engine again and pulled out on to the road. Skye cheered in evident glee. They raced away down the street.

Chapter Four

Skye's thighs still hummed from the vibration of the big machine even after she'd climbed off. She removed her helmet and handed it to Jack. He locked both helmets in a small carry box on the back of the bike.

Tank's pub looked like a classic all-male domain. The area was slightly seedy but safe enough if your clothing and stance didn't scream 'rich tourist, mug me please!' The awnings could do with a bit of a clean, and no upper class snob would have dared glance inside the door.

Skye decided it was one of the last bastions of manly refuge for the working class male who wanted a quiet pint, a few games of darts and decent food before heading home to the missus and kids. She liked it.

Side by side next to Jack, when she had taken in the measure of the atmosphere she fell a half step behind him, letting him silently take the lead. They made a beeline for the bar, winding their way around the scattered tables. Many of the men who were nursing pints glanced up.

Skye could feel their eyes linger on her for a moment. Then she would see them shift their gazes to Jack, take in his measure and look away. A part of her wanted to smile, though she kept the urge under control. As they moved through the dim room, she noticed they were drawing close to the bench.

Two rotund men in their mid-thirties worked behind the large wooden table. Dressed in white shirts and black vests, they carried a competent air as they pulled pints into glasses, each time cutting off the head of foam just before the ale overflowed. Further behind these men a tall, solidly built man stood. He watched over the entire room from a vantage point in the background, but was still in the open enough to make his presence felt.

Skye knew intuitively that this was the fabled Tank. At close to six-foot-five with bulky muscles barely concealed by a black T-shirt, the man exuded restrained menace. She decided only someone with a death wish would start a brawl while the owner was in the house. Tank's head was completely bald. She could tell he had evidently been trained in combat from his completely self-assured stance and the power he exuded. Skye struggled to not feel intimidated.

Tank's gaze tracked them as Jack led her to the bar. When he smiled at them, Tank's teeth glowed white against the darkness of his skin.

"Looks like you've finally found someone worth spending your time on, Berwick," the large man commented, amused.

Jack flashed an equally cheerful grin back at Tank. Skye could feel satisfaction radiating from her lover.

"Tank, I'd like you to meet Skye Adams," he introduced with relish. Tank's eyebrows rose and he did a double take. Slowly, he nodded as his eyes seemed to catalogue her every feature.

"Well, I'll be damned, you're Victor's daughter. Shit. No wonder he never showed me any happy snaps of the two of you. Any man with taste would be hauling you over his shoulder and carting you away. I'm Tank." The man leaned over the bar and held out his hand.

Equal parts amused and touched, Skye shook the proffered hand.

"I don't know, I'm not so easy to steal," she laughed.

"Victor spoke of you often, with evident pride. Jack here is a brave man to take him on. What can I get you both? First round is on the house."

"Actually this isn't a social call," Jack interjected apologetically. Leaning an arm on the counter, he moved closer and spoke in a lower tone.

To the unknowing eye his posture appeared casual. Skye could see in the tense set of his muscles around his jaw that Jack took this very seriously.

"We're here for Victor's box."

The two bartenders moved further away to give them privacy without a word or gesture from either Tank or Jack. Skye figured this sort of request was not an uncommon occurrence. Tank remained motionless for a moment. Skye got the impression he was waiting for something. Panic fluttered in her chest.

Of course it couldn't be this simple. Her father was a meticulous planner, always with two or three — or even more — contingency plans. He always remained a few steps ahead of everyone.

Was there a password they needed to give? A code phrase? Knowing her dad, Skye didn't think a single word would suffice. Possibly they'd need to recite a stanza from one of his favourite poems or a key phrase or pun he enjoyed. The possibilities were endless.

Skye sighed and decided maybe she'd take Tank up on that offer of a drink. This could take a while. When the silence stretched on between them, Tank appeared to think a moment, and then his mouth twisted down.

"You got the key?" he asked simply. Skye saw Jack blink, but otherwise nothing altered in his expression.

"Can you give me a hint?" she asked as she stepped forward and leaned on the bar so she, too, could murmur and not be overheard.

"Is it only a few words or a whole bunch of sentences? Or is it a series of numbers? My father can be complicated, not to mention downright paranoid. I need just a little context, but I should be able to work it out."

Skye turned to glance at Jack. She could feel his gaze weighing heavily on her. He had the tiniest smile twitching the corner of his mouth. She wondered what he was thinking. Her attention was drawn back to Tank as he cleared his throat.

"No, Skye. I mean a key. Literally. Let me show you."

Tank lifted a side panel in the bar and let them come around the back. He lowered it after Jack, led them into a small office, then further into what looked like a supply room.

"No one around these parts is stupid enough to try anything here. Most people don't even know I offer to rent space in these lockers. Sure as hell ain't no one dense enough to try and rob me. Here, this one is Victor's."

Tank stopped beside a small row of box-sized lockers. There were approximately two dozen in all, with various forms of padlock on them, evidently placed there by their owners. Second from the top, looking identical to the others around it, Tank indicated her father's locker. A shiny, brand new looking metal lock latched the door tightly closed.

"I guess I can't request bolt cutters?" Jack commented wryly. Tank chuckled but shook his head firmly.

"Bloody hell, no, would ruin my reputation. Even though Skye here is his daughter, the rules are simple but non-negotiable. You pay your rent, you can keep whatever the hell you want in there and nobody without a key can get in. Easy."

Skye frowned and stared at the locker. Whatever her father had put in there for safekeeping couldn't be much bigger than one of those old style portable TVs. Weapons of mass destruction, large cases of ammunition or enormous semi-automatic machine guns simply would not fit in the small locker.

Of course, that left all manner of things that it could be. Papers, reports, documents of any description, books, a small hand-held device to control a larger weapon. Almost anything.

"Thank you, Tank. Hopefully we'll be back soon with a key," Jack said as the silence again stretched out between them all.

Skye threw a smile to the large man and nodded.

"Any time," he replied casually. "Sorry I couldn't be of more help."

They returned to the main bar area and went to the front door in silence. A large group of men dressed in construction overalls filed rambunctiously into the pub. Many of them were loudly discussing what an arsehole their site instructor was and how the union was going to make him pay. Upon seeing Skye, they paused and shuffled aside, one gent doffing his cap to her and holding the door for her to leave.

Standing to the side to let the rest of the men slowly filter in for their drink, Skye dug around in her purse for her phone and pulled it out to check if she had any messages.

Jack moved his way through the crowd to stand next to her.

Her attention on her mobile, Skye still felt Jack freeze. Looking up, she followed his gaze to where they had parked the bike. Two men in black were walking down the street, steadily closing the distance to the large machine. A third one lagged a few paces behind, a small electronic device held in both his hands, which he studied intently.

He called something out to the other two, his head jerking upward. It took him a second to hone in on her, but he shouted again and pointed at her when their gazes locked. One of the other men pointed to Jack's bike and everything became clear.

The electronic box must be some sort of tracking GPS thing. Damn. My mobile.

Jack, a half second ahead of her, ripped the phone out of her hand and threw it against the brick wall of the pub, smashing it into pieces. About to do something similar, Skye took a second to stomp hard on the broken pieces of the phone as Jack caught her hand in his.

"We're still closer to the bike than they are. Run, Skye, we need to get out of here, now."

As he shouted the command at her, Skye saw Jack turn inside and wave at Tank, giving him some hand signal she couldn't read. Curious more than scared, she peered around the new influx of people and saw Tank react immediately to Jack's gesture. The large man ducked beneath the bar and returned an instant later with an enormous shotgun.

Skye could tell from the casual ease with which he held the weapon that it was one he was familiar with. Rummaging in her bag again, she tried to feel the grip of her own gun. She'd completely forgotten she was carrying it. Jack, she noticed out of the corner of her eye, already had his in hand, levelled steadily at the men who had broken into a run down the street towards them.

"Everybody down!" Tank boomed from inside the pub as he vaulted over the bar and ran towards the door. He carried the shotgun as if it were light as a feather.

Patrons who weren't fast enough to duck out of his way were barrelled over and flattened in his wake. Proving their sharp reflexes, many of the construction crew poured out of the door. Their haste was not solely to get out of Tank's way—from their excited chatter it seemed they were all incredibly interested in the action that was unfolding.

"The bike. Now, Skye!" Jack shouted. Not waiting for her to merely follow his command, Jack grabbed her arm high up near her shoulder and hauled her in the direction of the bike. Skye ducked instinctively as an ear-splitting boom sounded.

She turned even as she continued to run and tried to look behind them.

Tank.

And his shotgun.

Jack managed to get a few shots fired off, his arm outstretched and remarkably steady for a man on the run. Skye clung to her handbag and swore she'd find her weapon the moment they reached the bike and she could catch her breath. The shotgun boomed again from behind them, laying down covering fire.

The street, she noticed, had become a war zone. The three men crouched behind various forms of cover and were shooting in return. Tank stood tall in the middle of the footpath outside his pub as the exits flooded with the evacuating patrons. The construction workers huddled in a tight knot, smoking and jeering a running commentary at everyone else as they ran for cover. When Tank managed to down one of their attackers, shooting his kneecap out, an almighty roar cheered through the crew and they acted as if their footy team had just scored the winning goal in the dying minutes of the second half.

Jack lifted her up on to the back of the bike and hurled himself in front of her, twisting the key in the ignition as he simultaneously fired the last few shots from his clip. The engine growled to life and Skye wrapped her arms tightly around his chest, clinging on with all her might.

A tall, shadowy figure caught her attention in the alley to the right. From the corner of her eye, in her peripheral vision, she saw a glimpse of midnight-black hair and a neatly clipped black beard.

Garth?

As soon as the thought entered her head, she dismissed it. The man couldn't possibly be Garth. He would be at the Agency still, answering questions and filling out the usual mountain of paperwork.

And yet...

Jack kicked the stand away from the bike and revved the engine. Skye saw a long, slender cylinder pointing out from where the black-haired man had stood a second ago. The smell of gas filled the air. She heard a click as something ignited.

Her hands convulsively tightened around Jack, warning him instantly.

"Jack! No! Over there!" Skye shouted and pointed to where a staggering burst of flame blasted out of the small alley a dozen metres to their right. A long whoosh of fire leapt out and engulfed everything in its path.

"Tank!"

The warning was too little too late. For a moment, dead silence rang out across the street, then a deafening cheer rose as the construction crew gloried in the burning, crackling blaze. Tank fell back, not quite a retreat, but certainly a self-protecting move to the safety of the doorway of his pub.

The men scattered a good distance away, preferring to watch the flames lick upwards and grow as they consumed cars, trees and the timber walls of a nearby baby shop. Another click and the flamethrower once again expelled a hefty dose of fire, frying everything in its path.

Shrill sirens rang out all around them. Smoke began to waft across the footpath and on to the road. Windows burst as flames engulfed the cars parked on the side of the street. Tank slammed the door of the deserted pub closed. The onlookers dispersed to a safe distance.

"Hold on, Skye!" Jack shouted above the general roar of noise. The motorcycle engine revved once again and they squealed in a tight U-turn and left the scene in a big rush. Skye had to cling to her lover to keep herself from being thrown from the bike. Cold air rushed past them and anything she might have tried to say would only have got lost as they gathered speed and escaped yet another catastrophe.

Heart pounding, blood rushing in her ears, Skye could only blink away the tears that threatened to fall from her eyes. Every time she thought she'd got a handle on the crazy reality her life appeared to currently be, something completely freakish occurred.

A flamethrower?

On the streets of London?

What the hell?

Jack drove like a man being chased by demons. Right now, that suited her mood perfectly.

* * * *

Miles later, they drew to a halt at a red light. Skye leant forward and spoke in Jack's ear above the rumble of the engine.

"We need to go to my place," she told him. Jack shook his head and cast a quick look at her, seeming to think she was joking. Skye stared at him soberly, her silence heavy between them.

"They've been tracking your phone, they knew the registration and make of my bike. Darling, the only thing we are doing right now is muddying the track between them and us, storing my motorcycle in a random garage and paying cash so they can't trace it and then we're going under and hiding out until we get some answers."

Skye stirred restlessly.

She was scared. She was exhausted. She was sick and tired of death, destruction and decay following her around like a shadow.

How the hell did her father cope with this as a living and not go completely insane?

"I'm not asking that we stay there, nor am I suggesting we linger, but I'm not being funny. I need to go to my place and pack a bag of things. A change of clothes for starters, a shoulder holster my father bought me for my last birthday and a few possessions I will not let these bastards steal from me."

"Darling—"

Skye cut him off before he could try to talk her out of it.

"This isn't a request, Jack. I know I probably haven't struck you as the most courageous, blasé or stable person in the half day we've known each other, but I'm not some weepy virgin who can't handle the reality she's given. I know my limitations and I don't plan to play hero here. But this is not negotiable. Either you agree to take me to my flat for a few minutes so I can collect a single backpack of belongings, or I will get off this bike right here and now and make my own way there."

"Bloody damned stubborn-arse Adams family genes," Jack cursed under his breath. "Should have known you'd be exactly like Victor when he got some maggot-brained idea stuck in his head."

Despite his harsh words, Skye smiled. They were venting, no true anger lay behind them and his tone was resigned, not disgusted.

"If you take a right at the second set of lights coming up we can go through some of the back streets and save some time," she suggested sweetly.

Jack sighed.

"What's your address?"

Skye tried hard to not let winning the argument go to her head. It was fairly small as things today went, but she felt immeasurably better for it. She gave him her address and mentioned the main landmarks near her small flat.

"Only my father and half a dozen people know where I live. Dad pulled some strings and so most of my bills and other assorted documents show my work as my residence. It's as untraceable as humanly possible."

Skye leaned into the turns as they wove through the city streets. Her body glided fluidly and thrummed along in time with the hum of the engine. In the last day she had discovered a whole new world of pleasure with Jack, but she had to admit she loved his bike. It was a form of shared foreplay beyond anything else in her experience.

"I still don't like going somewhere so easy to ambush you," Jack insisted stubbornly. Skye leant forward and pressed a hot kiss to his cheek. She flicked her tongue teasingly out to stroke over his skin and nipped him with her lips, working her way down his throat until he began to pant for breath.

"I'm grateful," she replied throatily after pulling back to speak into the shell of his ear. "Why don't you focus on thinking of somewhere safe for us to crash for the night? I don't know about you, but I could do with a hot shower, a welcoming bed and a few hours' sleep. Of course, that's only after I explore every inch of your body with my fingers, lips and tongue. Then I want to feel your cock penetrate to the depths of my pussy at least another few times before we get some well-earned rest."

"Don't I get to explore every inch of your delicate skin with my lips, teeth, tongue and fingers?" Jack teased.

Skye grinned at him as he cast her a quick, sexy smile over his shoulder.

"If you have any strength left after I've had my way with you, I might be open to the possibility of letting you have your way with me," she promised huskily. Jack winked at her.

"I think I can manage," he laughed and indicated for another quick turn.

Burying her head into the warmth of his leather-jacket-clad back, Skye tried hard to stem her laughter, love overflowing in her heart for this gorgeous man.

Chapter Five

Twenty minutes later, Skye surveyed her bedroom. Jack stood impatiently out in the living area, halfway between the door and the window that looked out over the street. He had barely said more than half a dozen words to her since she had let him in. Every few seconds he went to peer out of the window and study the people on the street, then paced back to the door to listen intently for anyone coming. Forwards and back he moved like a sentry.

Knowing a lost cause when she saw one, Skye had packed a few changes of sexy underwear – a girl needed to be prepared – a complete change of clothes and a few necessary toiletries.

She quickly changed out of her grimy clothes and into a clean set of see-through red lace knickers and a matching bra, a dark, forest-green, long-sleeved cotton top, a well-worn pair of pale blue jeans, fresh socks and a warm, woollen, burgundy jumper. It took her a minute to choose between some sexy leather boots and her new pair of trainers. Finally she picked the trainers. She could run easily in them should the need occur. Considering the last few hours, she felt the chance of having to make a run for it was looking probable.

Sadness tugged at her heart as she looked around her tiny bedroom. Knick-knacks, well-loved books, bits and pieces of her life spread out all around her. Knowing Jack wouldn't give her much longer, she went to her small, cheap wooden jewellery box. She put on the thin gold chain with the butterfly charm on it that her father had given her a few years ago.

It was one of the few gifts she had received after they'd become far closer. Her father had always insisted that the charm reminded him of her, coming out of her cocoon and turning into a beautiful, vivid, free creature who could do anything. His words had touched her, as had the gift. She treasured it.

She also put two bracelets, a brooch and a ring that had been her mother's into a zip-up compartment in the inner lining of her bag. While she didn't like to leave any of her other personal effects behind, she knew she couldn't bear the thought of those being stolen or broken.

Out in the main room she lamented the lack of time. She couldn't pack up her bookcase full of books and she hated to leave them. Steeling herself, she forced her hand to zip up the backpack and slide it on to her back. About to tell Jack she was ready, her eyes fell on the two small photo frames that sat on her mantelpiece.

The photo on the left was a candid but stunning photo of herself and her father.

A little over eighteen months ago they had gone out to a very special dinner to mark the fifth anniversary since she had arrived at his hospital bed in Helsinki. Over a sumptuous dinner they had talked intimately, laughed and drunk a ruinously expensive bottle of excellent wine her father had purchased for just that occasion. Without actually speaking directly of it, they'd both celebrated the event that had not only brought them closer together, but had also saved their relationship as father and daughter.

Towards the end of the night the restaurant owner, a friend of her father's, had brought his son to their table with his digital camera, insisting that such a joyous evening deserved a keepsake. Victor had come around behind Skye, wrapped his arms around her shoulders and they had leaned into a close hug. They'd both smiled with obvious, genuine warmth. The picture was vivid, living proof of how expressive and loving they had become since that fateful night.

The photo on the right was far grainier, older and evidently from a different era altogether. Shot at the beach on a warm summer's day, a six-year-old Skye frolicked in the water with glee. She obviously had no intentions of coming out of the sea any time soon.

Lucy Adams stood at the edge of the water, a bemused smile on her face, an enormously large-brimmed hat shading her pale, delicate skin, but not hiding her classically beautiful features. Victor stood between them both, tall and proud. Despite the relaxed set to his shoulders—looking very much like a man on holiday—it was clear to anyone who studied him closely that he stood ready to dive into the water and rescue Skye should she get into trouble.

The photo of herself and her father was the only decent shot she had of the two of them since the change in dynamic of their relationship. The negatives of the photo from the beach had been lost years ago in a move. It would be difficult if not impossible to replace either of them.

Skye unzipped the backpack and gently placed both frames in amongst her clothes so that the glass wouldn't shatter and possibly tear the pictures.

"You look amazing in both pictures," Jack commented while continuing to stare out of the window. "You glow with a beauty I've never seen in another woman in the picture with your dad, and that shot of you and both your parents at the beach shows just how much courage and guts you still have to this day. I was planning on suggesting you add them to your bag myself."

"Thanks, that's a sweet thing to say," she replied, touched.

"I'm loath to ruin this moment, but I've been thinking about that birthday card from your father," Jack said as he turned around to face her. Skye frowned and glanced at the mantelpiece where she had dropped her post after collecting it on their way in.

"My card? But we felt the envelope. There isn't the indentation which would signal a key being in there."

"I've got a feeling," Jack insisted in a quiet tone. "Humour me, please, Skye."

Skye paced over to the mantelpiece and gathered the handful of envelopes. Sorting through them quickly, she shoved the assorted bills and notices into her bag and studied the thick, cream-coloured envelope. Her father's distinctive, neat handwriting lettered her name and address across the front. There was no return address, but it had been postmarked almost a week ago in Germany. Skye nibbled her lower lip.

"My father posted this almost as soon as he arrived on his mission," she commented. She carefully slid her finger into the back flap of the envelope and prised it open. Pulling the card out, she opened it carefully, but found nothing inside except the greeting her father had written.

"To the most amazing daughter a man could hope to have. You have always been the sun and moon in your mother's and my world. Our love for you is as endless as the ocean. My miraculous Skye, never doubt I love you more than life itself."

Skye felt tears well in her eyes as she read her father's words. He'd signed it 'Always, Dad'. Her heart pounded. Her father always had protected her, watched over her, even when she'd thought he didn't pay attention to anything but his stupid 'important job' — she now knew better.

"Hand me your beach photo," Jack said. Skye blinked her eyes hard to get rid of the tears. It only took her a second to put two and two together.

"You think my dad is even more paranoid and has more contingency plans than a mastermind, too." She ignored the faint wobble of emotion in her tone. Skye closed the card and sucked in a quick breath, as if bracing herself.

Regardless of the double meaning, the words he had written meant an incredible amount to her. She wanted to keep this card and cherish it.

Skye placed the card inside her backpack, unwilling to let it and the extremely subtle clue fall into anyone else's hands. She pulled out the framed photo of herself with her parents that day at the beach. Turning it over as Jack hovered, she carefully unhinged the cardboard backing of the frame and removed it.

A large, folded piece of tissue protected the back of the photo from being indented by the small key her father had placed there for safekeeping.

"Well, maybe I shall have to stop teasing Dad about his paranoia and addiction to contingency plans. This time it might have paid off," she said in awe.

She took the key and held it out to Jack. He shook his head.

"No, darling, you keep a hold of it. Your father left it for you, not me."

Skye slipped it into a pocket of her jeans and carefully put the backing on her frame, returning it to the safety of her backpack. Slinging it over her shoulders, she took a final look around her small flat.

"Okay, I know how on edge you are. I'm ready to go if —"

The phone on the kitchen bench rang, jangling her nerves. Jack spun around, his gun steady in his hand as he levelled it in the direction of the phone. A heartbeat passed, the phone rang again and Skye huffed out a small laugh, more nerves than actual humour.

"Please don't shoot it — the way trade people charge nowadays I can't afford to renovate my kitchen."

Jack shot her a bemused glance and holstered his weapon. She could see in the tension that vibrated along the line of his muscled body that he was on edge. Making a snap decision, she decided not to tell him of her own fear. Practically no one had this number. Her landline almost never rang. Everything came to her now-destroyed mobile.

Her father knew the number.

Hope and fear surged through her body. She ran into the small kitchen nook, reaching for the phone and praying she hadn't left it too late. Snatching up the receiver, she huffed out a breath, caught between hope and fear.

"Daddy? Daddy, are you there?"

Her entire focus was on the other end of the line.

When he spoke to her, she trembled. Hearing his voice, the familiar, soothing tone reassured her he was fully in control, calming the quavering deep inside her soul.

"Sweetheart, I need you to listen to me. You need to get out, go somewhere and let me handle this. Everything will be fine but you can't let them use you for their own evil purposes. Do you hear me? Don't—"

A thump followed by a grunt of evident pain followed.

"Daddy? I can't do that, you know that. I'm not alone, Jack's helping me. I'm not going to leave you there. You'd never even consider that if our positions were reversed."

"Sweetheart, this is complicated. You can't rely on the Agency. There are m—"

Her father's voice grew faint then cut off entirely as the phone seemed to be removed from him.

"Ah, Miss Adams, I feel like I already know you, really. I'm trying hard to not be too cliché here, honest, I am. Despite your father's lack of conversational skills—his resistance to our...persuasion is an accomplishment to be proud of—his sparkling wit returned with a vengeance once we added you into the equation."

"I don't suppose you'll stop torturing him, now that you have my full attention?" Skye replied. Even to her own ears her voice sounded hard, flinty. She was always amazed by just how much her father's daughter she could be on occasion.

"Oh dear, you are an innocent, aren't you?" the man laughed. "Skye—I do hope you don't mind if I take the liberty, I really do feel as if we know each other—

after all these years nothing could entice me into missing such an opportunity as this. The great Victor Adams, at my mercy and pleading like a little girl—"

"No! Don't you listen to him, Skye! Don't you dare give in to—"

A harsh, electrical sound sang through the air and her father fell silent again. Tears leaked from her eyes, ran down her cheeks. Biting her lip hard enough to draw a thin trickle of blood, Skye held her breath and refused to let the man on the other end know how deeply he was affecting her. Not daring to breathe for fear she'd cry or scream, Skye remained motionless. A warm hand cupped her jaw and she looked up to Jack. He watched her with a stony glance, clearly as deeply upset by her emotions as she was at hearing her father being abused.

Electric blue eyes seared into her and Skye drew strength from this warrior she'd found.

"How very touching," the man drawled sarcastically on the other end of the phone. Skye drew in a deep, silent breath and got a hold of her shattered emotions.

"I want my father back," she insisted. Despite the tremble in her tone, the force she put into the demand still rang clearly through.

"I really do hate how predictable these sorts of demands are," her father's captor insisted. "Still, there's a reason they're clichés. They work. I'm certain you know the ground rules. No calling in the Agency, no police, no heroics. I'm willing to exchange whatever remains of your father for the hard drive he stole from me. I do hate the whole routine of meeting at dawn, though. So very Regency-duel-for-honour-esque. Let's say, then, at noon. High noon. Far more appropriate, I think."

Skye's eyes flew to Jack as the man so casually mentioned what must be hidden in her father's locker at Tank's. Jack appeared grim—determined in a steely way she'd not witnessed before. This was the man her father trusted to guard his back and assist in his work upon occasion. For the first time, Skye truly saw this other side to Jack and was incredibly impressed.

"Where?" Skye bit out. As the man named the location of a small park area she grabbed a pen and jotted notes on the pad beside the phone. She tried hard not to focus on the scuffling and muted grunts she heard in the background.

In her heart she knew her father was wrestling with his captors, determined to convey to her his need to keep her safe. She adored him for it, but this time she refused to buckle under and obey his commands. Her father was sacrificing himself and she would not let him do so. Not when she could help.

To her mind there was no option but to save him, regardless of his feelings upon the matter. Her father would not ever entertain the thought of running away and staying safe were she in trouble. She would not do less for him, no matter what he wanted.

"I understand. We'll be there at noon," she concluded when the man had finished giving her directions.

"I look forward to it. Skye, it's been a pleasure."

The phone cut off and Skye allowed her body to finally react. She replaced the receiver and started shaking violently. Jack wrapped solid arms around her and she clung to him. Sobbing softly, she buried her head in his shoulder and let the fear, adrenaline and worry pour from her to leak on to his shirt.

"I could hear," Jack intoned gently. "Your father is a strong man—he'll hold on until kingdom come if he needs to. They need him alive – they know he is their only bargaining chip when it comes to you."

"I need to digest this." She finally got a hold of herself. Rubbing her hands over her eyes to wipe the tears, she scrubbed her cheeks and went to get a tissue and blow her nose. Splashing water on her face in the small bathroom, she tidied herself as best she could and returned to the living room. Jack stood by the door and she smiled tremulously at him.

"I wish we could take the bike. Speeding and weaving through the streets would be wonderfully cathartic right about now. Still, it's safer to leave it in my garage under the building. After the recent break-ins, security is really tight down there. It's as safe as it could be anywhere else."

"We'll go for a night ride together once we have your father back," Jack promised her. Skye walked into his arms and they kissed passionately. His tongue probed inside her lips and she groaned hungrily as she sucked him into her mouth.

She twined her arms around his shoulders as she pulled herself flush with his body. Jack's hands cupped her arse through her jeans and he lifted her into his warmth, the heat of his cock penetrating his black jeans. The thick ridge of his need had her crying out softly as she arched her body into his.

The sound of a car driving by on the street had them both alert.

"Not here. As soon as I get you safe," he promised thickly. Skye nodded, understanding. He took her hand and she linked her fingers through his. Opening the door and looking carefully up and down the hallway, Jack led her out. Skye set the locks behind her and followed him into the darkness of the night.

She trusted him implicitly. Even though she had no clue where he led, she knew she would be safe. Excitement sang through her blood as they walked.

* * * *

Skye waited outside the cheap motel room as Jack checked every inch of it. She shivered in the cool night air and rubbed her hands over her arms to ward off the biting wind.

"Okay, come on in." Jack's voice came to her from within the room. Skye entered and closed the door behind her. Muted sounds came from the patrons in the next room. The murmur of indistinct conversations, whistles, cheers and noise she assumed meant the TV or radio was on.

The walls were evidently incredibly thin.

Jack had drawn the curtains against the glowing lights from the street. A lamp cast a warm glow over the threadbare room.

"You've been really quiet," Jack spoke, concern creasing his brow. Skye dropped her bag on the chair leaning against one wall, toed off her trainers and crossed the room to her man. He opened his arms and she moved directly into them as easily as if they had done this a million times.

He wrapped her in his comforting embrace, the feeling of coming home nearly overwhelming.

"I'm okay, just been thinking too much. I'm hoping you can help me with that."

Jack pulled back slightly. Skye tilted her head up to soak in the sight of him. His grin was lopsided, wry.

"You want to talk about Victor? Anything you need, darling."

Skye remained silent, not able to form words just now. She lowered her hands to release the top button of his jeans.

"I was thinking of a different sort of help," she replied huskily, her voice thickening with her need.

"Ah. Perfect. Like I said, darling. Anything you need."

He lowered his mouth to hers and their lips fused together passionately. Tingles immediately erupted all over her body, need searing her blood like an intoxicating drug. Flames of desire licked over her skin, threatening to consume her whole.

They stripped one another with hasty greed. Jack moaned in appreciation of her sexy lingerie, but that, too, promptly fell into a crumpled heap on the floor. Jack pulled the duvet back from the bed, baring the clean sheets and gesturing for her to join him. He dug into the pocket of his jacket and pulled out a strip of foil packets, placing them on the bare bedside table before climbing onto the mattress.

Kisses filled her blood hotly with a drugging intensity. All her fear, worry and uncertainty melted away as heated love penetrated her heart and soul. Skye lifted her leg to wrap her thigh warmly around Jack's waist, opening her slick pussy to him. Lifting herself partially over him, she took control of their series of kisses and rubbed her body along his firm length.

Thick, fully erect and tempting as sin, his cock called a wicked siren song to all of her senses. She hungered for him with a sensual need she'd never felt so severely before.

"Jack," she murmured, loving the taste of his name upon her lips almost as much as she enjoyed the hot press of his soft mouth on hers.

"Fuck, Skye, you're stunning," he groaned, seeming almost in pain with the level of his arousal.

Their hands raced over each other, skimming soft skin sensually. Heat flared between them, the powerful chemistry that had been present since he had opened the door to her. His thick, skilful fingers pinched her nipples exquisitely. Skye's back arched, her body bowing as her head fell back at the erotic torment. Soft curls brushed over her shoulders, heightening her already inflamed senses.

"Please," she pleaded, incoherent as she lost herself to his touch. Jack continued to play with her body, strumming it with a master's reverent care.

Her breasts were heavy, full and unbearably sensitive. His touch sent chills of pleasure racing to her fingertips and pulsing down to her wet pussy. Skye spread her legs further, grinding her damp heat over his naked erection as they moved in time with one another.

Jack leaned his hands on her shoulders, a small exertion of pressure pushing her on to her back. She arched into him, craving his touch and needing the fulfilment only he could give to her. Warm hands cupped her thighs, spread her wider. Jack dipped his head and laved his tongue over the curve of her labia.

Murmuring his appreciation for her taste, he lapped at her, threatening to devour her whole. The hard pressure of his tongue rolled over and over her clit, sending pulses of pleasure up her torso. Skye's head pressed into the mattress as she struggled to contain the rising pleasure.

"Oh, yes," she hissed in approval. "Right there. Please, Jack. Harder!"

One thick finger, slick from her own juices, rubbed against her tightly puckered anus. Skye jerked, the shock of the probing surprising but not entirely unwelcome. She'd never done that before, never shared such a dark intimacy with any of the previous men in her life, though a few had asked.

"I—" Breath escaped her as the tip of his finger penetrated her, barely a few millimetres inside her virgin passage.

The pressure was painful, but electrically so. Thick heat washed over her in waves, nerves she had never known about were actively screaming, her senses were almost overwhelmed with the dichotomy of the pleasurable pain.

"That's it, darling, accept me," Jack murmured before returning his attentions voraciously to her pussy and clit. Thrilling sensations balanced the full, burning pressure of his penetration of her ass. The rough glide of his tongue over her clit spiked her lust.

Skye arched up into his ministrations, then pressed her bum back on to his finger to accept more of the painful joy. Heat flooded her cheeks, breath eluded her and Skye had never felt an orgasm as powerful as the one growing within her right now. Clawing her way up the pinnacle, she could feel it moving, consuming her every sense. She struggled to remain in control, not wanting her body to overload on the magnificent sensory input her lover was giving to her.

The wet penetration of Jack's tongue flickering up inside her pussy nearly sent her over the edge. Eagerly he ate her out, sounds of pleasure and grunts falling from his lips as he hungrily devoured her. One hand continued to caress her clit, keeping her inner fire burning brightly as his other finger twisted around, corkscrewing the decadent, forbidden dark pleasure radiating out from her arse.

Skye clutched at the sheets, her body heaving and twisting as she accepted wave after wave of lust rippling out between them. The chemistry humming in the air—always potent—exploded as he started fucking his finger in and out of her tiny back hole. Her orgasm, a powerful blend of pain and sensuality, ripped through her, eliciting a scream drawn from the depths of her soul.

"Oh, yeah," Jack moaned, clearly unable to restrain himself any more. She heard a crinkle and his cock moved fully inside her on the first thrust. His finger still reamed her arse, in and out with blurring speed as he possessed both her entrances.

Still shuddering, her body felt hyper-sensitive with every nerve raw. She'd never experienced the level of arousal racing through her just now. Skye wrapped her legs tightly around Jack's waist and lifted herself higher so he could penetrate her fully. He pounded into her, his thick prick plumbing her depths even as his finger screwed in and out of her rear passage.

Inarticulate noises fell out of his mouth. She could tell he was almost insensate with his own overwhelming need as he took her fiercely. Tears blurred her vision, not from the pain, but as her body struggled to absorb the sensations she received. Gasping, she shuddered and fucked her arse back on to his finger, pressing him more deeply inside her as his cock filled her pussy.

"Oh, fuck, oh, Skye, yes, yes," Jack shouted hoarsely as his body convulsed in release.

Skye could feel her own orgasm building again. Her body arched up, seeking more. Even in the grip of his climax, Jack sensed this and added a second finger into her ass. His fingers lightly twisted her clit to fuel more pleasure and Skye flew apart.

She screamed, her body shuddering in release as his fingers pumped hard in her rear. Tingles raced along the edge of her skin as heat flooded her insides, melting her completely. They both shook together, panting and gasping for breath. They collapsed back onto the bed, limbs tangling together as they wrapped themselves together tighter.

Jack cradled her in his arms and she curled into the embrace. His body radiated heat against the cool night air. Skye snuggled into him, content and at peace.

"I love you," he whispered. The words were distinct, but muffled as his head was buried against her curls. She tilted her head, pressed a kiss to the edge of his jaw. She breathed in his scent, the faint musk of their mingled juices, and let a few heartbeats pass to show him she wasn't merely mimicking the words back at him.

Letting her teeth graze his sensitive skin, she flicked her tongue out to swipe along his salty body.

"I love you, too," she murmured huskily.

"We should plot our strategy. We'll need backup and—"

Skye put a finger to Jack's lips, silencing him. "Let's get a few hours' sleep. We have plenty of time for that later when we're rested."

His eyes roamed her face hotly, but after a moment's thought he nodded. Reluctantly he climbed out of her embrace and padded over to the bathroom. She heard the water run in the basin and she stretched languorously. Leaving the bed, she straightened the sheets and covers then joined Jack in the bathroom to clean herself up.

Minutes later they were spooning under the duvet, the lights out and the covers drawn up to their chins.

Skye sighed, happier and feeling more sated than she could have dreamed possible.

"I trust you to find him," she whispered in the darkness, knowing her lover was not yet asleep from the pattern of his breathing. His arms tightened around her and she wriggled back, pressing her naked skin into the warmth of his body.

"With us both working together, we'll get my dad back and I know he'll be okay. I'm not sure I could believe it would be possible without you. Regardless of how awful the last day has been, I'm so glad it brought me to you. I can't imagine my life without you in it any more."

"You don't need to try and imagine that," Jack replied, his voice firm. "From this day onward, you will always have me in your life. By your side. I'm not going anywhere. You're mine, Skye, and I'm yours. It's as simple as that."

Smiling, Skye turned slightly, tilting her head up, and pressed a kiss against Jack's lips.

"I love you," she repeated. Jack murmured to her, clearly on the edge of falling asleep. Skye snuggled back, content. In moments she, too, was asleep.

Chapter Six

"You guys certainly know how to throw a party," Tank commented wryly as he led them into the back room of his pub. "It's been quite a while since I've had such an entertaining evening. Do you play with the rough guys frequently, Skye? Victor always led me to believe you weren't involved in his area of expertise."

Skye laughed quietly and shook her head.

"Heavens, no. Last night was a first for me. I'm not involved in the same business as my father."

Tank glanced at her sideways, a small smile twitching the corners of his mouth. He seemed amused. Skye wasn't certain whether he believed her or not. Halting in front of the lockers, he turned to face her and Jack fully.

"May I see the key, please?" he asked. His tone seemed formal, as if this were part of some ritual.

Skye dug her hand into her pocket and drew the key she'd found in her picture frame out. She held it to him and he took it.

Turning it over, he squinted at it, then nodded as if satisfied.

He handed it back and she frowned and looked at the metal. Etched into the top was a series of six numbers.

"Sorry, had to be sure," Tank apologised. With a tilt of his head to Jack, the large man left the room, giving them privacy.

Skye frowned, perplexed.

"Shouldn't he remain behind to make sure we don't do something dodgy?" she questioned.

Jack snickered.

"I have a feeling Tank is far more worried about retaining plausible deniability should it ever come to that. No one in their right mind would even consider stealing from that man."

Skye had to admit her lover had a good point. She stepped forward to the locker and inserted her key into the shiny new lock. It turned easily. She pocketed it and opened the metal door.

A small black box roughly the size of an old-style video cassette tape sat within. Seconds before she reached to grab it she paused, her father's voice echoing in her head as strongly as if he stood beside her.

'Always make something important look easy. Your enemy will be so driven to grab it they won't notice the trap you've set until it's too late. A clever person always assumes if it looks simple it rarely is'.

She snatched her hand back as if she'd been burned.

"What is it?" Jack snapped, his arm whipping around her and drawing her back protectively.

"I just remembered this is my dad we're dealing with," she replied. "I should check for traps before I stumble blindly in and lose a finger."

"If this were anyone but Victor I'd insist they'd never have given it a thought. I think most people would assume the measures they'd made so far were enough protection for anything they wanted kept safe. But I know your father too well to believe that would be the case. Ever. Maybe I should do this."

"No, I have it. I should just think before I act," Skye insisted. Carefully she checked around the opening of the locker for trip wires or any indication there was a security device or explosives connected to the box or the locker itself.

Satisfied that the locker was clean, Skye removed the small box. Turning it over in her hand, she discovered, as they'd been told, that it was indeed a hard drive. She noted the portals where connections could be plugged in.

"It's a portable hard drive," she declared, but then sighed as reality hit her. "Which means it could contain practically anything at all. We're still not really any closer to understanding a blind thing about this."

"We're loads closer," Jack insisted. "We know some very bad people want whatever information is on this drive. We also know it's in electronic format, which means it should be fairly straightforward to encrypt it."

"Why don't we just corrupt it, keep them from accessing it. Hell, while we're at it, why don't we just destroy this entirely? Whatever is on here is not something we want to fall into terrorist hands."

"It's quite possible whoever was smart enough to take Victor by surprise and abduct him is smart enough to test the hard drive before handing your father over to us. We can't risk destroying the data in case they kill Victor—and us—because we tried to play in the big boys' league."

Skye digested that, her stomach sinking. She knew in her heart her father would be angry when he saw she was prepared to hand over the hard drive for his safe return. She couldn't even blame him — his outrage would be justified. But he was her dad and that fact stood out, far more important than any vague terrorist network, than any unidentified data he'd worked so hard to protect. She couldn't give him up for something as stupid as intelligence data.

She knew he'd be frustrated that she'd willingly handed over what he'd give his life to protect — but he was her dad. She adored him. His life was more important than countless strangers who might possibly be affected by her actions. Besides, she and Jack were no slouches — they'd figure something out.

"We need to slow them down without destroying the data," she insisted. "You're right, we can't corrupt or destroy it, but we should be able to buy time. I'm not tech savvy enough to do it myself, are you?"

Jack shook his head.

"Not properly enough that they'll do their tests and scans, deem it clean and hand your father back to us without realising what I've done. We'll need professionals for that."

For what felt like the dozenth time that morning, Skye tried to bring the image of the dark-haired, bearded man from the alley back into her mind. Had it been Garth? Was he really involved in this or had her overactive imagination been working overtime yet again?

She was almost positive it hadn't been Garth's voice on the phone, but that was easily explained. He could have had an underling make the call. Even with her father there, he couldn't have risked identifying Garth to her over the phone. But at the same time her father hadn't been shy about risking their wrath to convince her not to hand over the hard drive. Skye looked up, caught Jack's electric gaze in her own.

Putting the moment off, she closed the metal door to the locker and slowly replaced the padlock, clicking it shut and securing her father's box once again. She put the key in her pocket as Jack watched her, waiting patiently.

"Before the flamethrower ignited last night I thought I caught sight of a man. Tall. Dark-haired. Clipped beard. My initial instinct was it might have been Garth, but then I thought not. I honestly don't know whether to believe my gut or my following certainty it wasn't him. We can't contact the Agency directly, my father is convinced this can't be trusted to them, but we can't stall these people without some extra help."

"We need to trust someone. Victor felt Garth was a good man. He trusted him enough to mentor him, take him on as a partner," Jack reminded her. Skye nodded.

"But he went alone on this mission, not trusting anyone from the Agency," she pointed out.

"I think we can hedge our bets with Garth here," Jack insisted. "Calling the Agency means involving the mole for certain. We have a chance of not having our plan leaked if we go with Garth here. Added to that, even if Garth is the leak he will already know about the exchange. He might slip up and give us evidence to have him prosecuted if we bring him in now."

"Assuming he doesn't kill us or my father."

"Does your instinct think the man you saw last night was Garth? Your gut reaction to the thought?"

"No," she said, though she frowned as she still debated within herself. "I really can't be certain, but I don't believe it in my heart. Not yet, not without more proof."

"I say we call him," Jack replied. "He will have access to toys we can't imagine and will be handy as backup for the exchange itself. Victor is your father, though. I'll leave the final decision up to you."

Skye weighed the portable hard drive in her hand, thinking deeply. She wasn't prepared to let her father suffer for whatever resided on the drive. That was certain. Neither did she want to let classified or dangerous information fall into enemy hands. The compromise would be to risk trusting Garth only to be proven wrong in the hope that they could stall their nemesis long enough to rescue her father.

The plan held weight. Sure, it had holes and could backfire, but it was the only middle road she could think of at such short notice. She would have to trust her own inner instincts as well as those of her father. It would have to be good enough for now.

"We've lost my phone and I don't want to linger here and possibly get Tank in even more trouble than we've already brought to his door. I say we call Garth from somewhere else, preferably somewhere we can talk."

"If Garth has access to a discretionary Agency slush fund similar to the one I've seen Victor use, he can pick up the tab to a much better hotel room than we could ever afford," Jack suggested.

Skye chortled.

"I bet he could even hand in receipts and get repaid legitimately if we pull off the rescue of my father," she agreed, amused by the thought.

Skye slid her backpack from her back, unzipped it and carefully placed the hard drive at the bottom, underneath her clothes and photos. Shaking the bag to be certain it was balanced and some jostling wouldn't upset either the drive or her precious photos, she nodded.

Shrugging the bag back on, she straightened her shoulders, satisfied with the solid feeling of the small but noticeable extra weight.

"Feels good," she murmured as they headed for the door.

"What does, darling?" Jack asked.

"The feeling that we're making progress, achieving something, getting closer to rescuing my father, all of the above," she replied.

"That lump in your stomach, or your chest, that knowledge that we're moving forward? That's what I feel when I can tell a case is coming together, when I know I'm unearthing the truth and things are falling into place. It's addictive after a while, like when you can finally see the big picture, or when you're certain the puzzle is coming to a resolution."

"Garth and my father must feel it all the time, too, when a mission is solidifying, or going to plan. No wonder you're all adrenaline junkies," she mused.

Jack cast her a quick glance, a smile tilting his mouth upwards. "Oh, please, you can't possibly expect me to believe you're not running high, adrenaline surging as you can feel this speed up and really get moving? I can see the bounce in your step."

Skye exchanged a quick smile with him as they came back out into the main bar area.

"Well, maybe. Doesn't mean I'd like to get addicted to this rush, though. The highs are wonderful, but I have a feeling after a while the lows would crush me."

"It's why most of us retire after only a handful of years," Jack replied, his tone gentle. "It takes an inner core of pure steel, or a really soul-deep motivation to keep on going in this industry."

Even if Skye had a response to that, she'd not have been able to reply. They came to where Tank stood, stacking glasses in their places. He raised an eyebrow at them.

"Found what you were searching for?" he asked, not seeming overly interested in the details of the answer, but more asking from manners.

"We did, thank you," Jack replied and held out his hand. Tank shook it warmly and Skye followed her lover's lead.

"Glad to be of service. I hope whatever you're working on goes smoothly."

"Thanks, Tank. We appreciate your help," Skye answered with a smile.

"Come on back one night. I'll cover your drinks. I'd love to hear some of your stories."

Both Jack and Skye promised they would, then headed to the door and back out on to the street.

Without needing to speak, they both turned in a random direction and walked for a while in companionable silence. After a distance Jack reached down and took her hand in his. She moved almost imperceptibly closer so that their shoulders brushed and they walked side by side as if they'd done it a million times before.

The ease between them, the solidarity and sense of partnership warmed her.

When they came across a phone box. Skye dipped a hand into the pocket of her jeans and pulled some loose change out. Entering the cubicle, with Jack standing guard against the door frame, she dropped the coins into the slot and pressed a series of numbers to call Garth.

The tone rang, and rang, and rang.

Finally, as she prepared to hang up, Garth's voice answered.

"Yeah?"

"Garth, it's Skye. Is this a bad time?"

"Hey! No, no definitely not. Are you all right? Where are you?"

"I'm fine." She paused, wishing for a moment she'd thought through this conversation before having made the call. After a second she decided to plunge right in.

"Look, this isn't a good conversation to have over the phone. I might need a bit of help from you, but you can't make it official. Will that be a problem?"

"Well, it's not going to be easy, but it could be doable depending on what you need. Tell me what you can, but remember this line isn't secure."

Skye chuckled and rolled her eyes, her glance meeting Jack's. As soon as she'd dialled the number he had leaned in, crowding her within the box, but needing to be as close as possible so he could overhear the majority of their conversation. Besides, she liked his nearness—it made her feel secure, loved.

"We need some tech support, and possibly some backup," she replied in vague terms.

"We?" Garth snapped harshly. "Who's we? Skye, I told you at the restaurant to be careful whom you trust. Victor insisted there were…problems."

Skye frowned. She hadn't thought twice about Garth's reminder that the line wasn't secure—the number of times her father had made a near identical comment on his mobile while in her presence had taught her well that those in the industry took the threat of tapping seriously. His hesitation now, however, and the delicate way he phrased his words had her instincts flaring.

Without conscious thought, she lowered her voice to a whisper, as if she and Garth were speaking face to face.

"You're not alone there?"

Logically she knew whoever was in the room couldn't overhear unless they stood close enough to his phone, but her instinct was still to keep her voice lowered as if she could be overheard in person.

"Katherine and Tarek have been given babysitting duties," Garth replied wryly. Tension she hadn't noticed had crept into the set of her shoulders evaporated at his explanation.

"Oh." Skye frowned as she tried to weigh the ramifications of this new knowledge. Covering the mouthpiece with one hand, she whispered to Jack, "They're Agency people—turned up at the Thai restaurant to drag Garth back for questioning." A frown creased Jack's forehead as he, too, thought through this new glitch.

"I'm not the only one with company, am I?" Garth pressed again. Skye kept her gaze locked with Jack's as she worded herself carefully, Katherine and Tarek still question marks in her mind.

"A while ago my father recommended someone he trusted who I could turn to if I ever found myself in a bind and Dad was unavailable to help me himself. After what happened at the Thai restaurant he was the first person who came to mind."

"Who is he?" Garth demanded. "Skye, I told you, your father... There are more issues going on in the background here than you know about. Your father will skin me if something happens to you. You need to trust me."

Skye held her breath, her gaze steady on Jack. He nodded minutely and without a word she nodded in return. They needed to work on at least a little faith, otherwise they were sunk. Trusting Garth was a calculated risk, but one they both appeared to hope would pay off.

Besides, Jack's bike was safely stored in her allotted car park, neither were returning to their homes until after this situation had been resolved and they were not stupid enough to use their credit cards right now. Even if Jack's identity were to fall into the wrong hands, they would not be easily stopped before the exchange of the hard drive for her father needed to take place. The risks were hopefully minimal.

"Jack Berwick," Skye answered after a pause. "I'm here with Jack. He's been helping me unravel this mess and has done an amazing job so far."

"Oh, yes, I've heard Victor mention Jack. He's supposed to be a good guy," Garth's voice had returned to normal, much of the tension seeping out after her confession.

"I don't want to explain more over the phone," Skye added impishly. "This is an unsecured line, after all. Can you arrange somewhere in London for us to meet so we can go over everything?"

"Katherine and Tarek will need to tag along," Garth warned her.

Skye cast another quick look at Jack, who nodded again.

"That's fine. We're okay with it, but I'm trusting you to make sure they understand this can't get back to the Agency. What we're proposing isn't strictly sanctioned."

"We can discuss it when we meet. Let me organise things from my end and I'll call you back with the details."

"Um, I don't have my phone," Skye admitted. "That's why I'm using a payphone now, not just because I'm learning to be as paranoid as Dad. Even if you can't get us a room, make a meeting place now."

"Can you make it to the Four Seasons in half an hour?"

Skye checked her watch. That would make it nine a.m.

"We can do that. See you then."

Garth hung up, as did Skye. Jack moved out of the booth and she followed.

"We'll need a cab if we're to make it in time," he said. She nodded and they made their way towards one of the larger main streets.

"We'll be cutting it fine," she worried. "I hope Katherine and Tarek don't give us any trouble."

"It's at times like this you need to think positive," Jack insisted as he whistled to hail a passing taxi. "This will work out, I'm sure of it."

Skye's mouth twisted as they ran to the cab. Jack pulled open the back door for her.

"In the last twenty-four hours I've been introduced to a rocket launcher and a flamethrower — pardon me for not being quite as optimistic as you are."

Jack pressed a hot kiss to her lips as she brushed past him. She paused before entering the cab to suckle his tongue for a second. Her heart sang, her body tingled awake once again. The cabbie cleared his throat and she broke away, sliding into the back seat. Jack followed a moment later.

"The Four Seasons please, mate," he instructed. The cabbie rolled his eyes but didn't say a word as they pulled away from the kerb.

Skye struggled not to laugh.

Chapter Seven

Even though she'd been inside the Four Seasons before, Skye found herself staring at the elegance surrounding her. Walking across the large front foyer, hand in hand with Jack, she felt almost as if she were in a movie. Jack appeared as if he were on high alert. He glanced around them constantly as they moved. She presumed he was checking they weren't being followed.

Skye, on the other hand, searched the milling people for Garth, a knot of tension in her stomach. They were taking a gamble with this course of action, she knew. Oddly, she wasn't afraid for herself, but for Jack. And she was terrified her rash actions might hold terrible consequences for her father.

Despite Jack's earlier praise, Skye decided she certainly wasn't cut out for the life of a spy, no matter how thrilling and exciting it might be.

Before she could wallow too much in her own thoughts, she caught sight of a tall, dark-haired man and the flash of a neatly clipped beard. Panic surged through her stomach and she felt for a moment the painful edge of terror. It passed in the space of a heartbeat as she realised this was Garth, not the man from the alley.

Or she thought it wasn't the man who had burned down a large section of the street. Once again her instincts suggested that man hadn't been Garth, but the similarities were too close for her to be sure one way or the other. Jack had frozen, seeming to pick up on her fear and his head shot around. For a moment she wondered if he'd been a bodyguard in the past. He certainly acted how she'd expect a security guard to behave.

"Garth!" she called out, catching his attention.

Garth turned, saw her and smiled with evident relief.

The tall, buxom blonde she'd last seen in the crumbled ruins of the Thai restaurant and the solidly muscled, sandy-blond man melted out of nowhere to stand on either side of her father's protégé. Like an honour guard, the three of them kept pace with one another as they crossed over the large foyer to meet them.

"I'm so glad to see you, Skye." Garth spoke warmly, his black eyes showing clear relief. "I know things have been messy these last twenty-four hours, but things should be much calmer and safer for you from here on."

Skye exchanged a glance with Jack, the two of them holding their own counsel. Should Garth genuinely not be involved he might not have the same outlook once they'd explained everything to him. Jack glanced at his watch, and spoke hurriedly. Time was evidently running out.

"We have a lot to organise and not much time. Have you already booked us a room? We'll need to bring you up to speed and then start acting immediately."

Garth looked puzzled, his glance moving from Skye to Jack and back again. He seemed more than happy to utterly ignore both Katherine and Tarek.

"Uh, sure, we have a room, but—" Skye cut him off before they could get bogged down in explanations. She glared at Katherine and Tarek.

"You didn't inform the Agency where you were heading, did you? I made it clear on the phone those were our terms."

Katherine smiled with only a small hint of disdain. Skye got the feeling Katherine remained under the illusion she and her partner were still fully in control of the situation. Skye had nothing personal against the blonde, but a small spurt of defiance burned through her chest. It would be almost fun to watch that cool, calm, collected visage melt from her face once their true standing was revealed. Especially considering how she and Jack—and not her precious espionage Agency—had all but solved this problem.

Skye was definitely her father's daughter.

"No, for now we're off their radar. Once we bring you in, however, we will compile a full and cohesive report on—"

Skye cut the blonde woman off.

"It's a bit more complicated than that. Let's go up to the room, shall we? Like Jack pointed out, we don't have much time."

"There isn't much time until what?" Garth insisted as the five of them made their way to the elevators.

Jack pressed the call button and a set of doors opened immediately. After they had all climbed in and the doors had shut, Tarek pressed the button for level five and Skye spoke with fake sweetness.

"There isn't much time until the exchange for my father occurs. That's why we've been rushing you. We need the technology to encrypt a portable hard drive full of data without corrupting or destroying it. We need to buy time to get my father to safety and stall the kidnappers without all of us losing our lives in the process."

It was everything she could have hoped for. Tarek threw his head back and laughed, a delighted sound. Garth stared at her, his mouth falling open almost comically and Katherine looked as if she had bitten down on a lemon, caught somewhere between outrage and curiosity.

"You've been contacted by the kidnappers?" Katherine deduced, her voice sour. Skye smiled in what she hoped was an innocent and not gloating manner.

"And retrieved the portable hard drive my father recovered and hid. It's in our possession. Jack and I are just reluctant to hand it over to what effectively amounts as a group of terrorists without trying to make it hard for them."

"Where is the exchange to be?" Tarek asked. His tone conveyed little other than mild curiosity, but Skye was not convinced. She shook her head as the elevator doors pinged open.

"That's not part of our deal," she replied. "Or not yet. Help us encrypt the data—or at the very least make it difficult for these people to recover whatever it is they want—and you can come with us to the exchange. My father didn't trust the Agency for this matter and I'm not going to risk his life if you've got an unidentified traitor in your midst. Those are our terms."

Tarek threw a frustrated look to Jack as they exited the lift. Garth, ignoring the undertones in their group dynamic, led them to a room and pulled out a hotel key card. Swiping it, he held the door open for them. Katherine stalked inside first, clearly trying to retain some semblance of control over the situation.

Jack grinned widely at Tarek, his cocky attitude clearly taunting Tarek to make a comment or start a fight. Skye snickered, thinking Jack would probably enjoy the scuffle with the tension crackling in the air between them all.

"Our way is currently best, Tarek," she warned the sandy-haired agent. "I know it's not how you're used to doing business, but right now Jack and I hold the cards and, with my father as the bargaining chip in question, I'm not going to entrust his life to a group of people not even he currently trusts. Hell, if we didn't need your technical support we wouldn't even be having this conversation, Jack and I would be doing this ourselves."

They filed into the hotel room and Garth shut the door behind them.

Ego filled the small room and Skye sighed, shrugged out of her backpack and sat down on one side of the small love seat. She kept her bag in hand, resting it on her lap. Almost immediately Jack sat protectively beside her. She took his hand in hers and smiled. A fierce energy crackled around him. She was surprised he didn't growl like a guard dog. Skye let her gaze linger first on Tarek, then on Katherine and finally come to rest on Garth.

"Now you know exactly what we need and why, are you going to help? The meeting is for twelve noon and it will take us almost an hour to get there. We have to hurry."

Katherine and Tarek exchanged glances, seeming to consult with each other silently as long-standing partners do. Garth on the other hand studied her, then went to the room phone and dialled a series of numbers.

"Dave? Yeah, it's Garth. You up for a quick bit of work? Hour's turnaround with double your usual pay. I need it immediately, now, and it has to be custom-fit. You on board?"

Garth nodded as his contact appeared to give him a positive response.

"Come to the Four Seasons with your bag of tricks. Room five-nineteen. We'll need a small attachment for a portable hard drive." Garth made a hand motion to Skye.

She quickly unzipped her backpack, withdrew the box and walked to hand it over to Garth. He took the black item, turned it over in his hands a few times, studying it intently.

"Yeah, yeah keep your shirt on, I'm looking for that now. Okay, it's a regular black device, USB connections and a two-point-oh series. There's not enough time to make it external, so we will need to clip it to the connecting wires I'm thinking. Bring a couple of plugs that will be compatible with your baby. If we add an encryption device so that when they power the box up it merely scrambles the data instead of destroying it that will suffice for our needs. Make the encryption as difficult as you can in the time frame."

Garth remained silent. Skye waited beside him, unwilling to lose her only connection to her father.

After a moment he turned the box in his hands again and found a serial number.

He read the series of digits out and nodded.

"Yep, that sounds good. This is a delaying tactic. It's imperative whatever you choose to do doesn't destroy the box or the data stores within it. Am I clear?" Garth paused again and smiled. "Exactly, it will be your balls I fry for dinner if this blows up in my face. Oh. And if you can lay a passive tracking device in the wire I'll double the amount I pay you. It has to be passive, for at least twenty-four hours. Even then, if it can be discreet, on a low frequency maybe, I'll make it worth your while."

Garth laughed as Dave said something he found humorous.

"Of course I'll need a receiver or tracker of some sort, this isn't my first day on the job you imbecile."

Dave spoke again and Garth chuckled.

"Just be here with all of that inside the hour or you lose a per cent a minute. I warned you this was a rush job."

Garth said his farewells and hung up the phone. For the first time since she'd seen the man enter the restaurant, Skye felt the tension in her stomach start to relent. This crazy plan might actually work. She never could have guessed.

Taking the hard drive from Garth, she returned to her seat next to Jack and zipped it back up in her backpack.

"Dave will be here soon with everything we need. He's good, an old friend from my uni days. He's not my most discreet contact, but he's the quickest and one of the best. It's a calculated risk but, since we should have Victor back in a few hours, discretion isn't integral to the mission—speed and accuracy are."

Skye nodded.

"I appreciate this, Garth."

"Now do you mind explaining what's been going on, Miss Adams?" Katherine interjected, her hands on her hips and one foot tapping against the carpeted floor. "I suggest you start back at the beginning and leave nothing out. It seems I should have detained you back at the restaurant and not Garth here."

Skye smiled. Despite her clear aggravation, there was no menace or acid in the other woman's tone. She appeared frustrated and on edge, but not angry. Skye shot a quick look at Jack, who merely nodded at her.

"Well," Skye started, "last week was my birthday. When Daddy discovered he wouldn't be around to take me out to dinner, he promised me lunch at this new Thai restaurant we've both been meaning to try out."

She had no intention of revealing everything that had occurred, and she still didn't think she'd share her doubts about Garth, but Skye saw no harm in updating Katherine — and thus the Agency — on the basics of the last twenty-four hours. With almost an hour on their hands, going over her story would help pass the time.

Skye settled comfortably next to Jack, the warmth of his body pressed against the length of her own, and recapped the last day's excitement.

* * * *

"So you have no idea who Victor suspects is the mole?" Katherine spoke with clear scepticism.

Skye shrugged.

"I've explained how busy I've been lately. In great detail, I might add. When have I had time to interview people at the Agency?" Skye answered obliquely.

Skye studiously kept her gaze on the woman and didn't glance at Garth. A knock sounded at the door and instantly the tension level in the room skyrocketed. Skye immediately shoved a hand inside her handbag, her grip closing around the handle of the small lady's gun. Jack whipped his own gun out of his holster and turned his body to the side so he was shielding her from whoever was standing outside the door.

In other circumstances Skye would have been amused. A part of her brain sat back in awe at how a bit of tension and an unknown person outside the hotel room door instantly had her drawing a weapon that twenty-four hours ago she'd not even owned. A part of her wondered if her father would even recognise her when they had him back safely.

"Yes?" Garth called out, his body to the side of the door. Skye frowned and it took her a minute to work out why he wasn't standing behind the door itself, ready to open it. If someone with a shotgun—or a rocket launcher—waited on the other end and blasted through the door, Garth would remain relatively unscathed, standing to the side as he was.

The things she was learning on this adventure boggled Skye's mind.

"Garth, it's me man, Dave. Open up. I only have five minutes left of that timeline you gave me. If I'm late and it's your fault, I'm charging interest."

Garth's stance relaxed as he seemed to recognise either the tone or word choice of the other man. He opened the door and peered out cautiously, checking up and down the hallway to make sure his contact was alone.

A slender, scrawny young man with a mop of brown hair entered the room, a satchel-like bag slung across his chest. Skye watched as he took a quick measure of the room before heading over to the coffee table. A swift motion had the strap of his satchel lifting above his head and his bag landing on the wooden table with a thump. Dave opened his bag and began to remove electronic devices efficiently.

"You said you were in a rush?" he commented without looking at any of them. Garth had closed the door and had come closer to them. He nodded at Skye. She removed the hard drive from her backpack, stood up and deposited it in front of Dave.

"We need it to be functional enough to placate another group of people," she reminded the tech. "They seem to know what's on it and logic dictates they should be able to access the data on here to verify it's legitimate. Having said that, the more complicated you make the encryption, the longer they have to spend to interpret the data, the better it will be for us. Will that be a problem?"

"Trust me, curls, this is child's play for me. I can do this in my sleep."

Satisfied, Skye returned to sit next to Jack on the couch and watched Dave with interest. The young man had pulled out a bunch of sleek, metallic devices she couldn't begin to guess the uses of. Some looked like cylinders, others small adapters and box-like shiny probes, with pins to attach them to other things.

It was a cylindrical metal box Dave picked up from his pile. It was roughly the size of a ballpoint pen. Opening it, he carefully removed a tiny metal ring about the size of a fingertip. In one hand he lifted the hard drive and peered intently at the output plugs. Nodding, seeming happy, Dave replaced the hard drive on the table.

He dug once more into his satchel and withdrew two cords, one with a USB connection, the other a power cord. He carefully inserted both into the hard drive, satisfied when they connected perfectly.

"Okay," he began to speak in a quick tone as his hands remained busy. A pair of pliers appeared from nowhere and he began to remove the plastic outer casing of the USB connection with a delicate efficiency Skye found mesmerising.

"This little beauty is next gen. I know you only ever want the best, Garth, and, trust me, when you see my bill for having lifted it, you're going to weep. It's a combination tracker-encryptor and will blow your Agency techs' minds when you explain what I'm doing here."

As Dave spoke he stripped a section of the plastic casing from the cord and attached the small ring around the outside of the wires. Squeezing the ring tightly closed he used his other hand to dig in his satchel again and remove a tiny tube of adhesive glue. With quick motions he fit the removed plastic casing back around the wires and started to repair the damage with the clear liquid paste.

"The fibre optics in that baby will network with the connecting wires in the USB cord. They should be untraceable. As your goons download from the hard drive the ring will encrypt the data so everything they download will take them days, if not weeks, to unlock."

Skye watched, amazed, as the scene unfolded before her eyes. She could hardly believe something so small, so simple, would create such havoc.

"How does it act as a tracking device?" Katherine asked. She didn't sound convinced to Skye. "Garth insisted it be passive. Any fool with a brain cell in their head would sweep the living hell out of the hard drive for explosives and tracking devices. That's useless to us if they discover it before we get what we need from them."

Dave lifted his head and glared at the agent, not amused in the least.

"I'm not a novice here. I understood Garth perfectly when we spoke earlier. The ring is passive when it isn't plugged into a power outlet. As long as your goons check it by itself you're fine. Even when it's connected to a computer or power source — which I imagine they won't risk doing in your presence — it simply sends out a small signal over a specific frequency. It would be almost impossible for them to detect it."

Katherine nodded curtly but didn't speak further.

Dave sighed and shook his head.

"As long as you monitor the frequency I'll give you, it should be a simple matter for you to hone in on its output. But, since you specified it had to be passive, you'll only be able to do so while the hard drive is connected and being powered. It's a delicate balance between keeping something subtle enough so the bad guys can't detect it and active enough for you to trace. It's the best I can do and I believe it's a damn sight better than anyone else on your tech team could come up with at such short notice."

Skye stirred from her place on the couch as Dave finished reattaching the plastic casing and checked the integrity of the device he'd just implanted for them.

"I appreciate your help," she remarked. "Especially considering we gave you no notice. I have to admit I'm impressed."

Dave glanced at her then cast a wary glance at Jack. The young man grinned and shrugged his shoulder casually, accepting her thanks.

"You're either new, or not Agency," he commented wryly. "This is easy, nothing really. This time out in Tanzania, Garth and I were stranded in one of this group's underground refugee camps. We had nothing but an old crystal radio set and an electric toothbrush I'd managed to salvage. We hooked it up to a —"

"I really don't think Skye needs to hear our old war stories," Garth insisted, as Katherine shot him an evil glare. "Come on, I'll walk you to the lift. You've really come through for us, Dave. I owe you man."

Dave raked a hand through his hair and collected his gear, shovelling it back into his satchel. He grinned and winked at Skye, who struggled not to laugh. The man was incorrigible. Skye had the random thought that he'd started to tell the story purely to push Garth's buttons. She couldn't help but like the vivacious man.

"Been a pleasure, as always," Dave insisted with a wicked grin. He cheerily threw a mock salute to Katherine and Tarek, waved to Jack and Skye and left the room, Garth trailing him and pulling out his wallet as the door closed behind them. Skye took a deep breath and moved to the coffee table, lifting the small hard drive into her hand and examining the work Dave had so simply done. Under close observation she could see the tiny marks where the plastic casing had been cut away and re-glued, but it simply looked as if something had dinted the plastic, not as if it had been tampered with.

Besides, who looked at a USB cord in such detail? Skye felt certain it would pass any scrutiny her father's kidnappers gave it. She could hardly believe the time was almost here to meet their enemy and continue with the exchange. Butterflies twisted nervously in her stomach. With a quick glance to Katherine and Tarek, Skye picked up her backpack and placed the hard drive into the bottom of her bag again.

"I think we should take that," Katherine insisted. Skye shook her head.

"Not a chance. My father's captors expect Jack and I at the scene. This is my responsibility. You, your partner and Garth are only along for the ride."

The door beeped as Garth used his key card to let himself back into the room.

Katherine threw him an exasperated glance.

"Garth, please tell Miss Adams that we should be doing the exchange and not her. This is not a matter for a civilian to get messed up in. This should—"

"Civilian!" Skye repeated, outraged. "I'll have you know, Miss…whatever the hell your name is, that we two civilians not only discovered where my father hid this damn hard drive, but we are his only hope at being exchanged. You and your bloody Agency so far as I can see have not even lifted a finger in attempting his return. No wonder Dad doesn't trust any of you as far as he could toss you. You've got leaks all over the place, a mole selling you all out to the highest bidder and a threat to national security. Not to mention—"

"That's enough!" Tarek shouted. His outburst was so far out of her experience of him thus far that his interjection succeeded in halting her tirade. He smiled at her, seeming pleased by her compliance.

"We're agreed that there are a few, erm, minor issues back at headquarters just now, but that doesn't mean we're playing for different teams. Protecting Queen and country is what we are all still trying to do, albeit in our own ways. Let's keep that in mind," he reminded them all.

Skye deflated, her outrage washed away, and she nodded.

"I think Skye and I should lead the exchange." Jack broke the silence lying thick in the air of the room. "It's what they will be expecting and shouldn't make anyone trigger happy. They will likely also assume we will have backup. The park is large so you should all be able to maintain at least a few hundred metres' distance away from us to be backup, but not make anyone shoot us for double crossing them."

"The exchange is happening in a park?" Garth replied, surprised.

Jack nodded.

"One of the old duelling fields. Since they will be bringing Victor with them, I think it's a safe bet there will be at least four or five of them, possibly more. Us bringing you three might not make them happy, but should not be too far over the line."

"Considering they brought a rocket launcher to their initial attempt to obtain Skye and this damn hard drive, I think it's a safe bet that, unless we had half the Armed Forces with us, they'd still out-power us weapons wise," Katherine said, seeming to capitulate to their plan.

"Can we at least use our transport?" she asked wryly. "The body of the car is armoured and the windows are tinted."

Skye turned to Jack and caught his grin. Her lover nodded his assent.

"Sounds like a plan. Shall we move on out? The last thing we need is to get stuck in traffic and lose this chance."

Katherine, Tarek and Garth turned towards the door. Jack and Skye stood up and faced each other for a moment.

"You okay?" he murmured so the others couldn't overhear easily. She moved into his arms, enjoying the warmth and solid security in his embrace. She lifted up on to her tiptoes and whispered in his ear.

"I've got nerves in my stomach. I'm scared they're stringing us along and have already killed my dad. Otherwise the adrenaline seems to be kicking in and I'm fine. You?"

Jack kissed her tenderly. The press of his lips on hers sent electric passion coursing madly through her blood. Her body heated, her nipples peaked and for a moment she longed to forget their audience, forget their mission and pretend nothing at all was wrong in her world. His tongue flicked out and stroked inside her mouth. She longed to drag Jack to the bedroom, to test out a real-life, honest-to-goodness Four Seasons bed and have her wicked way with her man.

For a heartbeat she could see it—stripping him naked, bending on her knees in front of him and sucking his thick cock down her throat. He'd clench his hands in her hair, fuck her deeply and spill his hot seed down into her belly.

She'd lick every ounce he gave her and still beg for more.

But this wasn't the time or place. Reluctantly, Skye pulled away from the intimate kiss and glanced towards the door. Katherine turned in the door frame to raise her eyebrows at them, the silent, 'Are you coming?' as vivid in her look as if she'd spoken the words aloud. Skye pressed herself against Jack and tried to absorb his strength into her body.

"Love you," she whispered into his ear.

"I love you, too," he murmured back before they let each other go.

Silently, they followed the agents out the door and down into the street. They had a mission to perform and Skye didn't want to compromise that.

Chapter Eight

Skye straightened her spine as she walked across the isolated park. Grass blew in the gentle breeze – the sun shone warmly down. The gorgeous weather proclaimed that summer was only around the corner. The sky appeared endless, blue and calm, but Skye couldn't find it within herself to relish the rare beauty of the day. Jack kept pace beside her, his shoulder barely touching her own.

Had they been in almost any other circumstances it would have been the perfect setting.

The three armed men keeping guard around a black car with darkly tinted windows managed to keep the sickening twisting of her stomach rolling dangerously around, shattering her nerves.

'Even if you don't feel it, portraying confidence and not letting your enemies know how badly they've hurt you is always the most important aspect of battle, sweetheart', her father had whispered in her ear. 'Never show your nemesis how greatly they affect you. That simply hands them another weapon. If you portray an in-control attitude then you hold an edge over them'.

Her father's advice had worked all those years ago back in school against the bullies he had been counselling her about. Skye knew the advice still rang true today. She lifted her head, tilted her chin to a stubborn angle and straightened her back as if she were walking into a battle.

With some effort she managed to push down all her fear, her heart-wrenching concern for her father's safety and even the doubts that crowded her mind, the worry something horrible was about to go wrong and destroy her entire world.

At her insistence they had left Garth, Katherine and Tarek with the car on the other side of the park. Jack and she had decided to walk into the middle of the clearing and wait, forcing their enemies to meet them halfway.

"What if they won't budge? Will we lose face if we end up having to walk all the way over to them? Do you think they have my father in their car?" Nerves had Skye almost babbling, questions overwhelming her mind. The action of walking at least helped give her some form of release. In one hand she carried the small black box, clearly visible to their enemies as a sign of good faith.

Her free hand strayed to the small of her back, where hidden in the waistband of her jeans and under her sweater sat the small lady's gun. Determination raced through her blood. Skye knew without a shadow of a doubt that she would shoot to kill if the need came. She wanted her dad back. Whole. Safe. If that meant she had to shoot these evil bastards, even if she had to end up killing some of them, that was a price she was willing to pay.

"We hold something they need," Jack replied calmly, his warrior's mask firmly in place. Skye nodded, struggled to mimic the cool demeanour he portrayed. She recalled her father's face, how he could look in control no matter what the circumstances. She schooled her features carefully and lifted her head higher, determined not to show even the smallest hint of the fear that coursed through her body.

"They have Victor, true, but this is an exchange. Both parties are vulnerable and need to meet halfway. While we won't push them on something so small, exerting this level of control merely evens the playing field for us both."

Jack stopped speaking as they both came to a halt dead centre of the park. Katherine had not been pleased with their decision to leave the three agents behind, but as their enemies' men stood outside his car, guarding them but making no move to become further involved in their exchange, Skye had been adamant. Finally she had pointed out that if Katherine, Tarek and Garth joined them then their guards would follow, and there would be far too many people in a knot for a simple exchange. The situation would be incredibly fluid — things happen in the space of a heartbeat. Some of them could die.

"If your stubborn need to be a part of this costs my father his life I won't rest until every branch of the Agency and even your government competition knows of your arrogant fuck-up," she had shouted at Katherine, her patience at an end. "I don't care if I need to organise an interview with the Queen herself, I will make it my life's mission. This is my father and my operation right now. Am I being clear enough?"

Katherine had given her the evil eye, but nodded stiffly. A part of Skye felt bad for her over-reaction.

Katherine was the professional here, and if Skye was being honest she'd dealt rather well with 'a civilian' stomping all over the mission. Skye just found the safety and protection of her dad was a hot button and she would not let anything mess with that. Not even a professional agent.

Skye resisted the impulse to fidget, refusing to give in to the urge and show their enemies just how ill at ease she felt. Jack remained by her side, his gun in hand, though lowered and pointing to the ground. She held the hard drive in her hands, clearly in view but just comfortably in front of her, not on show.

The seconds dragged by endlessly. It took every ounce of her patience and strength to not jiggle, pace or move more than strictly necessary.

"This isn't going to work," she murmured, though everyone was far enough away so that even if they had they spoken normally no one would've been able to hear a word. "They aren't going to come meet us. We have to go to them. Oh, Lord, have mercy. What if they don't have my dad here? What if this is a trick or a setup? I shouldn't have trusted Garth. He must be involved. What if they just shoot us here and now and come take the hard drive? Who will rescue my father? We need to—"

"Skye Adams, stop that right now," Jack whispered firmly. "I can see movement inside the car. Look. Someone is climbing out. Take a breath. This will work. You'll see."

Skye's head whipped around to watch the car and sure enough Jack spoke the truth. The back door opened and one of the guards stood protectively at the side and raised his gun defensively. At first she couldn't see more than the shadow of a man climbing out of the rear seat. When he stood, she gasped.

Tall with midnight-black hair, the muscled man filled out his black suit and jacket powerfully. When he turned, Skye caught a glimpse of a neatly trimmed beard and confusion flooded her. Superficially, he resembled Garth, and she could understand how from only a split-second glance she had mistaken the two and been so uncertain. This man, however, had a good twenty if not thirty years of age over the young man. Relief flooded her mind, followed quickly by the sharp sting of guilt for not trusting her father's protégé.

From such a distance she couldn't hear the words the dark-haired man spoke, but clearly he was giving orders to his men. After a moment he slammed the car door closed and began to stalk across the grass, evidently meeting them halfway. One of the men followed, his sub-machine gun held ready and with what to Skye's eyes looked like a professional stance.

She eyed the weapon warily, suddenly feeling extremely under-protected and out-classed.

"I don't recall seeing any Uzis or the like in your gun safe." She tried to lighten the ambiance with a half-hearted joke. "You call yourself a professional?"

"I'll buy you one as a belated birthday gift—or for our first anniversary if you wish," Jack promised solemnly. "Victor and I can teach you how to use it properly. Right now you're as likely to shoot yourself with something that powerful."

Skye nodded and conceded the point. Jack was right, though her mind lingered hungrily on the promise of a first year anniversary.

"I'd rather travel or get a nice house for our first wedding anniversary," she replied. "So it will need to be a belated birthday present, if that's okay with you."

"It's a deal, though you can break it to Victor. I got the strong impression he's a lot more protective of you than you've ever realised. I'm not sure how he'll feel knowing I plan to give you weapons as well as take you off his hands and marry you once this mess is dealt with."

Skye laughed and threw Jack a delighted look. For a moment everything faded into the background and she simply stared at the man she had come to love more than life itself. He met her gaze warmly, love shining in his electric blue eyes. Skye had to remind herself she couldn't lean over and kiss him right now.

This really was the wrong moment for such thoughts, but at the same time it had all fallen into place so perfectly she knew she'd never regret a single thing the last few days had brought her. Not the pleasure and not the pain, either.

Jack broke their contact and she watched the suit-clad man halt a dozen or so metres away from them.

"I'm Jennings. You must be Skye Adams," he said. Skye recognised his voice from their earlier phone conversation. "You look a lot like Victor. The resemblance is strong. In many ways, I gather. I don't know many women who would be exchanging top secret government data for their father and still be able to laugh with such delight at something their companion had just said. I could use someone like you. I don't suppose you're in the market for a job? You'll learn I pay quite well."

Skye shook her head.

"I'm already spoken for, but I'm willing to continue with our deal. No," she added hastily with a raised hand as the bodyguard with the Uzi began to take a step forward. He halted the instant she raised her hand. "Not until I see my father. You can see the hard drive—I've been up front about that. I want you to bring my father out here and stand him with you."

"This isn't how things are done," Jennings insisted, his tone dangerous. Skye nodded. Even though her stomach was twisting in fear, she refused to let any of it show on her face.

"You know I'm not with the Agency. Think of me as a freelancer. I don't mean to be insulting, I promise. But neither am I stupid. Have one of your guards bring my father out here and stand him with you. I'll give you the hard drive—you can test it right here and we can complete the exchange."

"You know," he mused, "I really could do with someone like you in my company. Are you sure you're not interested? Nerves of steel, just like Victor. You'd be astonished how rare it is."

Not waiting for her to reply, he turned around and made a hand signal to the two guards still out by his car.

Skye was torn. Either they were all about to die in the next few seconds, or her bluff had worked and he was about to bring her father out. Tension mounted inside her and she almost passed out from the stress of waiting those last few seconds.

The back seat door on the other side was opened by one of the armed guards. Roughly he leaned into the car and dragged a bound man out.

"Daddy!" she cried out, the word heartfelt and instinctive. In that second she could not have pretended to be the cool, collected agent any more than she could have spread her arms, grown wings and flown to the other side of the park.

Her gaze drank in the sight of her father and her voice shook with emotion.

"What the fuck have you done to him?" Her eyes burned with anger and the fierce need to kill this evil man.

He shrugged, an amused grin on his face as he didn't bother to reply, the answer evident on her father's battered, blood encrusted face.

Jack's hand fell on her shoulder and Skye sucked in a breath and tried to compose herself.

"He's fine," Jack murmured so softly she had to strain to hear him. His voice soothed her as little else could. Her gaze soaked up the heart-wrenching sight of her father.

"Look at how Victor can walk," Jack continued, the soft monologue obviously meant to calm and distract her so she could get her boiling emotions under control once again. "He's limping, yes, but he can walk. All his fingers are intact, though the strapping means a few are broken, but bones mend, they are all attached, as are his other limbs. His shoulder is broken, probably the collarbone, considering the way his bound hands are linked to support it at one elbow. His face is beaten badly, but the dried and fresh blood makes it look far worse. See how the bruising around his eyes is dark black-purple? That means he's been spared long enough to begin to heal. Chances are once they called us they've left him be since then."

Skye breathed heavily, her chest heaving as she struggled to contain herself. Her father looked as if he had been badly battered in a pub brawl to end all brawls. But Jack spoke the truth. Her dad was bruised, beaten, hurt, but not broken. Neither had they truly done irreversible, permanent damage to him. Skye figured they had been leaving that as a last resort and quickly pushed the thought aside.

She didn't care if she had to kill every one of their enemies here, she was not leaving without her father. He could walk and so she knew he could escape. She refused to even acknowledge there was an alternative ending to this scenario.

As her father and his captor halted a good dozen or more paces behind their nemesis, the bearded man held out his hands as if to prove what a good, friendly guy he really was.

"I know he's not pretty to look at right now, but trust me when I say we've treated him astonishingly well, little Skye. Now, you said I could test my hard drive? If you please?"

Skye ground her teeth together, refusing to rise to the bait and snap back at him. She longed to shoot Jennings just for the hell of it, his reference to how much worse it could have been for her father no comfort at all. She caught her dad's glance and held it. One eye was swollen fully shut, thin tape held together two bad splits in his face, one on his cheek, the other on the edge of his mouth where it looked like he'd been severely pistol-whipped.

Regardless, his light brown eyes met hers. Even considering the immense pain he must be in, she could swear he was actually trying to reassure her with his gaze. It took everything in her to push down the molten hot hatred she felt for the abuse he'd suffered. Pouring as much love as possible into her eyes, she tried to silently explain to her dad how very much she loved him. She smiled tremulously, as best she could, given the situation.

Breaking her gaze away before she started to bawl like a baby and ruined the image she'd worked so hard to portray, she straightened her spine, injected as much pride into her bearing and walk as possible, and stalked over to the man, the box held out in her hand.

Jennings took a few paces forward and met her, grasping the hard drive with an eager greed. Pulling a hand-sized PDA out of his inner jacket pocket, he plugged the USB cord in and powered the device up. Skye tilted her head and saw the screen light up as it read the various folders on the hard drive. The man flicked through the folders, seeming satisfied with their names — which looked to be in a form of code to her, letters strung together, not making coherent words, like LRFEAGDT3d4.

After a second he powered down his PDA and nodded, satisfied. Skye breathed easier. She'd been worried he'd try to download or open the individual files, not just be satisfied by seeing the data there in the folders. That would have made the encryption programme kick in and things could have got dicey.

"Now here's just one more, small thing," Jennings explained.

Skye frowned, thinking it really had been too easy up until now.

"I need to know none of you will impede my retreat, follow me or try to nuke my car on the way out. So Tennent and Dixon here are going to remain with you and guarantee I make my extraction connection. I do hope that won't be an issue?"

Skye took a step to the side, ensuring she had a clear view of her father and the guard whom the man had indicated as Tennent, who still held his unbroken shoulder. A glance at Jack showed his gun now was trained on Dixon, while the final guard stood protectively in front of Jennings, clearly willing to shoot them to ensure his retreat.

"You have the hard drive and, if Tennent lets go of his shoulder, we will have my father," Skye tried to stall. "Why don't you let him go instead of making this more dangerous and complicated?"

"Ah, my dear, while I think it might be that simple for you, things rarely are so when the masculine ego is involved. And just for the record, nothing is ever simple when Victor is in the mix."

As he spoke he slowly retreated without turning his back to them. Obviously, even with his personal guard, he didn't trust them a bit. Skye could grudgingly understand. Jennings continued to move and watch them both warily as he did so. Step by step, Skye came closer to her father until Tennant lifted his machine gun level on to her.

"No closer," he snapped as she was just a bit more than an arm's length away. A shout from the edge of the park split through the air and all hell broke loose with a roar. The guard who had remained back with the car had shouted, lifted his gun and started to shoot. Jack and her father dived for the grass, as did Dixon. Skye, untrained enough that ducking for cover was not as instinctive, instead pulled her gun out and aimed it at Tennent.

They were all literally caught in the crossfire, out in the open. Skye didn't like their chances and with her father's hands restrained it was still two against two, and their enemies could all too easily overpower them or re-kidnap her dad.

Time stood still for a moment as she weighed the decision that burned through her. They could all too easily be killed, here and now. For the first time ever, her dad couldn't protect her. She needed to defend him. Skye hesitated for a heartbeat, but, as gunshots rang out again, she forced herself to act. She aimed for the upper shoulder and shot Tennent, the short distance making her aim true.

Blood welled in his shoulder. He dropped his gun to the grass and fell like a downed tree.

"Skye! No! Damn it, get down!" her father shouted at her, clearly wild with worry.

Skye fell to her stomach. She lifted her head and could see Jennings crouched but racing for the car, his guard laying down covering fire. Shots came from behind Skye and Jack, Garth, Katherine and Tarek evidently getting in on the action. Skye crawled towards her dad, her body shaking with delayed reaction to everything that had happened.

"He's got keys in his left-hand pocket and you'd better tie something around that wound or he'll bleed out and be of no use to us." Her dad spoke with astonishing calm. The car's engine revved and tyres squealed as it peeled out of the park. Skye looked up just in time to see Jack punch Dixon out. The man fell to the ground, unconscious.

"Good to see you, Victor. You look like shit," Jack said with a grin as he moved to Tennent. Jack ripped the fallen man's shirt, bunched it up into a tight wad and pressed it down hard on his wound to stem the bleeding. The man grunted but she saw Jack just exert more pressure, not fussed by how much it might hurt. Skye dug the keys out of his pocket.

"I'm doing fine. Germany was a bit of a bust, though. I was annoyed to miss Skye's birthday. How was the Thai, sweetheart?"

Skye levelled an admonishing glare at him.

"These goons turned up and destroyed it. I've never seen a rocket launcher before. You have the most unsavoury friends, Dad, I have to say."

"Rocket launcher?" Victor repeated. His shock only lasted a second, quickly replaced with wry amusement. "I miss all the good parties. Well, sweetheart, you can't say I never show you a good time."

Skye shook her head, caught somewhere between laughter and tears.

"I missed that one," Jack replied as Skye found the key and unlocked the handcuffs around Victor's wrists. Jack assisted Victor to his feet, the gunshots having ceased when Jennings had made his escape.

"Of course, I got to personally witness the flamethrower out front of Tank's. I think that almost makes up for it. That was a party you'll be ashamed to have missed."

Victor grunted, his shoulder paining him as he stood.

Katherine and Garth raced up to them, guns drawn and cuffs out. Garth cast a fleeting glance at Victor, surmised he was fine for now and crouched to restrain Dixon and Tennent. Katherine appeared shaken, the thin set to her lips showing something had seriously upset her. Skye looked behind them but couldn't see Tarek.

"Is Tarek bringing the car around?" she asked, puzzled and not understanding why Katherine looked as if she were barely holding herself together. The agent shook her head.

"No, those assholes got him. I don't think they even meant to. They were shooting as a distraction, to assist in that bastard's escape. One of the bullets ricocheted off the side of the car and caught him in the side of his neck. We've stopped the bleeding, but he's unconscious. Backup should be here with the paramedics any minute now."

A stunned silence greeted this announcement.

"I'm so sorry," Skye replied in a small voice, feeling awful. Katherine nodded, but managed to hold herself together, though her gaze flitted around, unable to rest on anything for very long. With a curt nod to Victor, she bent down and helped Garth pick up the wounded Tennent. Without a word they both carried him back to the car.

Jack wrapped an arm around Skye and she buried her head in his shoulder. They held each other tightly, fiercely for a moment, unwilling to relinquish one another.

"Told you it would be okay," he mumbled against the top of her head. Skye chuckled and nodded.

"It's all still a bit surreal."

"It will be for a while," Jack informed her gently. They kissed, a soft, fleeting press of lips on lips. Skye's eyes fluttered and she flicked her tongue out to taste his mouth. He drew her back again, sucking her tongue into his mouth and they kissed more deeply, a promise of what would come later.

With evident reluctance, Jack pulled away and drew out his phone.

"I'll call for backup — we won't all fit in the car and I want to take Victor to a medic I know. You fine with seeing Evans?" Jack asked with a glance to her dad. Skye flushed, a little embarrassed to realise the show they must have just unwittingly given him. He didn't appear fazed in the least.

"Evan's is good," Victor replied, "but I'll be right for a while. Make sure the backup get here for Tarek, Katherine and Garth first. The Agency will want to question the two guards, even though Jennings will be long gone from where they all held me."

Jack nodded and moved away to make the calls. Skye wrapped her arms around her father's waist and he hugged her tightly with his good arm. Despite the fact that she wanted to cling to him like she was six again, she carefully made sure she didn't jostle his bad shoulder or hurt him. He sucked in a deep breath, winced and indicated his ribs.

"Got a few broken, but damn that felt good, sweetheart. I'm so sorry you got dragged into this."

Skye shook her head and pressed a featherlight kiss to his cheek.

"No, don't be, Dad. I'd do it all again in a heartbeat. I know sooner or later the Agency would have found you, but I could see you weren't their first priority and I couldn't bear to sit back and do nothing. Besides, it led me to Jack. I love him, Dad. We're going to get married down the track a little."

Victor chuckled and shook his head.

"He got my postcard, I assume?"

"Oh, no, we found that later. After I escaped from Garth, Tarek and Katherine at the Thai restaurant, I didn't know where to turn. I'd kept Jack's card that you gave me. I called him. The rest just fell into place."

"Fell into place?" Victor laughed. "Sweetheart, you two were made for each other. I've been working on a plan to bring you together for the last six months. I was going to instigate it as your birthday present after lunch. This wasn't quite what I had in mind, but, broken bones and battered pride aside, it still seems to have worked out wonderfully."

Skye just stared at her father, amazed. She shook her head, not sure she even wanted to question it further.

"We've bought a little time for the Agency," she explained as Jack came back, his gun back in its holster and his phone in his pocket. "When they plug the hard drive in to download it there's an encryption programme on it. Hopefully the Agency can track it from there."

"The Agency have a car nearby," Jack continued. "We'll have one hell of a debrief to go through, but they shouldn't be too upset when all is said and done."

Skye frowned, stared at her father thoughtfully.

"I think we should commandeer the car," she suggested. "If we can get Dad some medical attention first, Garth and Katherine can give them the big picture. Then we can fill in the blanks once we know Dad's going to be all right."

Jack stared at her thoughtfully, then turned to tilt his head at Victor. He nodded and they set off towards the car. Jack hurried ahead to explain their plan to Katherine and Garth, who were soon nodding. Skye helped Victor settle into the back seat. He sighed once he was finally as comfortable as he could be.

"I knew you and Jack would make a great team," Victor said faintly. His words were slightly slurred from exhaustion and pain. Skye took his hand and squeezed it gently.

"It's okay, Dad, we can talk later. We have the rest of our lives for that."

"I want you to know how very proud of you I am," he insisted. Skye felt tears leak from her eyes as emotion overwhelmed her. "You've always been such a precious little girl to me, sweetheart. But you've grown into the strongest, most capable woman I could have dreamed of. I love you, Skye. I'm glad you and Jack have found each other, even without my help."

Skye sniffed and dashed a finger under her eyes to collect the tears falling down her cheeks.

"I love you too, Dad. You're going to be fine. We'll take care of you now."

Victor sighed and fell into an uneasy doze. Jack climbed into the driving seat and had a double take when he saw Skye was crying. His gaze flickered to Victor and fear crossed his features. Skye shook her head and touched his shoulder with her free hand.

"No, no, he's just passed out—he's exhausted. I think he must have been holding out until he was safe and now it's just got too much for him. He's fine. Let's go, love."

Jack nodded and pressed a kiss to her fingers. She traced his lips as he started the engine, but then he turned around to drive. Skye shook gently as the adrenaline continued to course through her body.

It had been one hell of a morning, but against all the odds she was not only safe, but her dad sat beside her, safe and mostly whole. Skye trembled but held on, not willing to let everything go until she was sure things were under control.

* * * *

Skye leaned heavily against Jack's strength. His arms were wrapped tightly around her and their bodies fit together as if they had been created precisely for this purpose. Contentment surged through her and Skye never wanted to move ever again. They stood in the doorway of a small room, the thin cot bed comfortable enough that her father slept peacefully on it, dosed to the gills on morphine.

Iodine had been lathered over his cuts, a few stitches neatly closing his wounds, his shoulder taped and bound firmly. It had been Skye who'd cringed at the antibiotic shot he'd been given, Victor barely flinching at the painful procedure. By the time Susan Evans had handed Victor a couple of morphine pills with a glass of water, he'd taken them without blinking his eyes and practically passed out before they could lie him down.

Skye had covered her father with a couple of blankets, kissed his cheek tenderly and now they watched him to make sure bad dreams didn't mar his rest. Satisfied, Skye turned to her lover and partner and wrapped her arms enticingly around his neck. They shared a deep, hungry kiss, their passion barely restrained.

"Do you really think the Agency will notice if we disappear for a while and celebrate ourselves before coming in to give our reports?" she asked.

Jack chuckled and nipped her lips gently.

"They've probably already got both our flats staked out to make sure we don't do exactly that. Hell, it wouldn't surprise me to know they have a few agents outside Susan's with orders to frogmarch us back to base the instant we leave here."

"Hmm, then maybe we should find our own cot bed and hole up here?" she teased. Instead of responding, Jack kissed her again, stealing her breath. She reached out and caressed him through his clothes, itching to feel his naked skin. With a groan Jack pulled back and took her hands in his.

"You are the most enticing distraction I have ever come across, darling. Promise me you'll keep me up all night once we've squared things away with the Agency."

Skye huffed, more in mock anger than genuine pique. She knew they had to go, she just didn't like it. Blowing a curl out of her eyes, her gaze fluttered as

Jack twisted one spiral around his finger and tugged it gently.

"Okay, okay," she grizzled. With a puff of laughter she stole one last kiss.

"Dad said he was going to set us up." She changed the subject with a wicked glint in her gaze. "He said he'd made this whole convoluted plan and was going to set it in motion yesterday morning for my birthday. You were worried about nothing—he's pleased we've found each other."

Jack raised his eyebrows. He appeared both pleased and surprised.

"Really? Well then, maybe we can organise something quick." Skye laughed and shook her head.

"Not a chance. I plan to enjoy every moment I can with you, though I do get all weak in the knees thinking about spending forever by your side. We make a good team, don't we?"

"The very best," he murmured. Their lips found each other again and heat seared through her body. Satisfied beyond her wildest dreams, Skye gave herself up to the passionate feelings Jack brought out in her.

Happy beyond measure, she kissed him in return, this man who held her heart. Never would she have guessed how such a disastrous lunch could lead her to the man she would spend the rest of her life with.

Skye kissed Jack as if he were the elixir of life. And, for her, he was.

COURTING
PASSION

Prologue

Katherine Hitchens knew she'd been acting like a ball-busting bitch, but she couldn't bring herself to change her attitude. At heart she was a rule follower, a by-the-book shining example of what a product of the Agency could be. She hated how the rogue, cowboy-like antics of agents such as Garth Spenser put others' lives at risk.

Now Garth Spenser was in deep water. His mentor and partner, Victor Adams, had been kidnapped and was likely dead. The equivalent of a terrorist's Rolodex and lifetime's collection of blackmail material was missing.

Anyone who possessed this intelligence held untold power over countless judges, politicians, barons, lords and heaven knew who else. As if that wasn't enough, they now held an unimaginable source of contacts. There were details for underworld figures, protocols for getting in touch with everyone who could supply any need or desire—no matter how reprehensible.

And this was only what they knew was in there. All sorts of other possibilities could be laid out in intricate detail.

To their knowledge the bad guys now had it all.

Blasé, fly-by-the-seat-of-their-pants agents such as Garth might make the impossible a reality once in a while. But without the maturity and seasoning long-term work gave — the sort of experience Victor used to keep his own inherent cowboy tendencies in check — disasters such as those they were facing now were almost a certainty.

Katherine knew the other agents looked askance at her. That they whispered that she was too rigid, too by the book. She'd even heard tales behind her back that she didn't have the adaptability a real agent required. Right bloody now she wanted to wave Garth Spenser in front of all those naysayers. He remained solid proof as to what happened to those with a cavalier attitude.

Not fame, glory and respect for Queen and country. No. Gung-ho, wildly wicked agents such as Garth always ended somewhere in the shit.

With a kidnapped, tortured and probably dead partner. With a missing piece of intelligence so priceless it could mean anarchy and the death of the world as they knew it, should the wrong people wield its power.

And now she and her partner Tarek had finally brought Garth in to be questioned about his knowledge. They'd found him making contact with Victor's daughter at a local Thai restaurant. Once again, when Garth was involved in the simple pick-up and retrieval of a presumed rogue agent, things had gone straight to hell.

They'd been fired upon by unknown assailants.

Before she and Tarek could get control of the situation, Garth had shouted at them to evacuate. They'd barely made it away with their lives. A rocket launcher had decimated the restaurant. The formerly beautiful, old-style building was now nothing more than a smoking mess of dust and broken bricks.

Katherine didn't even want to think about the paperwork. She had a headache just imagining what her summary report to their team leader would be like in a few hours, once word from the street hit the manager's desk.

Tarek leaned against one wall, his muscled body full of barely repressed power, his sandy hair clipped military short. His gaze caught hers and he tilted his head a tiny bit, giving her the silent go-ahead to start their questioning. Garth sat behind the thin aluminium table, cool as you please.

Katherine knew he'd had a chance to speak with Skye Adams, Victor's daughter, though she didn't understand why he'd sought the girl out. She wasn't an agent, wasn't field trained and, to Katherine's knowledge, didn't have a clue about what was happening.

Part of Katherine assumed Garth wanted to warn Skye of the potential danger. Victor's love for his daughter was common knowledge. If Garth was optimistic and felt his partner had a chance of survival it made sense he'd protect Skye to the best of his abilities.

Garth lounged in his seat. No tension showed in his languid pose, his black gaze was calm and the epitome of cool. His short, dark hair spiked up from his scalp. A thin, neatly trimmed beard covered his jaw and chin. Dressed in his standard black slacks and black button-down shirt he looked as if he should be working for the opposition, a black hat and he'd be every movie-goer's dream bad boy.

Katherine wasn't certain that Garth didn't play fast and loose with those who worked against them. While she didn't feel he was a traitor literally, she'd known men like him who would use both sides against each other for their own, personal means.

She let her thoughts wander as the silence drew out. Every agent was trained to withstand questioning, to understand the interrogation process. It made situations like this difficult, if not impossible. Add Garth's ego, and Katherine knew she had her work cut out for her.

She tried to keep all emotion out of her eyes and resisted the impulse to check that every hair of her chignon remained in place. She knew she could break him, get Garth to tell her the truth of what really was going on under the surface of Victor Adams' disappearance and the ruinous mess of the Thai restaurant. It was just a matter of using the right method with this man.

Instead of dancing around the situation, she decided that the direct approach would be the best place to start. She sat primly down on the uncomfortable chair opposite Garth, Tarek still guarding the door and acting as her spotter. She'd need to focus on the man in front of her. Tarek — as always — would guard her back.

"For now, I'm going to pretend that you didn't ignore Agency protocol and elude our custody. You're a big boy, Garth. You understand how running only makes you look more guilty. So, for the time being, we will act on the assumption that you had an urgent need to see Skye Adams, to inform her of her father's status as MIA and give her whatever protection you managed in the ten minutes you were alone in her company. Let's start this round of information gathering off on the right foot, okay?"

Katherine didn't expect Garth to speak or acknowledge her in any way and she wasn't disappointed. He stared at her with his hot, black gaze and didn't move a muscle. Katherine smiled and pushed the unfurling lust in her belly out of mind. No wonder women all over the world craved and fantasised about the bad boy, each and every time.

Sitting here, pinned by Garth's gaze, she could feel electric chemistry rise hotly between them. Garth dipped his eyes to her cleavage and she felt as if a laser beam had settled on her nipples. They pressed behind the crisp white linen of her low-cut, business shirt. Years of training and iron-hard restraint kept her from letting the flush of heat searing through her body being reflected on her face.

Her buxom curves had always been a problem in the Agency. Whenever they needed 'bait' in the form of a seductive woman, or a lusty wench to cause a distraction, she was always their first call. It wasn't her fault she had a rack that could grace the covers of *Penthouse* magazine. For years it had pissed her off. Katherine's body was considered more of an asset in the Agency than her brain or her numerous other skills.

Eventually she'd got over it. Instead of fighting for every inch of respect, she had used this need other agents had for her and worked it to her advantage. It didn't mean she didn't still feel the sting of being thought of as the 'bait' rather than an equal member of any team she joined.

Finally, after scrabbling for every case, she had been given command of a few smaller jobs. It wasn't a lot, but she was determined to work her way up, even if she had to claw herself there.

Annoyed now, Katherine's temper spiked. Crossing her arms over her chest, she snapped angrily as she lost some of her self-control.

"You realise we have witnesses," she said. The momentary loss of her cool angered her even more than Garth's lazy, and thorough, perusal of her breasts. Regardless, she ploughed on, the damage already done.

"There are witnesses from the airport. You were seen tailing Victor and making a call once he got into the cab," Katherine spoke far more calmly. "Initial reports from the destruction of the restaurant also put a tall, dark-haired, lightly bearded man in the alley behind where the attack was based from. Obviously, this was a few minutes before you joined Skye inside the restaurant, but we're slowly closing the net over you. So this is your one and only chance to not be facing certain death, Spenser. Explain to us why you've stolen the terrorists' intelligence and not handed it directly over to the Agency. Tell us where Victor is — and even more importantly — why you kidnapped him in the first place. Was it a ruse? Does Victor have proof you're dirty? Have you already killed him?"

Garth chuckled and shook his head as he crossed his arms over his chest. Anger flashed in his black eyes.

"You have got to be kidding me," he drawled as if they were discussing the latest statistics from his favourite football game. "Victor is my partner and, more importantly, my friend. Surely you know how hard it is to come by a genuine, bona fide friend in our industry. If we killed them off then we'd all be nutters — on a one-track path to the insane asylum. I haven't a bloody clue where your precious intelligence is. I was searching for it in tandem with Victor before word reached me he'd disappeared. I knew he'd made lunch plans with his daughter and needed to warn her."

Garth pressed his lips together and Katherine had the feeling he weighed every word before speaking again. She remained silent, one of the oldest tricks in the book. Garth seemed to recognise exactly what she was doing. A light of what she thought might be approval shone in his eyes for an instant before he hid that, too.

He seemed about to start speaking again a few times, drawing his breath in before he changed his mind and stayed silent. Finally his lips opened, then closed silently, until at last he started again.

"If you've asked even a few people, you know Victor's love for his daughter is near legendary. I've met the girl a few times, seen them interact together. Despite their evident and very mutual love, their relationship is rocky. Hell, what father-daughter dynamic isn't? But she loves him and he adores her."

Once again Garth stared at her. With a sigh he continued, as if he was explaining something very simple and she wasn't getting the point.

"If I knew Victor was in trouble and I hadn't tried to protect Skye, he would happily carve my heart from my chest. Aside from that, I'd be a poor friend if I didn't try to keep her safe, wouldn't I? If I refused to even try to safeguard his most cherished possession? No, Agent Hitchens, I have no idea where Victor is or where the Rolodex is and I haven't a clue who is behind this or why your so-called eyewitnesses claim to have seen me."

Katherine watched Garth's every nuance with unrelenting attention. She had to admit, either he was the best liar she had ever come across, or he was telling the truth. Irritation surged through her. She couldn't be wrong, she believed they'd found the mole they'd been searching out for weeks. The recollections of their witnesses—"a tall dark-haired man with a thin, clipped beard"—had all pointed to Garth, especially since he'd been known to be in the vicinity of both sightings.

But a man this arrogant, an agent this sure of himself would be giving out a different vibe had he been guilty. He'd be smug, self-satisfied, cocky. Garth radiated a high level of confidence, but he also seemed genuine, his answers honest and logical. It didn't jibe with him being the turncoat they sought.

She hoped her growing lust for the man was not clouding her senses or swaying her judgement.

Katherine leaned in closer, her hands flat on the cool table, tilting her face so it almost touched Garth's. She lowered her voice and murmured in what she hoped sounded like a firm, commanding tone and not the sultry, sexy whisper she longed to use instead.

"We're going to nail your ass to the wall. Betraying the Crown, directly causing the death of a fellow agent, fraudulent espionage, not to mention thievery and assisting acts of terrorism. Those are the charges I can list off the top of my head. I'm sure, with a bit of creative thinking and time, I can double that list. Make it easy, Spenser. Confess."

Garth mimicked her posture, pressing his hands onto the table, leaning his face in until mere millimetres separated them. She could feel the warmth of his breath caress her face and smell the spicy scent of his cologne. Need surged through her body. Her belly tightened and her nipples peaked anew, hard against the lace of her bra, which strained against her tight shirt.

"Check with the techs," Garth whispered back, a wicked light in his gaze. Katherine had the strong impression Garth's mind was full of very naughty ideas, which had nothing to do with her questioning of him.

The dark light in his eyes and the electric tension between them had her heart pounding. The image of what it would be like to kiss him seared through her brain. She lowered her eyes for a split second to his lips. Would they be soft? Would he tilt her head to access her mouth better? Need slammed into her, electric currents arcing from her tight nipples to her wet and dripping pussy. She had to stop herself from moaning there in front of God and everyone.

"My cell emits a signal that should be easily traced through the satellites. That will clear me. Whoever your witnesses saw in relation to these terrorist activities wasn't me. I'm a lot of things, but I'm not a bloody terrorist."

Tarek's phone beeped. Katherine's heart pounded. Chances were it was the test results—and confirmation from the techs that Garth's words were true. They'd already set those tracking tests in motion before starting this interview. Tarek pulled his phone out of his pocket and scrolled through his messages, distracted for a few brief moments.

Garth's hand cupped her jaw intimately for a moment. Katherine's breath caught, her attention reverting back to the darkly sexy man.

"We need to work together on this, not be at each other's throats," he whispered. "I know you don't like my style, but guess what, sweetheart, it gets results.

My partner is missing, his daughter is out there, unprepared and undefended. We are on the brink of an international incident the likes of which we've never seen before. Now, I'll admit I want to get into your knickers something fierce. The number of things I want to do to your mouth, your breasts and those luscious long legs you keep so well hidden probably would have you screaming for weeks, but I'm man enough to put that aside and get the job done. So how about it?"

Katherine felt her face flush at the raw sexuality of his words. Heat pooled in her pussy, her lips slick with the need to feel him ramming inside her, filling her to bursting point. It took a second for her brain to catch up with everything he'd said, her mind wanting to linger over the potent, dark sensuality of his words.

"How about what?" she replied in a low tone, wondering what his wicked brain had come up with now.

Garth shot his hand out. He held her chin in a firm but not painful grip and he tugged until their lips pressed together.

Heat and sensual lightning arced through her body. Her clit sang with the desire to be touched, her breasts pressed forward needing the contact of his hands, his chest, anything. His lips were soft but firm, better than she could ever have imagined, even in her most erotic fantasies. Katherine's blood surged as lust slammed into her, painful with its intensity.

Her body blossomed, her nipples craved stimulation and cried out for the intimacy of his touch. She nearly wept and begged him to take her right there, on the table, on the floor, pressed up against the wall. He could have had her anywhere he chose in that moment, so overwhelming was her need.

In a second it was over. Garth pulled back, his dark eyes flared in lust and surprise, seemingly as taken aback as she was by the potent chemistry that had exploded between them. He gasped, but then managed to get control of himself again.

"Get me the hell out of here!" he insisted.

Katherine gulped and shot a quick, worried glance at her partner. Tarek seemed amused as he waved his mobile at her.

"He's clear," Tarek said. Katherine couldn't decide if she was excited that Garth's supposed innocence had been proven, or irritated that he'd been right and she was in the wrong. Something told her that nothing was simple when it came to this handsome, devastatingly sexy man.

"Well then," she spoke, but had to pause to clear her throat. Her voice was low, husky from her need. She lifted a hand to push back an invisible strand of her hair. Getting herself under control, Katherine knew, without a doubt, the next few hours and days would be interesting, if nothing else.

"Let's discuss where we should begin," she continued, in what she hoped was a professional manner. Garth grinned wickedly, and Katherine felt heat and moisture once again pool in her knickers.

Ah yes…interesting might be an understatement.

Chapter One

About twenty-four hours later

Garth locked the two goons into the back seat of their car. Tennent had a bullet in his shoulder so, with his wrists cuffed, there appeared to be no fight left in him. Dixon—currently unconscious—was similarly restrained but posed even less trouble. With both men secure, Garth watched as Jack Berwick assisted Victor into the other car.

Victor, his mentor and one of the few people on earth who truly mattered to Garth, paused as the back door opened. Garth caught Victor's gaze as he looked up at him. Garth nodded at him. Victor acknowledged it and tilted his head in return before making slow, tender progress into the car.

Victor's face was badly cut and bruised from repeated beatings. One eye was swollen shut. Caked blood stained his face. He cradled one arm, the collarbone having been broken, probably in multiple places from the bruises that were already blossoming.

Garth noticed his mentor also walked stiffly, with a noticeable limp as if he wanted to curl in on himself, but still refused to show even a hint of weakness. Garth had a feeling there were other broken bones and internal damage not easily visible. Regardless of all this, Victor was alive and that was the important thing.

They had exchanged a hard drive with all the sensitive data Katherine had mentioned during Garth's 'interrogation' for Victor's life. Their enemy had escaped. Superficially, Oscar Jennings resembled what Garth might look like in twenty or thirty years' time. From the front, in clear light, Garth believed the resemblance between the two men was passing at best.

Despite that, Garth could understand why a few brief glances had the witnesses making statements that pointed fingers his way.

Garth returned his attention to Katherine. Her lower lip trembled as she assisted her partner's comatose body into the back of the ambulance. Two medics crouched on either side, monitoring Tarek's vital signs. With the medics in control there was little he or Katherine could do to assist her partner in any way. Garth had moved aside to give her some time and privacy to say her goodbyes before she handed Tarek's care over.

A ricochet had caught Tarek in the neck during the firefight exchange. They had rushed to stop the bleeding, but it had been touch and go. Tarek clung to life, he needed a hospital's care.

That's the way this industry worked, Garth thought, not unsympathetically. One day you're here, the next you might not be.

Katherine stood and Garth couldn't help himself, he let his gaze linger over endless curves. Soft hair the colour of spun gold was pulled back into a tight chignon. She knelt beside her partner, her large, expressive brown eyes filled with unshed tears.

Desire hit Garth hard. Katherine's full, round breasts strained against the buttons of her shirt. His hands itched to cup them, to hold her luscious body close, to press those silky mounds together and thrust his hard prick up through them.

With effort, Garth pulled himself back under control as Katherine clambered to her feet, pressed her fingertips to her lips then transferred the kiss to Tarek's cheek. She climbed down from the ambulance and waved to the driver that he was clear to go. The siren wailed as they pulled away, the vehicle moving at a fast pace.

Unsteadily, Katherine crossed over to him. Garth rested a hand on her shoulder and guided her away from where the van had stopped. They walked out on to the grass and between the shrubbery that had been planted to separate the green fields from the parking lot.

"Back-up will take at least another ten minutes to get here because of the traffic," he said. "Let's sit on the grass. The place is deserted now. Tarek will be fine. He's in the best possible hands."

"He can't go through all of this for nothing," Katherine insisted. "I won't let this be a waste. He's my partner."

Garth smiled, though it wasn't a humorous gesture. He understood all too well the mixture of fear, anger and overwhelming duty Katherine grappled with.

"Ready to throw out the rule book?" he teased.

She nodded. "Absolutely. It hasn't helped a damn bit on this bloody case. Why not toss it aside?"

Garth's heart twinged for her. He wanted her badly, yes, but more than that—she touched him. Her fierceness, her warrior's courage. She could match him, blow for blow and keep up with him stride for stride. Without conscious thought, he palmed Katherine's jaw, turned her mouth to his and kissed her passionately.

Fire exploded between them, hot and potent. Need slammed into Garth's body and his cock hardened painfully. He had meant it to be a brief thing, a touch of lips and show of solidarity. That thought flew right out of the window the moment their flesh fused together.

He wrapped an arm around her waist and drew her curvy body up against his. Her mouth opened on a low moan. He snaked his tongue inside, tasting her as they tangled together. They parried, vying for dominance in a battle as sensual and old as time.

Appearing to surrender to the passion flaring between them, Katherine arched her luscious body into his, her large breasts pressing into the thin material of his shirt. He didn't know if it was his imagination or not, but he thought he could feel the hard peaks of her nipples against his chest. Garth stroked his thumb over the tender skin of her jaw, caressing her and tilting her further so he could plunder her mouth and claim her with his tongue.

Their lips pressed against one another, lust making his movements languid. Garth moved his hand slowly down the long column of her neck, his grip firm. He loved the feel of her as he caressed down her slender throat, her skin silky beneath his rough hand. Her pulse beat wildly at the tender juncture where neck met shoulder.

He flicked his thumb out, stroking over the flutter as if he could soothe it. Her blood pounded more furiously. They broke apart, each gasping for air, her dark eyes wide and rich with passion. Her pale cheeks were flushed, her pupils dilated with pleasure. She looked wanton, drunk, and utterly ravishable. Garth couldn't contain his need for her. He didn't know how he could possibly wait to be inside her.

"We can't," she murmured, her tone thick with lust and need.

"Of course we can," he chided. "You're throwing out your bloody rule book, remember."

He took her hand and guided her down onto the soft grass behind the shrubbery, well out of sight of anyone who might happen to pass by. Katherine didn't raise any further objections, though he could tell from the set of her jaw that she wasn't wholly on board with him. Yet. From the flush of her cheeks and the rapid pulse in her throat he knew she was not unwilling. It would be simple to convince her to dabble on the dark side, just a little.

He laid her on her back in the grass. With quick motions he released her pants and tugged them over her hips to give him free access to her lacy knickers.

"Garth," she reached a hand down to cover her partial exposure. He leaned over her, covering her body with his own. Kissing her, he waited until her fingers quivered and reached to thread up through his hair.

"The moment we hear someone I'll stop, my word on it," he whispered, pulling a small distance from her. He brushed his lips over her mouth. He paused, not wanting to take her against her will, but prepared to coax as much as she required. Katherine nodded and he continued.

He lowered his hand and dipped into her lacy underwear. She groaned at his touch and canted up into it, her hips lifting off the ground. Garth slid two fingers inside her pussy, his thumb seeking through her trimmed blonde curls and discovering her small, hard clit. Rubbing over the sensitive nub, he stimulated her. Her back arched and she cried out in pleasure, her body jerking up into his as his fingers pumped steadily.

"This is what throwing the rule book away is all about," he spoke into her ear, wanting to make her ache with his words because he could not explore her body as fully as he craved. So, like any inherent fighter, he used the weapons he did have. In this instance they were his voice and his hands.

He cupped one large breast in his free hand. He popped open three buttons in the middle of her shirt, making enough room to insert his fingers between the folds of her crisp linen. Smooth lace met him, restraining warm, silky flesh. Garth almost moaned at the feel of her full, heavy breasts.

Like any red-blooded man, Garth enjoyed a gorgeous rack as much as the next bloke. Katherine had a luscious, enormous set of tits and he'd been daydreaming over them since the moment he'd laid eyes on her. The reality, he discovered, offered even more than the wicked fantasies he'd been conjuring.

Her nipple pebbled in his fingers and he twisted it with careful calculation, wanting to give her the maximum enjoyment with only a minimal amount of pain. She gasped, her back bowing. She pressed her breast further into his hand as he inserted a third finger into her clasping cunt. Her body sucked down on him like a warm vice.

Garth wanted to sink his cock inside her more than his next breath. He restrained himself, not wanting to press Katherine too far too fast. Besides, their back-up would soon be arriving, so it wasn't as if he could linger.

"You have no idea how decadent you look," he murmured as he enjoyed every second possible with her body. "Your eyes sparkle, your skin is flushed, your breasts are every man's wet dream come to life and your cunt squeezes down on me so hungrily you couldn't possibly convince me you don't want this as much as I do."

"Harder, Garth," she panted as she lifted her hips. He groaned, able to penetrate her more deeply with the change in angle. "Please, I can feel it coming."

"Would you like to come, beautiful Kate?" Garth spoke sweetly. Her gaze met his, her eyes a burning chocolate pool of need. He lifted his head and kissed her lips chastely. He moved his hand from one breast to the other, not wanting it to feel neglected. Her eyes fluttered when he pinched her nipple a little harder.

He could tell from her reaction and the increased speed of her gasps that she loved it as much as he enjoyed giving it to her. He caressed her breast harder and pinched it again. Katherine's flush deepened to a rosy pink and her hands clutched at clumps of grass.

Fingers wet and slick from her flowing juices, Garth pumped harder inside her. His thumb stroked over her clit and he flicked it with the corner of his nail. She cried out, a lusty sound that was music to his soul. His cock strained against the confines of his pants and he craved being inside her with a burning intensity he hadn't experienced since his youth.

He lifted up so he could watch her as he brought her pleasure. Katherine lay splayed out before him on the grass like some pagan sacrifice. Her blonde tresses had started to come out of her chignon, her skin showed signs of her heated blood, her breast strained against his hand, filling it to overflowing.

Her pussy felt slick and needy, hungry as she tried to swallow him whole. Garth pumped harder and deeper within her, his manipulations of her clit firmer now as she seemed accepting of a stronger touch. His warrior did not need coddling or a delicate hand — she seemed to blossom and thrive on a bit of pain.

Garth reluctantly released her breast and pushed aside the scanty, lacy knickers that covered her mound. Nudging her legs wider to grant him better access, he sniffed the delicate aroma of her passion.

"The moment I get you alone I'm going to strip you down," he insisted. "Then I'm going to lick every inch of you, taste you and bite you, mark you as mine, sweetheart. If you're lucky I might even spank you a little, rosy your arse for me. Have you ever taken it up the arse, Katherine? A body like yours, it was created for sinful pleasure such as this. A man could fuck those breasts of yours and lose himself. Much as I'm going to enjoy your slick pussy right now, it's your other passage I'm craving to possess."

She moaned at his words, cupping his face and threading through the short strands of his hair. Garth looked at her and their gazes clashed. She watched him, her gaze not wavering from his face for a moment. She nodded and tugged with her hands, brought his face closer to her crotch and all the delicious secrets that lay within.

"Please," she pleaded. "I'm nearly there."

Garth felt satisfaction unfurl within him. She hadn't run screaming at his words, nor had she denied him outright. He could work with that. Eagerly, he buried his face in her pussy and licked her like a starved man. She tasted spicy, musky. Her legs widened further as she accepted him to her.

Pressing his fingers deeply inside her, three long, thick digits fluted and fucked her hard as she pleaded for more. He curled his fingers and found her G-spot. Her body bowed and she screamed as her pussy clenched hard and release washed over her.

Garth ate up every drop her body wept, pumping steadily through her orgasm as she shuddered. His thumb flicked out over her clit again and she trembled, the sensation too much for her overloaded body. Gently, he nibbled on her plump, soft labia, enjoying the short hairs and the faint rasping over his stubbled chin.

When her body stopped shaking and she lifted up on to her elbows, Garth looked up once again to meet her gaze. She looked astonished, sated and rumpled. He could have happily stripped her there and then and begun again, this time with utter penetration and possession of her body as his goal. His cock leaked in his pants and he wanted to fuck her until they both couldn't move.

The faint sound of cars coming down the access road came to them. Reluctantly Garth sat up and pulled his shirt out from his pants, letting the tails hang low and cover his bursting erection. When he glanced at his colleague he noticed Katherine had buttoned up her shirt and was fixing her slacks.

Before he could speak, to reassure her everything would be all right, Katherine surprised him. She took his face in her hands, drew their bodies flush together and kissed him deeply. Shocked, but more than interested, Garth closed his arm around her and he held her next to him. When she moved her mouth over his chin and she sucked her own taste from him, heat pooled low in his belly.

"Fuck, be careful how you wield that," he warned her.

"Wield what?" she asked, appearing confused.

"That sexy, wanton power you hold over me. I'm primed to burst already. You push me any further and I bloody well won't care half the cavalry is here. I'll lean you against this tree and fuck you blind in front of every man and woman present, professionalism and our reputations be damned."

Katherine's eyes widened, though Garth knew enough about her now to sense the desire his words elicited. She couldn't fool him any longer. She might be surprised, but she wasn't offended or turned off. Indeed, he could swear the gleam in her dark eyes indicated willing consent and interest, not revulsion.

"Welcome to the dark side, Kate," he grinned evilly at her. Kissing her one last time, he checked that his rumpled, stained shirt covered his groin and stood up, gallantly offering her a hand for assistance. He helped her to her feet, brushed the grass from her mussed hair and gave her arse and one breast a squeeze each.

"Don't make me wait too long," he murmured as six cars raced into the car park. Doors slammed as agents spilled out everywhere. "I'm hot and hard for you, sweetheart. Next chance we get I won't be such a gentleman. I'll fuck you raw and keep going until you plead for mercy."

"Promises, promises," she replied with a grin. Garth felt rich, utterly masculine satisfaction roll through his blood. His prick ached, he needed release or he was sure to explode. For all her prim, by-the-book external preachings, Katherine Hitchens appeared to be a seriously kinky soul.

He loved that. Indeed, he could see himself becoming addicted to her.

Life had just got incredibly interesting.

* * * *

Katherine's body still hummed hours later as they finished a quick dinner of takeout, greasy boxes lying scattered over her and Tarek's desks. She and Garth had eaten fast from necessity. Other agents could smell fresh takeout from two floors in either direction, and came running to steal what they could.

"So, I've set the laptop to scan the frequency you've mentioned for activity every thirty seconds," Scott said as he ran a hand through his scruffy red hair. Tall and skinny, he was the Agency's best tech. Katherine was glad they'd managed to bribe him with a chocolate milkshake.

Katherine and Garth leaned close as they watched the small screen of the slim laptop. Scott showed them how to run the scan and how to search different frequencies and change the parameters, should they need to widen their net. He then flicked a switch and explained the tracing unit he'd factored in to the scanner.

"It's similar enough to your average GPS device, so it shouldn't be too difficult to work with," Scott added with pride.

Katherine tried to keep her mind focused but it was impossible with Garth so close. On a subconscious level, she retained Scott's advice, warnings and explanations, but, had she needed to recite his words back, she'd have been lost.

She imagined she could smell her musky scent on Garth's lips. His cologne was something elemental and masculine, spicy and intriguing. She wanted to touch him, taste him, strip him bare as he had done so easily to her out in the park. Garth nudged her and she came back to their cubicle with a snap.

"I believe that's a detailed enough explanation for now, thank you, Scott," Garth said.

Picking up the thread of conversation once again, Katherine nodded.

"Yes, thank you," she added, in what she hoped was a calm tone. "We don't want to cramp the night shift's groove. I think we'll head back to my apartment soon. Can you stay on call?"

A distasteful grimace crossed Scott's face.

"Sure thing. I guess I can trust you to not call me out six times through the evening because you're too simple-minded enough to remember things such as plugging in the battery or turning off the sleep mode for your screen. You have my mobile number—call if something goes down the crapper."

Katherine relaxed. Scott hadn't appeared to find anything amiss with her tone or distracted air. He cast them both quick glances, seeming to watch for when they were finished. Raking a hand through his unruly hair, he collected his equipment in a rush and all but fled.

"Do you really think it wise we head back to your place?" Garth asked.

Katherine turned to face him and noticed his face was in profile to her. He'd leant back onto the desk and was looking at the laptop. She realised that, outwardly, it appeared as if he were merely chatting idly about whatever he was working on the computer.

A small smile twitched the corner of Katherine's mouth. It was quickly replaced with a frown as she noticed how easily the casual deception appeared to come to the dark-haired man. Uncertainty spiked through her. She leaned her palms flat down on the table and bent close to him, her eyes on the screen though her entire focus was on her new, temporary partner.

"You're awfully smooth," she snapped, more harshly than she had meant to. "Are you so used to playing games that it's become second nature to you?"

"Ease back," Garth responded. "In case it has escaped your notice, sweetheart, we're spies. Multitasking is supposed to be second nature to us. Just as you thought quickly on your feet to warn Scott we wouldn't be hanging around here all evening, so too was it an easy enough thing for me to try to protect your reputation and not stand here staring at your gorgeous breasts and talking dirty to you."

Katherine flushed, embarrassed at how she'd let her suspicion overwhelm her good sense.

"Now, every other bloke in this room would understand if I began talking to your chest and ignoring the fact you are a decent agent and have a brain in your head, but really I didn't feel the need to lower myself in such a way," Garth continued. "Are we going to have a similar problem every time we open our mouths to each other, or are we good?"

Katherine stood up and nodded.

"I'm sorry," she apologised. "I'm on edge. After thinking you're a traitor, then the speed with which Victor's rescue took place, now Tarek lying comatose, so close to death's door, and losing the hard drive…"

Katherine let her words trail away and shook off her maudlin air.

"I'm not making excuses," she added. "A lot has happened in the last day or so. Forgive me. If we're going to work together we need at least a minimal level of trust. I'll try to not jump down your throat again. This is a big change for me. I'm not adapting as well as I could."

"Sweetheart, you can jump down my throat any time you like," Garth riposted with a wicked grin. He turned to look at her, the laughter in his dark eyes making her belly roll with lust.

Damn the man was sin incarnate.

Katherine huffed out a low laugh and punched him lightly in the shoulder. Warmth spread through her chest, grateful acknowledgement of how easily he had let her sharpness go.

"I've been thinking about how we can try to narrow potential suspects for who the traitor might be," Katherine said. "Now you're firmly crossed off the list, of course, it takes us back to square one."

Garth stood, an intrigued look on his face. His hands rested on his hips as they talked in quiet tones to each other. The sexual chemistry still burned between them, but the serious note to their conversation distracted her.

"I presume word of Oscar's identity has filtered through the rank and file?" he stated more than asked.

Katherine nodded and tilted her head towards a small group of agents clustered around one workstation on the other side of the large room.

"Walters and Peterson are leading. I think they've got three different pairs rotating on shifts to get everything they can within the next day or so."

"I'm sure the overtime will be welcome," Garth inserted. "Have you heard from Henley yet?"

Emma Henley was the team leader, responsible for overseeing each of their partnerships and coordinating everyone's missions. "No, I haven't seen her since I left yesterday to pick you up for questioning," Katherine replied. "I've emailed her a brief update after our interview yesterday to clear your name, but things have been hectic since. I haven't seen or heard from her."

Garth looked around the office. The hum of activity was evidence of contained chaos. After perusing the large room his gaze came to rest on hers again. Katherine chuckled, no words needed to be said.

"Yes, I know. It is rather crazy around here right now, isn't it? I can just imagine how upper management has their knickers in a twist over events so far. Even with Victor safely returned to us, an unknown terrorist organisation has the resources and competency to not only kidnap one of our own, but instigate an exchange of data so valuable we don't fully understand how deeply it reaches into our government. Then, of course, there's the insult added to the injury that an untrained civilian and an external PI managed to crack the case and instigate Victor's return, practically unassisted by us. Yes, I can imagine how heads will roll soon."

"We need to get our hands on a copy of whatever Walters and his men have on Jennings," Garth suggested. "We can go over it, maybe do some data mining ourselves while we wait for our chance to trace where Jennings and his goons are hiding out."

"Do you want to go over and organise that while I pack up, or should I?" she asked, her mind flickering ahead to the potential of what the forthcoming evening could bring.

Garth's gaze lingered on her lips, then lowered to her chest. Katherine felt her cheeks heat. She felt as if he were caressing her, his nimble hands tracing over her skin tantalisingly, his fingers once again pinching her nipples with that exquisite blend of pleasure and pain.

Finally, his eyes lifted and the naked need she saw in those black orbs stole her breath away.

"I think Walters will be far more susceptible to a suggestion from you, sweetheart," he purred. "I'll pack up the laptop and gather our things. I'll meet you out front when you've sweet-talked poor, unsuspecting Walters into emailing the file to you."

Katherine grinned and squeezed his shoulder in an innocent gesture of camaraderie. She tilted her head so she could whisper in his ear.

"Who knows? Maybe I can be persuasive enough to get him to print me out a hard copy."

Garth growled low in his throat, the sound one of masculine defensiveness.

"Don't go overboard, Kate," he warned her with a harsh snap. "My patience only extends so far. I've been rock hard for you all this time. You don't want to see me snap and lose control."

Katherine released his shoulder and stepped back, her gaze thoughtful. Despite her initial distrust of him, she knew he wouldn't let her down. They could rely on each other to cover each other's back and arse. Indeed, her arse was safest with Garth rather than anyone else.

The thought made her smile.

"I trust you," she replied. "You might snap, you might even cause me some...discomfort, Garth, but you'd never harm me, not irreparably. I know that."

Surprise flared in his eyes as his eyebrows rose. Throwing him an impish grin over her shoulder, she added an extra sway to her hips as she stalked across the room. The men were gathered together over the other side, discussing Jennings and dissecting possible connections to others within the Agency.

Her sway was purely for Garth, though she noticed that, one by one, the other agents took note of her sultry walk. She'd never thought to use her charms on her colleagues, it had seemed beneath her. As the mental image of Tarek lying bleeding and dead on the ground burned behind her eyes, she knew her attitude had been permanently altered.

She still didn't trust the cowboy, borderline rogue methods, but if they worked she'd use them now. Justice was not as black and white as she had always believed. If a bit of a smile and slutty kink to her walk helped her get the results she needed, then so be it.

"Hi, guys," she upped the voltage of her smile. "You're working on Jennings? I have the biggest favour to ask."

She didn't need to pretend to add the tremble to her smile when she thought of her fallen partner. Despite overplaying her hand right now, her grief for her friend remained deep and true.

After a pause, when she knew she held their attention, Katherine continued. "You know he's responsible for harming Tarek, don't you?"

The men nodded. Katherine pressed her lips together and restrained herself, reluctant to press.

"I don't have to tell you I want this bastard badly, along with the possible traitor – if we have one internally. I promise to not step all over your feet, but I'm hoping you'll agree to share everything you've found with me."

Katherine met each of their gazes as they stared hard at her. She tilted her head. The innocent gesture turned one of her shoulders and, in a smooth motion, pushed one of her breasts against her shirt.

"He has been my partner for five years," she reminded them. "If the situation was reversed you know I'd do the same for you."

One of the men nodded, then Peterson joined in and glanced at Walters. With a sigh he waved a hand, conceding defeat. Katherine grinned, relieved.

"Can you email it to me?" she asked as she moved in to glance at the screen they'd all been discussing. She brightened her smile once again, thinking of Garth and their teasing.

"And maybe I could print out a hard copy? Just for the road, you know."

Chapter Two

"I can't believe how little data there is on Jennings," Katherine said, amazed. Garth returned from the kitchen holding two mugs of tea. "In this day and age it should be impossible for a man in his late fifties to have so little in the way of information against his name."

"Maybe his name isn't really Oscar Jennings?" he hypothesised.

Katherine took the mug Garth offered her and cupped it in her hand to absorb the warmth. The night had turned cool. It had been almost forty-eight hours since she'd been in her flat, the rooms had become uncomfortably chilly after a long stretch without the heating on.

She cast a quick gaze at the laptop. They had set it up to one side of her coffee table. It emitted sporadic hums and pings as the programme cycled through, searching for any indication the frequency they sought was being used. Katherine had set up her own laptop in the centre of the table so they could both view the data Walters and the other agents had collected so far on Jennings.

"Victor recognised him as Jennings, though," she answered with a frown. "So either it's an alias he uses a lot and is commonly known, or he's deleted any background information held on him. Wiped himself clean."

"Gee," Garth replied with a sarcastic grin. "No one in our industry ever does that."

Katherine laughed, drank some of her tea and placed the mug down on a coaster.

"If I were in Peterson and Walters' shoes I'd get some of the techs on to unearthing his background," she commented. "What we really need is to find a connection between Jennings and someone from the Agency, a link we can use as proof to get another interview set up."

Garth rubbed his eyes and Katherine saw him glance at the frequency scanner before returning his attention to the files she scrolled between. She found it interesting she had tuned into his personal ticks and mannerisms enough that she could feel the impatience radiating from him. She wondered how long it would take before he'd break down and pounce on her.

Just as she figured she had ten or fifteen minutes, he sat back on the couch and snaked a hand under and up the bottom of her shirt. In a swift motion, he unsnapped her bra and reached around to cup one of her breasts as it spilled out of the soft lace. He sat up again, his chest pressed into her back, his other hand at her neck, unbuttoning her shirt.

Stepping out of her pumps, Katherine lifted up, turned around and swung a leg over Garth's thighs so she straddled him. Cupping her hands to his jaw she ground her dripping pussy over his pants to show just how ready for him she was.

"I could hardly pay attention when Scott explained everything to us," she confessed, panting as she dipped to cover his mouth with hers. Katherine had no clue where her shirt fell as Garth pulled it from her arms. She slid her bra off and tossed it to a corner of the couch. Garth moaned as he palmed both her breasts.

"Bloody hell, I could spend a whole day doing nothing but playing with these," he said, his voice rough with need. Katherine gasped as he bent his head and suckled her right nipple, his tongue flickering over the tight nub as his teeth latched firmly on.

Her back arched and rational thought fled from her mind as intoxicating pleasure radiated from her nipples down to her clit, electrifying each nerve on its way through. It took her a moment to get her hands working again and, with fumbling fingers, she undid the buttons of his shirt. Finally, she opened each side and exposed his chest to her view.

Garth played her body to perfection. His teeth and tongue worked her to a fever pitch. Moving his fingers delicately over her breasts and nipples, he made sure the luscious peaks didn't feel neglected. The tingling deep within her stomach grew, her clit thrummed and she knew she couldn't last.

Katherine didn't want to come too soon, though. She'd already climaxed once today because of this man's wicked fingers. It was his turn. Rising up on her knees, she inserted one thigh between his legs, and nudged them apart. Tugging gently, she urged Garth to scoot forward on the couch and she turned to move the coffee table back to give herself room.

Kneeling between his thighs, she felt her excitement skyrocket as she unfastened his pants. Garth toed off his shoes, bent to remove his socks and lifted his hips as she pulled his trousers and boxers off. She lifted his sac with one hand and wrapped her other around his girth.

Closing her hand around his shaft into a fist, she pumped her hand up his length, swiping her thumb over his tip to collect the fluid already leaking from his slit. Garth rocked his hips up, thrusting his cock faster through her hand. Rolling her fingers beneath his balls, she explored him with a decadent slowness, to further inflame him.

"Kate..." he growled at her. She looked up to catch his gaze as she continued to stroke along his shaft. He was warm beneath her touch, his head slick as she toyed with him.

Kate needed to assuage her curiosity. She lowered her head and feathered her lips around his tip. Caressing his cock with her tongue, she taunted Garth with how close—and yet how far—he was from her mouth enfolding him.

"Suck me," Garth demanded as he canted his hips towards her. His tone demanded, brooked no argument.

With a small smile of private victory, Katherine complied. She'd discovered within herself a hitherto unknown desire to push this dark man's buttons.

All of them.

She shivered at the thought of what it would be like to truly feel him lose control.

Katherine opened her lips and swallowed down around Garth's thick cock. She breathed through her nose, focused and relaxed her throat muscles to take him even further down as he pressed inside her.

Sitting down on her heels, Katherine lifted her gaze to catch Garth's. She stared at him innocently, her expression clearly asking, "Is this what you wanted?"

"Yesss, just like that," Garth hissed between clenched teeth. His hand cradled the back of her skull. He pulled a dozen or so pins from her hair and the tresses fell just below her shoulders.

Immediately, his fingers twisted in the strands and he groaned his approval. His hips set a driving rhythm and, once she'd acclimatised to it, she began to bob her head in time. Her tongue flicked out and she laved at the pre-cum that leaked from his tip.

Katherine found she had to focus on keeping her breathing regulated, her excitement warring with her racing heart and threatening to make her lose control. After a moment, her eyes fluttered closed and she massaged her breasts, squeezing the nipples in mimicry of what Garth had done earlier in the day.

"Let me," he said, his voice thick with lust. Garth covered her hand with his and he took over from her with evident pleasure. Katherine's head fell back as much as it was able and a moan of deep satisfaction rumbled through her, vibrating in her throat and caressing his cock with the sound.

Garth pumped his prick faster into her mouth, the usually fierce grip on his control clearly slipping. With one hand he guided her head down in an ever increasing pace while the other fondled her breasts with skill.

"Oh, that's perfect, right there, yes," he shouted, his voice rising in pitch as his face and upper chest flushed with arousal. On a low, muted roar he climaxed, his cock hammering the back of her throat as thick, salty seed shot into her mouth. Katherine swallowed as he emptied his balls into her.

Garth's grip on her hair loosened as he rode through his release, his cock only going partially soft. Clearly, he wasn't close to finished with her. When he'd come down, she ran her tongue around the tip of his head, pleased with herself for not flinching as his thick cock all but suffocated her, bruising her throat with his enthusiasm.

When she was certain he'd relaxed, even though he hadn't softened much at all, she lifted her head from him and licked her lips like a very satisfied woman.

"That was a delicious appetiser," she purred. He lifted his hands to her shoulders and held her. Guiding her back onto his lap, he kissed her and plundered her mouth with his tongue.

She shared his taste with him, eating at his mouth as her own arousal spiked. His cock stirred beneath her slacks and heat radiated from him. Katherine unfastened her suit pants and wriggled her body as she slid the smooth material down her thighs to her knees.

Pressing Garth back onto the couch, she continued to kiss him as she stretched her legs behind her. A few tugs and she managed to slip the trousers off. They crumpled into a pool on the floor.

With her palms flat against the muscles of his chest, Katherine pushed herself reluctantly to her feet. Garth sat forward, his hands reaching for her. Chortling, she ducked his hands and grinned at him.

"If you want me, you'll have to catch me."

Garth raised his eyebrows at her. With a sexy swish of her ass, she turned and fled. Loud, thumping footsteps followed her as she fled into the kitchen. Racing around the island bench Katherine sucked in a breath as her bare feet slapped on the cool tiles.

Bloody hell, her juices were flowing. Excitement sang through her blood. She shot a quick look over her shoulder and saw Garth barely two paces behind her. She feinted right, as if she were about to run out into the back yard but dived left at the last moment.

A thump sounded as Garth pushed himself off the back door. The mental image that it brought to mind made her chuckle, his curses filled the air. She dashed down the hall towards the bedroom. The smooth floorboards felt slippery under her feet. She could feel the vibrations of his heavy step catching up with her. Unable to restrain herself, Katherine laughed in sheer delight as she crashed through the bedroom doorway and felt warm, solid arms wrap around her.

Garth's momentum lifted her and they both fell into a heap on the bed. She wriggled and tried to see if she could get free and really make him work for it. He slapped her arse, the minute sting thrilling her even through the lace of her knickers.

"Damn, that made me hot," Garth said breathlessly. "Nothing gets the fires burning more than chasing a naked, hot woman around. You'll be lucky if I can do justice to you, sweetheart."

Katherine laughed, certain that no matter what Garth ended up doing to her, it would be amazing. They were both too worked up to be left partially satisfied now. She flipped on to her back and tried to squirm free. Garth chained both her wrists in his iron grip and pressed his hot, hard body along the length of hers.

"Enough, you wench," he snapped. "I'm on the very edge here. If you run again it might not end as prettily as you want."

The whip in his tone caught her attention and she met his gaze with her own. Dark and burning, she saw he was serious.

"Garth," she said, her smile gone as she absorbed the fact he wasn't joking. "It's very difficult to rape the willing. I don't mind some rough play, indeed if what we did together back at the park was any indication, I get off on it as much as you do. I want you to ream my arse, and I am craving to explore this darker side you've opened up in me. You don't need to be afraid I'll tease you, lead you on a merry dance then scream, point a finger and cry rape."

Garth studied her a minute and she willed him to see how honest she was. Satisfaction and something far more intoxicating shone in his black eyes.

"Shortbread," he rumbled as he nuzzled the sensitive spot at the base of her neck. Katherine shivered, delight spiking through her blood as her body heated and wept for him.

"What?" she choked out, the word making no sense to her as a lusty haze swept through her brain.

Garth looked around, then she saw him spot the second drawer of her bedside table open a crack, half a pantyhose leg dangling out the edge. She'd dressed in a hurry and not had time to be neat. His eyes lit up as if he had spotted a shilling on the street. He bent over her, tugged the stockings into his hand and wound them around her wrists.

Her mouth opened silently, unable to stop him when something deep inside her craved this. He watched her with a steady gaze as he bound her wrists. Katherine weighed the risk verses the reward.

Should she truly become desperate or fear for her life, the restraints would not stand to a dedicated assault. That gave her confidence, but she didn't think it would matter to Garth. He wanted to hold her steady and likely give her the feeling of being tied up, restrained, not in control. That thought thrilled her, so she didn't utter a word in argument.

"If I get too close to a line for you, if I push you too hard, you can stop me by saying the word 'shortbread'. You have my word on it."

Katherine thought for all of two seconds before nodding.

"Okay," she agreed. "Shortbread it is. I hope you don't expect me to break easily, though. I'm not some tame little virgin, you know. I'm not going to whine and cry if you slap my arse a few times, or if you pound that lovely thick cock as far into my pussy as you can reach. I'm an agent, just like you, trained and tested by fire, bloodied and true. I'm not some vanilla little debutante looking for a quick thrill. You want me to beg for you? You want me to scream and plead and cry for you to stop? You'll have to earn those pleas from me, Garth Spenser."

Just as she'd hoped, her words inflamed him, she could see his reaction as she verbalised her own wicked fantasies and likely hit more than a few of his own hot spots as well, if his rapid breathing was any indication.

Bloody hell, just looking at him made her wet. Here, in her bed kneeling above her was the bad boy of her dreams and most sensual, secret fantasies. Garth was a man she knew who could match her pace and not break. He could take all of her, every aspect of the complicated person she was and demand more, push her harder and further and not lag behind.

He was the perfect counterpoint for her own stubborn strength.

More than that, she trusted him implicitly.

He must have read something in her eyes, for he hesitated, glancing at her. Not wanting to talk, wanting to feel him penetrate her every orifice and wash away the serious nature of her thoughts, she teased him once again.

"What's the matter, Garth? You getting a little bit of stage fright? I didn't know you suffered from performance nerves. How about you untie me and I'll give you a hand, or even two if you prefer. I can guide you along, lead you by the cock."

Garth snorted, though Katherine got the strong feeling he saw straight through her tough words and saw her worry beneath. She had a feeling he'd not let that train of thought drop, but he appeared to shelve it for later and she was grateful for that.

"Oh, sweetheart, you've proven that luscious mouth of yours has such better uses. I won't waste my erection on another showing of the true talents of those lips. Instead I think I'll have a look at your other secrets instead."

With a hard yank he ripped the delicate lace of her sheer undies, tossing the scrap aside. Willingly, she spread her legs for him, her bound hands lifted high above her head as she arched her back under his hot gaze.

"You have a body built for sin," he murmured appreciatively.

Katherine laughed and shook her head, a flicker of competitiveness searing through her as she tried to push him harder.

"You have no idea, lover," she purred. "Why don't you test it out? See which one of us cries for mercy first?"

Reacting with eagerness to her challenge, he plunged three thick digits into her pussy. Katherine gasped at the stretching penetration, but accepted all he had to give. Her feet pressed down into the mattress as she braced herself. His thrusts were hard and deep, exactly what she craved. Her body blossomed, opening for him and sucking hungrily, demanding more.

Her eyes fluttered shut as he stroked his other hand between the folds of her labia and caressed her clit. Katherine moaned, heat and need burning inside her as her arousal grew.

"More," she croaked, her voice raw with passion. The fingers tweaking her clit worked faster, the digits fucking her pussy moved harder within her and already Katherine could feel her lust tie a knot inside her stomach.

Suddenly, the exquisite playing of her clit stopped and she cried out with the loss. Garth stroked those fingers around her dripping cunt, the sensitive lips of her labia shuddering with the attention he paid them.

"Patience, sweetheart," he murmured. "We have all night."

"You might have all night," she panted, though her taunt was only half-hearted as she watched him. "I've got some bad guys to hunt and chase down."

Garth didn't reply, appearing too focused to vocalise anything.

"You have no idea how beautiful you are to me like this. Open, braced, soaking wet. I want to see how you deal with all of me. Open wider, little girl."

Before she could guess what he meant, Garth pressed the slick, free index finger of his other hand to her tightly furled anal passage. Katherine sucked in a harsh breath as the closed muscles refused to budge. Garth continued to force his way inside her until the tip of his digit pressed deep in her passage.

Slick with her own cream, he twisted the finger left and right, coating the lubricant inside her arse. The tight channel burned with the alien penetration. She'd never done this, not wanted or felt the need to share such an intimate possession with any man. Katherine gulped for air as he continued to push the wet finger deeper, to the second knuckle.

"Hurts, doesn't it, sweetheart?" Garth purred. Katherine's legs fell wider apart as she surrendered to him. It was true, the painful pressure was close to unbearable. As he continued the steady thrust of his fingers in her pussy, however, the fierce possession slowly blossomed into something darker, more wonderful than she had ever experienced before.

The blending of pain and ecstasy mingled until it was impossible to separate them from each other.

"Garth," she pleaded. He tutted and bent to kiss her lips. Not for a moment did either of his hands slow down. Pumping one hand inside her cunt, pushing her higher and closer to her peak, he reached the other finger as far into her as it could.

And then she felt the hard press of his middle finger, prying at her entrance, looking to see if it, too, could squeeze in and join in the party.

"I don't think—"

She couldn't even finish the sentence before the tip of his middle digit pressed inside her small hole. Her back bowed off the bed, her head pressed down into the softness of her mattress and a cry escaped her lips, caught somewhere between abject pleasure and unbearable pain.

Her orgasm built, the roiling emotions uncontainable. Katherine had never experienced such a perfect blend of diametrically opposing feelings. On the one hand she sat on the knife edge of pain, almost but not quite more than she could bear. On the other hand she knew the orgasm building within her was bigger, stronger and far more intense than anything she had ever been through. The intoxicating level of her feelings defied description.

And still Garth pressed her buttons.

More slowly this time he eased his second finger inside her arse. He scissored his fingers to stretch her tiny, virgin passage and stars burst behind her eyes. Incoherent sounds fell from her lips as Katherine lost control of the power of speech. Shuddering, curling upwards to feel more of him she recalled her hands were bound and she couldn't grab a hold of him.

"Untie me, Garth," she pleaded. Opening her eyes, she shot him a hot look. His cocked eyebrows dared her to push him further. She used hot words as she had previously, the only weapon remaining for her.

"I want to hold you, mark you, bite you and claim you as mine," she insisted. "Just as you're claiming me, I want you to know this is an equal partnership."

He looked at her for a moment and she held his hot gaze. Finally he nodded and pulled the fingers out of her pussy, licking them, taunting her by taking his time.

"I don't really have the patience tonight to do justice to your arse anyway," he spoke with a wry glance to his erect and pulsing shaft.

Katherine lifted her head and stared at him. Slick, clear juice leaked down his shaft. He obviously was in near painful arousal and only sheer stubborn control kept him in check.

With clear reluctance he gradually removed the two fingers from her ass, giving her a pat when she lay there feeling empty and irrationally abandoned.

"Next time, sweetheart, my oath on it. Tonight, I believe I need the feel of you and release far too much."

Katherine held her hands out to him and he untied them, the ripped stockings dropping to the floor as he tossed them aside.

"The top drawer," she murmured. He moved to the side and she heard the soft crinkle of foil. Seconds later he returned and she pounced on him, pressing him back into the mattress and straddling him. Eagerness surged as she finally—after a seeming eternity—had her lover exactly where she wanted him.

Not for the first time he surprised her. As Katherine sank down on his thick, pulsing shaft he cupped his warm hand across her arse and helped pull her until he was fully sheathed. As she caught her breath, adjusted to the enormous penetration, he slapped her arse with a quick, hard spank.

The sound of his open hand striking her flesh resounded through her room and she stared in shock. Her eyes widened and she caught his gaze. Smug, utterly male satisfaction shone in his eyes.

"You didn't think I'd let you off so easily, did you?" he murmured. Katherine lifted herself from him and started to ride him hard. Garth alternated, sometimes stroking over her tight asshole, sometimes rubbing her clit, and sometimes spanking her arse until her cheeks were hot and tingling. Katherine clenched him to her, her short fingernails digging into his back and shoulder as she grappled for purchase. She ran the pads of her fingers up and down the long, smooth length of his back. Now and then, when he delivered a particularly strong slap or the tip of his finger would penetrate its tip into her arse and shock her, she would dig her nails into him in reaction, small scratches marring his smooth skin.

All too quickly she felt her peak approaching, the stimulating blend of stinging arousal and languid pleasure melding until the boundaries blurred.

Shuddering, Katherine could no longer hold on. As her head fell back in ecstasy she uttered a fierce cry. She screamed her release as her climax washed over her. Her pussy tightened and electricity raced through her bloodstream. Pounding hard, she drove herself upon him, riding out her orgasm.

She hadn't finished coming when he shouted his own climax. Garth twisted her to the side and she fell, splayed wide open for him on the bed. He thrust himself between her thighs, his huge cock ramming into her with blurring speed over and over, as waves of release overtook him.

Panting hard, sweating and gasping for breath, Katherine trembled as her body ached in all kinds of places. Emotionally and physically drained, she lay in a heap on her bed. Garth pressed her into the covers.

Warmth suffused her as she caressed Garth's short, spiky hair. She let her mind wander, coming to the conclusion that, if she was going to throw the rule book out in her professional life, she might as well throw it out in her personal life as well.

She'd never seen any of the Agency's men socially. Any fool knew how tricky mixing work and play could be when lives were constantly at stake. The 'no dating' rule was a cliché only because it was so true. Personal agendas did not mix with making life and death decisions. Katherine was honest enough to know, however, she couldn't give Garth up. Not now.

She shied away from just how important he was to her, at just how easily she could fall head over heels for him.

Garth lifted himself to the side, careful to support his weight and not bear down upon her. Resting an elbow on the mattress he leaned his chin on his hand. They studied each other for a moment, his eyes far too penetrating and knowing for her peace of mind. She knew it was ridiculous, but she had the unusual idea her cool, savvy mask no longer worked with this man.

"You've been thinking an awful lot," he commented in a low voice.

Katherine gave him what she hoped was a mostly innocent smile. "Not really," she replied. She skittered her eyes away from that too-knowing gaze of his. Garth reached out and took her chin between his fingers, turning her to face him once again. Katherine lifted her eyes to meet his. This time she tried to hold it.

"What are you thinking, sweetheart? No secrets, okay?"

Katherine thought for a moment, not even close to being ready to bare her soul. In what she hoped was a teasing, joking tone she decided to tell a partial truth wrapped in a jest.

"I was just thinking that if you shatter my heart into a million pieces because I'm throwing my precious rule book aside that I will not just break every bone in your body in retaliation, I'll bury your body and deny all knowledge."

Garth grinned at her words. Katherine smiled, pleased and disappointed he'd taken her words as she'd hoped. The twinkle deep in his eyes showed her, inside, he laughed and found something amusing. He held up a finger to indicate he'd be right back.

Climbing from the bed, Garth went to the adjoining bathroom. She heard the water run as he cleaned himself up and she glanced at the alarm clock on the bedside table. It was only nine thirty but the past two days had been hell, with barely more than a few hours' sleep.

Katherine scooted from the bed and turned the covers down, then recalled the laptop. Hurrying out into the living room she collected the computer and its battery, unplugged them and brought them back to the bedroom. The ping of the alarm would be audible if she kept it on her dresser. Plugging everything back in place, she went to the bathroom and tidied herself up once Garth had come back into the bedroom.

When she returned, Garth had climbed into bed but left the covers turned down for her. He patted the space next to him on the mattress. She grinned and took a few hurried steps then bounced into bed with him. She pushed all her serious thoughts, all her worries and concerns to the back of her mind and admonished herself to take this one day at a time.

As she curled into Garth's embrace, he leant forward and kissed her tenderly. Katherine felt her heart overflow with warmth and she tried to clutch it all back. She couldn't resist him, though. She kissed him back passionately, her emotions building into sensual intimacy. When Garth pulled back she saw his expression was smug, arrogantly masculine in some way that eluded her.

"You keep on thinking so hard, sweetheart," he murmured. "I can see it all clear as day over your face."

Katherine tilted her head, not certain she understood him. It sounded like he was answering a question she hadn't asked yet. He yawned, covering his mouth and checking the time on her bedside clock.

Garth wrapped an arm around her and drew her close as he shuffled into a comfortable position. Resting his head on the pillows, he settled down. Katherine, still caught feeling bemused, lay facing him, enjoying the comfort of his embrace.

He threw a final look at the laptop, then turned to face her once more, his eyes closing.

She settled herself, finding that once she'd stopped, exhaustion washed over her as well. Garth's body exuded heat and strength. Katherine enjoyed the feel of sharing her bed once again. Just as the fog of sleep came close, Garth spoke drowsily.

"You know I love you too, sweetheart," he murmured thickly. "So there's nothing to be scared of. Looks like we're both in this together."

Katherine struggled to respond, but by the time she'd put together a coherent—and faintly cutting—reply she was too far gone. She fell asleep, once again caught somewhere between amusement and exasperation.

Chapter Three

Katherine woke up, instantly aware of her surroundings. Garth's muscled arm lay around her waist, chaining her to him. They'd shifted during their sleep and now were spooning on the bed, her back against his chest.

The low hum of the laptop had her head lifting from the pillow. Her eyes searched the dark monitor, tiny lights flashing to indicate the search programme still ran. No alarm sounded to indicate anything had been found.

Her room was dark, she knew it wasn't yet dawn. Katherine glanced at her alarm clock before resting her head back on her pillow.

Almost five in the morning, she mused.

They'd been exhausted, not just from the intensity of their marathon sex session, but also from being on the go almost forty-eight hours straight. Most missions — especially since she'd joined the Agency — were like that. Periods of calm followed by bouts of madness that could last for days without break.

Over the years she'd grown used to it. Now it was a way of life for her. Katherine knew she could never give it up. Carefully she untangled herself from Garth's tight embrace without waking him. Chances were, once they hit the ground running that morning, it could be another day or two before they had a chance to catch some sleep. She didn't want to wake him, even if he did look delicious fast asleep in her bed.

Resisting the urge to bend over and kiss him, or even lick him awake, Katherine stood on the cool floorboards and debated between breakfast and a shower. Feeling grungy, despite her quick hand wash before crashing the evening before, she decided on a long hot shower, then some food. Besides, from memory there wasn't much in the way of enticing breakfast supplies in her fridge or cupboards. She thought she might have some milk and cereal but, other than her ever-present boxes of various teas, that was about it.

The shower held far more appeal at that moment.

Katherine padded on silent feet to the small bathroom and closed the door behind her with a soft snick. She dug fresh towels for herself and Garth out and laid them on the side of the basin as she turned the hot faucet on as far as it could go. As the water heated and steam filled the tiny room, she brushed her teeth.

Finished, she climbed into the shower stall, adjusted the temperature until it was the perfect heat and let the hot spray massage her aching muscles. Water ran in rivulets down her body. As she shampooed her hair and soaped her skin, she cast her mind over the events of the last few days.

Thinking of Tarek, she blinked hard, her good mood taking an instant nosedive.

Katherine wondered if her own inflexibility had been a partial cause of her partner and good friend's close call with death. She and Tarek had never been lovers. In that sense the chemistry had never been present between them. A deep, abiding friendship had bound them together, tested true by all manner of deceit, temptation and trials over the years. Their partnership had been unshakeable by the end. It was the subconscious understanding Garth could prove to be another such partner and friend — not to mention lover and help mate — that had her shying away from just how deeply her feelings ran for the man.

Katherine pushed the ever-present thoughts of Garth aside as she rinsed her hair and began to condition it. She went over every movement, every decision, every link in the chain that had resulted in her partner lying comatose in a hospital bed. Katherine could not bear the thought that her stubbornness, her insistence on playing by the book, may have been a significant factor in Tarek's current position.

It wasn't until she gasped, her head lowered under the needling spray, that she found herself crying, finally releasing the pent-up emotions of the last few days. Katherine pressed her lips together and struggled to stem the flow of tears, unwilling to indulge in something she thought weak and useless. Tears would not assist Tarek. Weeping would not solve the puzzle, return the hard drive and stop Oscar Jennings.

None of those profound, logical thoughts helped in the least. Katherine pressed her palms down on the cool, slick tiles of the shower wall. Resting her forehead against her hands she bowed her head and in the privacy of her shower allowed her emotions to roll over her.

She wept.

For her friend, her partner. For the guilt she carried, wondering if she could have done more to protect him.

Katherine sobbed until her arms and stomach shook with the wrung-dry feeling of release. She lifted her head to let the spray wash away her tears and cleanse her face as it had her body. She drew in deep breaths and got a hold of herself, the first peak of her grief having now passed.

She knew sooner or later that the reality of Tarek's wounds would blindside her, but for now she focused on what she could do to avenge him. Wallowing was not her style. Katherine scrubbed her hands over her head and body, washing the water over her skin. With a twist of the faucets, she switched off the shower, squeezed the bulk of the water from her hair and sluiced it from her body.

Stepping onto the bathmat, she reached for the towel, only to freeze and crouch defensively. The split-second recognition of Garth was the only thing that saved him from being tackled through the door and pounded into the floor. Shaking her head, she made a face at him as he handed her a towel.

"You're lucky you aren't on your arse nursing a sore back," she commented. Garth laughed.

"If I'd been an assassin you'd be dead about now," he riposted.

She acknowledged the verbal hit by raising her eyebrows. Pride didn't let her actually say he was right. She'd been so consumed by her own thoughts, she hadn't heard him enter.

"Guess it's a good thing you're here to watch my back and not stab me in it," she grinned as she towelled herself dry. Garth tilted his head, studying her face. She nervously skittered her eyes away. She was not one of those women who glowed beautifully when she cried. Her eyes became red rimmed, her forehead splotchy. Thankfully, Garth didn't comment on her state. He merely drew her in for a hug and kissed her damp hair.

"Will you be all right?" he asked.

Katherine wrapped her arms around him and held him close. She took a shaky breath and nodded.

"Yes, I'm okay now. I just needed to get it out of my system. I've been going over every step we took, trying to see if my rigidity might have been partly responsible for Tarek's — "

"It wasn't," Garth said.

Katherine grimaced and shook her head.

"You can't know that. Hell, I can't know that for sure. But it will be okay, I'm dealing with it and we'll tear Jennings a new arsehole, especially for Tarek. We'll balance the scales for him."

Garth kissed her passionately.

Katherine felt the tingle begin in her belly and unfurl through the rest of her body. She lowered her hands to clench his tight arse, scraping her nails lightly over his skin as she pulled him closer. The towel fell to the floor and they moved against one another.

"You're such a fuckable distraction," Garth laughed. "Let me get clean and then we can get sweaty and dirty together all over again."

Katherine kissed his lips one last time and ducked out of his embrace. Picking up the towel from the floor, she whipped his butt with its edge, grinning at him as she did so. He winked at her as he turned the shower on. Katherine left the bathroom before she was tempted to join him.

After she'd hung up her towel, she returned to the bedroom and opened her drawers and rummaged for some clothes. Slipping on a lacy thong and matching bra, she stepped into a pair of black jeans, then pulled a T-shirt over her head. She shrugged into the shoulder holster with well-practiced ease.

Katherine carefully placed her gun in its holster, then concealed the weapon by shrugging into a jacket. Shifting the holster and gun over her T-shirt until it was comfortable, Katherine made small adjustments while studying her reflection in the mirror.

Satisfied with her look, she bent and laced up a pair of running shoes. She tried to remember if she had anything in the cupboard that would be decent to fry up for breakfast. Her musings were broken by the sound of the shower being turned off. Deciding she could rummage after turning the kettle on, she started out of the bedroom until she heard insistent beeping from the laptop.

All thoughts of food fled as her attention focused on their mission. Turning back, Katherine rushed across the room and nearly collided with Garth as he raced out of the bathroom. His short hair spiked up in every direction, still dripping beads of water down his neck and back. He wiped his face and skin with a towel as he strode over to the laptop.

Standing side by side, they scanned the monitor. It took only seconds to understand what was going on.

"This has to be them," she said as she typed in the commands to activate the tracer.

"Unless it's some other poor schmucks using the same frequency," Garth cautioned. Katherine shook her head.

"Scott said the frequency is too low for anything else, maybe a homemade crystal radio or something. But come on, what are the chances, at five in the morning, that some kid is trying to send messages to aliens on his science project?"

Garth laughed and moved to dress himself. For all of a minute Katherine kept her gaze locked on the tracing programme as it ran. But she couldn't resist. The magnetic pull of Garth's electric sexuality drew her eyes. He'd pulled dark jeans up over his hips. They were zipped but the button still gaped open showing a delicious hint of olive skin. He pulled his arms through the sleeves of his shirt but left it unbuttoned as he checked his weapon.

Katherine felt a thrill course through her body as she watched the ease and familiarity he used in handling the large gun. He ran through the checks, cocked it and gauged the weight again in his hand, though it moulded to him like they were created for each other. He settled it in the waistband of his jeans at the small of his back.

The laptop forgotten, she watched, mesmerised as he dipped into the small overnight bag. He pulled out a small ankle holster and a tiny clutch piece.

"Is that a twenty-two?" she asked, curious.

He nodded and checked it as thoroughly as he had his main weapon. The gun looked tiny, almost like a toy in his large hands. If he held it at an angle to his body Garth would almost be able to palm the weapon and keep it invisible.

"It's my Plan B," Garth spoke as he fixed the gun around his ankle. "Victor always insists the way to stay alive is to have a Plan B and, where possible, a contingency Plan C."

"Sounds logical," she conceded. "So what's Plan C?"

"Turning the fuck around and running like your arse is on fire."

Katherine laughed as Garth stood up. A frisson of sadness arched through her as he buttoned his shirt closed. He had a magnificent chest.

When Garth had finished dressing, he shot her a wicked glance. "Satisfied?" he asked.

Katherine grinned. "Absolutely."

It didn't really matter how he meant his question, her answer held true in many respects. Katherine licked her lips, finding the mere act of watching Garth suit up for battle hot. With those eyes and the prime condition of his body, he was smoking by himself. But watching a warrior prepare himself for the coming scuffle, knowing she'd be by his side and guarding his back — as he would hers — got her juices flowing.

The laptop hummed and drew her attention back. She turned to watch the coordinates narrow further and further down. Garth slung his bag over one shoulder as he stood next to her. She leaned into his side and he wrapped an arm around her shoulders. They pressed close together. The map closed in on the beacon.

They waited in silence. Katherine felt so comfortable with her lover — it was as if they'd been partners for years, working together on dozens of missions. The level of ease between them astonished, but pleased her.

"Looks like the industrial section. Stratford, maybe," Katherine said. Almost as soon as the words had left her mouth, the coordinates honed in on Stratford and continued to close on the frequency.

"Do you have a spare clip?" Garth asked. Katherine lifted her head and jerked her chin towards her dresser.

"I was going to pick it up on my way out. It's in the second drawer. I can fit it into my back pocket. My ID should be next to the clip, can you grab that too, please? Since we'll probably end up breaking down a door or two, I should carry that as well."

Garth moved to the dresser and pulled open the drawer. Katherine's attention remained on the laptop. She bounced on the balls of her feet as she waited for the final destination to be revealed. The screen narrowed to a single block, a red flashing dot representing the building the frequency emitted from.

"Got it," she beamed.

Garth came up beside her and handed her the clip and her wallet. She tapped the screen before reaching for both items and placing them in her back pockets. He studied the screen. She presumed he was memorising the cross-section and building placement.

As he began to stride towards the door, Katherine reached out to stop him, her hand curving around inside his elbow.

"Do you think we should call this in?" she asked.

She could think of serious pros and cons to both sides. The possible traitor weighed heavily on her mind. The last thing she wanted was to tip them off or, worse, give them a golden opportunity to kill more of their number or create havoc. At the same time, entering an unknown situation such as this was lunacy with no back-up except each other. Despite her earlier resolution to cast the rules aside, it didn't mean she wanted to ignore basic safety precautions.

"Are you saying you really want to call the Agency?"

Katherine couldn't read what Garth was asking. He didn't seem annoyed or angry, but neither did he radiate a keen desire to inform their colleagues.

"I want to tip our hand to the traitor even less than you do," she reassured him. "But I also don't want us to enter a firefight, or worse, with no one except each other aware of our movements. Would you and Victor rush into something like this with no safety net? With no one else having a clue what you were up to?"

Garth tilted his head and nodded, seeming to acknowledge her point. He moved back to study the satellite map in more detail.

"Do you know this area at all?" he asked, his attention riveted to the screen. Katherine crouched beside him, her gaze also focused on the map.

"Not well, though I'm sure I've passed through dozens of times. Over here there are some factories, and a block down, in this direction, are some newly built business parks. There shouldn't be too much in the way of collateral damage, certainly no residences that I can recall or schools, parks, nothing like that. The fact this shows basically warehouses, factories and small businesses has me leaning to believe nothing much has changed."

"It looks rather like a rabbit warren around here, though. See how there are almost a dozen small outbuildings in this particular block? Makes me think they've taken those old, large factory lots, knocked the original structure down and subdivided it into many smaller blocks, all on the one piece of land."

"One-one-three-two A, B, C," Katherine agreed as she switched from satellite view to street-map view. "I think you're right. So, with the exact address and hopefully a fair bit of privacy, I think we can take them on. If Jennings is holed up in there we should have everything under control with a minimum of fuss."

"Now you've made me sit and wish we had blueprints," Garth replied with a frown as he switched back to satellite imagery. "How many rooms do you really think the building could have? It doesn't look that big."

Katherine pointed and counted the windows visible from the different angles they could see.

"Being generous, I'd say there couldn't be more than six or so rooms. More likely three main ones and maybe a few windowless rooms. A bathroom, toilet, closet, that sort."

"We do recon as soon as we arrive," Garth insisted.

Katherine nodded. "If we get a whiff it's larger, or more complicated, we can call in a few favours. I've assisted Peterson a few times, a few of the other lads owe me from various other missions. We can keep this from being a legitimate mission until we've finished one way or the other. Keep the mole in the dark."

The grin Garth gave her made her belly roll in lust.

"Why, Miss Hitchens, I do believe you've come to the dark side."

Katherine chuckled and punched his shoulder.

"It's your corrupting influence, Spenser. You're dark and wicked by nature, I obviously have succumbed."

"Mmm, I'd like for you to succumb in other ways," his voice lowered, thickened with passion as he cupped his hand over her arse. He squeezed her cheek and she felt his fingers slide along the seam of her jeans. Had she been naked he'd have fingered her tight hole.

She moaned, hunger spiking through her at his sensual touch. Lifting her face to meet his, she pressed her lips on him. Eagerly, she kissed him back, the intimacy easy and natural between them. Panting hard, she pulled away. She laid a hand, palm down, over the thick ridge straining against the seam of his jeans.

"We have to go catch the bad guy," she murmured. He made an inarticulate sound that sounded something like a frustrated moan.

"Maybe if you're very good, once we've fried Jennings' arse and discovered the name of his contact within the Agency, I'll give you free access to my derrière. You can do anything you want to it and me, whatever you please."

Garth wrapped a hand around the base of her head, threading his fingers through her hair as he dragged her back for another devastatingly potent kiss. With a jerk, he pulled away. Her mind took a moment to focus again, the cloudy haze of arousal threatening to melt her brain entirely.

"You'll let me do anything I please to that luscious arse of yours anyway," he replied with fierce pride and a hungry smile. He patted her cheek again, this time in an arrogant, masculine way.

"But never let it be said I didn't rise to the promise of a sweet reward. You're on, sweetheart. Frying the bastard and locking him in a cage, discovering the rogue mole ruining the Agency and in return anything I desire, including unrestricted access to your body."

Katherine beamed.

"Deal."

"Well then, Agent Hitchens, lead the way."

Katherine patted herself down, going through her mental checklist as they walked towards the door. She checked her holster, her gun, the spare clip and her identification. She picked up her keys from the bowl by the door and jangled them at Garth.

"My car, I'm driving," she challenged. With a wry smirk, he nodded as she led the way outside.

Chapter Four

Katherine and Garth walked up the street, each carrying a steaming takeout mug of coffee. Their free hands were linked and, in the early morning light, they looked like a couple on their way to the start of a shift. They both smiled at each other and kept a close watch of their surroundings—this wasn't the type of area one would wander at night—but no one would recognise how carefully they surveyed the business park they passed.

When they were well out of sight and earshot, they paused beneath a lamppost and sipped their coffee. They'd swung by an early-opening food chain, grabbed a sausage and egg roll each and the coffee. Katherine had inhaled her roll but they had kept the coffee.

"What do you think?" she asked.

"Lights were on inside," he replied.

"Half a dozen cars parked in their bays, too. There must be at least a few people inside."

"The buildings on either side of our target were still dark, no cars. I think it's safe to assume the neighbours aren't home just now."

Katherine paused before replying.

"If we wait, call for back-up and the others to assist us there's a strong chance more people will arrive. Regardless of whether they're innocent or knowing conspirators, more bodies mean more potential casualties and a harder task keeping everyone under control."

"Agreed," Garth said as he sipped his coffee. "Whereas right now, with just the two of us, if we go back, walk in like we're starting a new shift and take charge there'd be a dozen people there tops. We know a short time ago someone was trying to decrypt that hard drive. If we wait and play it safe we might miss our window of opportunity."

Despite his words Garth watched her and remained silent. His opinion was clear to her, but he didn't push her either way. She smiled at him and felt a warmth unfurl in her chest, pleased that he let her make her own decision and didn't try to bully her.

"If the two of us can't handle a half dozen people — likely techs and civilians — then we don't deserve to hold this job," Katherine said before she drained her coffee cup. Retaining the empty cup, she shrugged her shoulders to loosen her muscles and bounced on the balls of her feet to warm her legs up.

"I'll take point," Garth insisted. "We go in easy, make a quick survey. If we can see the hard drive we go immediately for it before they have a chance to react."

"Resist only if necessary," Katherine added.

"Piece of cake," Garth grinned.

She chuckled.

"Because these things always go to plan, don't they?"

"That's why we have a Plan B."

"And C, don't forget turning tail and running."

In high spirits they turned around and walked back to the building. As they approached, Katherine could feel the weight of razor sharp awareness settle upon them both. Katherine noticed that both of their movements became graceful, fluid. Garth in particular appeared like he had released his inner hunter.

They stalked their prey.

With smiles on their faces, like any normal couple who were starting a new day together, they passed by, appearing to be completely unnoticed. But to the trained eye Katherine knew their movements would be recognisable. She remained alert, wary, coiled and ready for action.

"I count five cars," Katherine murmured. Garth shifted his head to indicate another parked out on the street.

"No other lights are around. I think that makes six. There's no condensation on the windshield or windows. It wasn't left there overnight."

"Still manageable," she reflected as they came to the front door.

Katherine reached out and pulled it open for Garth. She stepped to the side to let him enter first since he wanted to be on point. As he strode forward, confidence radiated from his body language. Nothing hinted he should not be where he stood. Katherine followed, with a quick check of their rear, making sure they were clear and not being followed.

Garth's head turned, surveying the large, open-plan reception area, greeting foyer and generalised waiting room. No posters or advertisements reflected the work performed here. Roughly painted bare walls were stark relief to the dark plastic tables. A few computer desktops were scattered around to create mini-terminals.

As they passed the receptionist's desk, Garth leaned over and dropped his empty coffee cup in the waste basket under her bench. Katherine noticed he used the change in his posture to continue his recon of the room. She mimicked his motion, also tossing her cup into the bin but using the act of leaning over the desk to make sure no one followed behind them.

More ambushes happened in the first few silent moments of an attack than at almost any other time, she had learned. She needed to make sure they weren't cut off from escape or blindsided by their enemies sneaking up them.

As they walked farther into the front room they could see two workers chatting in hushed tones, steaming mugs cradled in both their hands. The two women looked up as they heard Garth and Katherine enter. They relaxed. The blonde remained silent but the other, a brunette, stood.

"Can I help you? I'm afraid no one is really here just now. People won't start arriving until half past seven. Our office hours don't begin until eight."

Katherine smiled, in what she hoped was a reassuring manner, but remained silent, letting Garth take the lead. He dug a hand into his pocket and removed his laminated ID.

"I'm Garth Spenser, this is my partner. We're following a routine lead and discovered someone on the premises who is working at a terminal about now. Would you be able to show us to that person please?"

The women exchanged puzzled glances. Katherine's intuition hummed. They were on to something here. She could feel it in her gut.

"James and Robert are out back. They always arrive early to check the servers before the rest of the staff come in each morning. But our systems are quite strictly audited. I don't understand what possible trouble they could —"

"The company is not in trouble," Garth said quickly. "If you could take us to them please? We should be able to sort this out easily."

Neither woman looked convinced, but they left their mugs and indicated for Garth and Katherine to follow them down a small hallway towards a back room. The blonde pushed open a door along the corridor and entered, the brunette standing back to allow Garth and Katherine to enter first.

"James? Bobby?" the blonde called out through the large room. Many desktop terminals were lined up neatly in a row, the large flat screen monitors offering some privacy between cubicles, hiding people from view. The blonde halted mid-stride, seemingly taken by surprise.

Katherine's instincts screamed at her. Reacting unconsciously, she pulled her gun from its holster but kept it aimed at the floor so as to not appear too threatening.

"Oh! Hi, Connor," the blonde stammered. "I didn't know you were in so early."

A man peered out around the computer terminal. He had a shaggy blond mop of hair that looked unwashed and ratty. Young enough to pass for a college student, he didn't have the polished, professional edge most adults gained in the first few years of work. Connor took one glance at Garth, a second at Katherine and dived back behind the safety of his screen.

"Stop!" Garth commanded as he reached for his gun. Katherine pushed the blonde safely behind her and moved a few paces to the side to get a better view around the desk.

"Freeze! We don't want any trouble here," Katherine insisted in a loud voice.

"What the hell?" came a surprised shout from a different corner of the room. Two men stood up from terminals towards the rear of the room. They gaped at Garth and Katherine, then pulled weapons. Katherine glanced back at the door. The brunette had already left and the blonde—crouching and covering her head— was scurrying out of the room, shrieking.

"You can't stop us! It's our right to have these websites up for public access. We're doing the world a favour revealing the mysteries of the conspiracy within the House of Lords! No longer will they be able to pull the strings of our government!" One of the men shouted as he waved his gun about.

Katherine frowned and Garth scowled at them.

"I couldn't give a bloody rat's arse about your websites," he insisted.

Katherine moved around the desks, wanting to make it to Connor's cubicle. The blond shoved a pad of paper and memory stick into his satchel and all but ripped the USB connection of a small, black box from his terminal. She recognised the box as the portable hard drive. About the size of a video cassette it was unremarkable, except for the invaluable data stored within it.

"Garth, he has the hard drive," she called out and lunged towards Connor. He waved a gun he pulled from the satchel, his hand shaking so badly Katherine could barely believe he held on to the weapon. She reached out her free hand palm up to stop him.

"Just give us the hard drive, this isn't a joke. I promise it's far more serious than Jennings informed you of," she tried to calm him.

"Go, Connor!" his friends shouted as they fired their weapons randomly around the room. "We've got you covered man. Go, go, go!"

Connor ducked down and sprinted towards his friends. Katherine and Garth both cursed. Garth hunched down low and ran after Connor.

"We protect our own!" the hooligans shouted, firing wildly. They didn't seem to have any real understanding of how to use their weapons or the seriousness of what they were doing.

"Cover me," Garth snapped as he crouched, his gun raised and steady in his hand.

Katherine opened her mouth but didn't get a chance to caution her partner before he'd set off after Connor at a low run.

Honestly. Men!

She reached out a hand to shift a flat screen computer monitor to give her more cover. Sighting the men, she took careful aim, ignoring the banging of bullets around her. The only way those two would hit something would be by fluke.

Calming her breath, she judged her shot and winged the shoulder of one. He screamed. A spurt of blood blossomed through his shirt.

"I'm shot! I've been shot!" he screamed. His friend emptied his clip randomly around the room as Connor pushed past the men. Garth had closed in on the skinny blond, but he suddenly jerked back and lurched to his knees.

Scared, her instincts roaring, Katherine used the distraction of the wailing, shot man to circle the room, sneak behind the other stranger and cold-cock him with the butt of her gun. He sank to the ground unconscious. Oblivious, his friend continued crying and ranting, waving his arms about as he shouted for the secretaries to come in and assist him.

Connor had ducked out of the back door. Katherine saw him sprinting down the narrow hallway, his satchel bumping against his thigh and slowing him down as he tried to squeeze off a few shots, run and keep his balance all at the same time. Katherine threw a quick glance over her shoulder to Garth.

With one man unconscious and the other shrieking like a girl and trying to fire his now-empty gun, Katherine wondered what was keeping her partner. If they didn't move they would lose Connor and the hard drive.

"Garth, we need to — what?"

Her partner pulled himself upright with an obvious effort. Sweat beaded over his forehead and his usually olive tone looked grey. Wild-eyed she raced back to lodge her shoulder under his arm and help him get to his feet.

"What happened? Garth… Holy shit he got you. Here, sit down."

"Don't be stupid, it's barely a twinge. Go after Connor, Hitchens. Like you said, he has the hard drive.

When she hesitated, he added, "Don't worry about me, woman."

Katherine felt divided for a second.

"You fool," she replied with no heat. "I've lost one partner already, not twenty-four hours ago. Just think of the reputation I'd get if I ran off and left you here. Let me look at this."

"Don't be an idiot, we need —"

She cut him off with a dismissive wave of her hand. Her features were grimly set. He didn't think he'd be able to change whatever she'd decided.

"We found him once, Garth, we'll find him again. Now stop bitching like a little girl and let me see your side."

Garth strained his head around her, but, as she could have told him, Connor was long gone. She lifted the damp cotton of his shirt and sucked in a breath as she caught sight of his 'little twinge'.

The bullet had penetrated the flesh of his side, just under his ribcage. His back remained smooth and perfect but viscous blood was clotting at the edge of the wound, turning black in the air. If they didn't get it seen to straight away the risk of infection was serious.

"Go after Connor, I'll be fine," she muttered. "You're either demented or deluded. You need a doctor, Spenser. That bullet will need extracting, it's lodged somewhere deeply inside you. I bet you ten pounds you'll need stitches to close that wound. You're lucky that was a blind shot. Much lower and he might have penetrated your stomach, liver or kidneys."

While she felt certain an artery hadn't been nicked, there could be any number of internal organs clipped or damaged. She pressed down on the wound with care, trying to gauge how badly injured his muscles might be, and also whether anything internal had been hurt. She felt unwell at the thought. Katherine knew she'd have to move him, take him to a professional regardless of the pain it could cause. No way did she want to overlook anything by administering only the basic first aid she could give here and now. If she missed something the consequences could genuinely be lethal for her lover — and that was a risk she couldn't live with.

Garth sucked in a painful breath, his face strained and losing colour as she continued to put pressure on the wound. He didn't squirm or cry out, however. Katherine knew enough about field dressing wounds and basic gunshot care that if something had been seriously punctured he'd have screamed from the pain, not merely given her a death-stare.

That didn't change her opinion. He still needed to see a doctor.

Garth grunted in pain as she helped him stand up. The young man she'd clipped had rushed to the main office and was insisting the two secretaries call the police and an ambulance for him.

"You're citizens," he shouted at either or both of them. "Arrest that bitch!"

"Us? You're the one who wants her thrown into a cell. You're a citizen, too. If you're so worked up over this you do it. We didn't see her do a thing."

"I told you that stupid conspiracy website you tinker with out of hours would get you in trouble," the other woman chided him. "If you had half a brain you'd have listened to us months ago when we suggested you tone it back a bit..."

"I think we'd be wise to go out the back way," Katherine suggested. "Maybe Connor left a clue. We'd best see if we can spot anything on the way back to the car."

"Chicken," Garth chuckled. "I'd love to see them try to arrest you."

"'Try' being the operative word," she agreed as they moved down the corridor. "The day a scrawny kid like that can drag me into the local precinct is the day I start crocheting and give myself up for dead."

With remarkable speed, considering the severity of Garth's wound, they exited the building and made their way out of the business park by weaving around and between other buildings. As they came on to the street the sound of approaching sirens grew louder.

"You really shouldn't have let him go," Garth scolded as she unlocked the passenger side of her car and held the door open for him. He sucked in a harsh breath, then scowled darkly as he sat. His hand pressed his shirt over the wound. Blood seeped from it, despite the pressure he applied.

Katherine swore softly as she mentally ran through her list of contacts. From this side of the city it would still be a ten-minute drive to the nearest private doctor she could think of. She slammed her door shut, started the car and pulled out on to the street before she'd even clicked her seatbelt on.

"You're important to me, you great lug, so shut up about what I should have done. If you think this partnership is going to be something where you tell me to jump and I hear and obey then you can just kiss my arse."

"I don't just plan to kiss it," Garth replied with a hiss of pain as she turned a corner. He continued speaking, as if pain wasn't etched into his face. "I have plans for you and that delightful arse of yours. Plans a little projectile of metal won't dissuade me from."

"I'm sure Dr Hillon will just love that attitude," Katherine said with a laugh. Garth turned grey when she made another quick turn and appeared too busy trying to keep his sausage and egg roll in his stomach to reply.

"Damn it, I just knew you were trouble the moment I laid eyes on you," she swore, more to herself than Garth. "You haven't disappointed, Spenser. You're trouble all right. Sexy, wicked, bloody addictive trouble, but a heartache just waiting to occur nevertheless. I'm such a sucker to have got involved with you. You radiate sensual danger. I can't believe I'm in so deep with you."

"How deep, Hitchens?" Garth said through gritted teeth.

Katherine sent him a swift glance, trying to gauge how much she should—and shouldn't—say. He met her gaze, his eyes dark as night. Despite the intensity of how he watched her, small lines of strain were etched around the corners of his eyes. She could almost feel his pain herself.

She knew it would cost her, but she could no longer remain silent.

"I meant what I said back there, I can't cope with the thought I might lose you, Garth. We're equals, you're my partner. Not just in work, in everything. I want to see where this thing between us leads. I want to be with you."

"You proposing to me, Kate?" Garth tried and failed to tease her. Katherine shot him an evil look, laced with humour and love.

"Am I doing this wrong?" she asked, feigning innocence. "Should I be down on one knee? Offer you a ring? Gee, maybe I should call your dad and ask for his blessing, too. Take you out to dinner or something."

Garth laughed, then coughed as his side pained him.

Katherine frowned. "Should I break the speed limit? How bad is it?"

"I'm fine."

Katherine glared at him. Garth sighed, the tiniest smile twitching at the corner of his mouth.

"It hurts like a bitch, but a few good painkillers, getting the damn metal out of me and stitching me back together will have me good as new. Hillon will have some good Scotch sitting in a cupboard somewhere. A good slug of that, a handful of codeine and I'll be back on board as if nothing's happened."

"So stubborn," she muttered, more to herself than him. Even in the close confines of the car he must have heard, for he laughed.

The tension broken for the moment, a comfortable silence fell between them. Katherine grew lost in her thoughts as she skirted a few of the traffic laws to get them both at the good doctor's home in near record time. She pulled into Hillon's driveway and parked the car, not fussed that she blocked the doctor's vehicle.

Katherine unsnapped her seatbelt, opened the door and had half climbed out before she turned around to watch Garth. While he moved far more slowly than usual, he managed. The thought of offering him some help flitted across her mind, but then she remembered the man's pride and stubbornness.

Katherine climbed out of the car and waited until Garth was steady on his feet before she slammed the door shut and walked beside her lover up to the doctor's home.

"Next time you can get shot," Garth muttered in complaint.

Katherine rang the doorbell multiple times as she tossed her hair at him and sniffed in mock disdain.

"If I were shot you'd have not only killed those two imbeciles, James and Robert, but you'd have carried me back to the car and sworn a blood oath of getting revenge and making their lives miserable," she remarked. "I'd have put up a fight, but finally would've let your idiot masculine ego win. You'll note I'm not coddling you, not weeping and wailing and having feminine hysterics. Frankly I think you should be grateful for small mercies."

"That's a fair point," he conceded, seeming to think it over.

Before Katherine could speak further the front door opened. A short, round man with flyaway grey hair stood in the doorway. He glanced from Katherine to Garth, then lowered his gaze to the damp, stained shirt and Garth's bloodied hand clenched around his side.

"I'm glad I haven't made breakfast yet," the elderly man remarked. He stepped back and allowed them both entrance.

Katherine entered, followed by Garth. They stood in the front hallway as Dr Hillon closed and locked the door.

"Head on back, you know the surgery," he said. Katherine turned and began to walk back as Dr Hillion spoke to Garth, an amused tone in his voice.

"I'll expect you'll be grateful for a slug of my Scotch, young man? I'll need you to answer a few questions and then, once I survey the damage, I'll decide what I can give you."

"You mean this is one of those answer the question correctly and I'll give you the good stuff?" Garth asked with a chuckle. Dr Hillon laughed in reply.

"Heavens, no! If you lie to me I'll find out soon enough from your reactions to the dose of antibiotics or painkillers I inject you with. Once a patient lies to me I refuse to treat them again. Too hazardous. No, my boy, what I meant was depending on the dose and style of shots I will need to administer, there are varying risks of you losing your breakfast as well as my Scotch. There's no sense in my wasting the expensive drink if the chances are great you'll lose it a few minutes later. I'll give you the cheap stuff if that's the case."

The entire situation seemed surreal to Katherine as she entered the small, clean room Hillon used to patch up agents and other assorted acquaintances. He ran a pro bono day clinic sometimes, eager to do his bit. She moved over to one side of the room and leaned against the windowsill.

Garth climbed onto the padded steel gurney–style bed. He gingerly tugged his shirt up over his head, his face losing colour as the movement aggravated his wound. "That sounds fair, doc. Fire away, I need that drink right now. Or a shot of codeine. Preferably both."

The doctor smiled, pulled on a pair of gloves and moved a small lamp to shine it on Garth's bloodied side. He bent to study the wound.

"Let's start with the hour and items of what you last ate and drank, whether you've taken any drug — prescribed or non — in the last seventy-two hours and how the hell you managed to get shot at such an angle by a medium calibre handgun."

"Well…" Garth hesitated. Katherine had to look out of the window to stop the incredible urge to laugh. Her lover looked like a schoolboy at the doctor's office with a set of scraped knuckles and a broken nose trying to explain how it wasn't his fault he'd got into the scuffle. Sir, it was the other boy who'd started it.

Her partner was in excellent hands. The tightly wound ball of stress pressing against her heart eased. She'd been scared silly, though not able to show it. Dr

Hillon would not be taking this blasé, amused approach with Garth's wound had it been serious.

Everything would be all right now. She just knew it.

Chapter Five

"You can't possibly mean that. The moment I have some privacy the first thing I do is look at the damage," Garth insisted from his bathroom.

The door remained open and he called out to her in the kitchen, where Katherine was making a pot of tea. Adding in the leaves to steep, she placed the lid on to keep the water warm, added two mugs onto the tray and carried it into the living room. Careful not to spill any, she placed it on the coffee table. Her feet deliciously bare, she walked down the hall to lean against the doorframe of the bathroom and watched her lover.

He'd stripped down to his boxers, his jeans stained and his shirt ruined from the caked blood. The jeans were thrown half into the hamper, one leg still dangling on the floor. The shirt had been tossed straight into the bin. Garth had sponged the worst of the blood and iodine from his skin and now studied Hillon's stitchery in the large bathroom mirror that hung over the sink.

"I've never had stitches," Katherine admitted, almost embarrassed. "I've had plenty of cuts and scrapes, even got myself a few nice scars. But I've never been shot and never required stitches for any of the bumps and bruises I've collected over the years. So no, Garth, I don't usually dash off to look at the damage first chance I get. I will grudgingly admit, when I realised you'd been shot, my first concern was with how bad it was, but I put that down to the adrenaline."

She put a teasing twist on her final comment, it being true as far as the words went, but not the real reason she'd been near desperate to survey the damage to her love and assure herself it wasn't critical. Garth slanted her a hot glance and reached out to take her hands in his.

She let him pull her close, press her arse back against the edge of the porcelain sink and wrap his arms around her body. Tilting her head up, she met him halfway for a searing kiss that scorched her senses.

"What happened to my reward for being such a good patient?" he asked, a laugh in his tone. Katherine licked her lips, amusement crinkling her mouth into a smile.

"Considering the rich taste of Scotch on your tongue, my love, I would say you've been amply rewarded for being such a good boy."

"That wasn't what I had in mind," he insisted as he got busy unsnapping her jeans and pushing them down her legs. Katherine bent to help tug the pants over her ankles, though she was not convinced he was up to ravishing her just now. Surely he ached. Since Hillon had given him two shots, one of penicillin and one of codeine, Garth had been acting pretty much his usual self once again, just moving a bit more stiffly than she had become used to.

Frisky play, however, she figured must have been out of his reach.

Perhaps she was wrong.

"Garth, I really don't think —"

"Are you reneging on your side of the deal, Kate?" he asked. Kate frowned, perplexed.

"What?"

"Are you calling shortbread? Does the thought of having anal sex with me really not make you hot and jittery, because working on your earlier reactions I was positive that wasn't the case."

"What?" Kate repeated, then shook her head. "Of course I'm not reneging. But, Garth, you've just been shot. You should be lying in bed badgering me for cups of tea and slices of toast and whining about me not letting you have the remote or something. Not looking for the lube to give my arse a delicious reaming and chomping my anal cherry."

At her final comment, somewhat more detail than she'd been planning on sharing with him, his eyebrows rose.

"I get to chomp your cherry?" he repeated, sounding delighted. "That makes getting shot almost worthwhile, sweetheart."

Katherine couldn't help it, she laughed. He must've known very well that she'd have let him fuck her in the arse without getting shot, but to take such a view on the situation struck her as funny.

As she chuckled, Garth lifted the hem of her T-shirt up over her head and tossed it into a corner of the room. Katherine twisted her arms behind her and unclasped her bra, sliding the straps down and freeing her breasts. The lacy scrap dropped onto the floor.

Stark naked, she shivered a little in the cool room, but the heat radiating from Garth's body made up for the low temperature.

She cupped her hand around his hardening cock. Katherine dipped her fingers under the waistband of his boxers and felt the heat of his soft skin stretched over his thick prick. She stroked him from the base of his shaft right up to the tip, caressing him multiple times as he moaned his approval.

A few tugs and his boxers fell to the floor. Garth stepped out from them and leaned over to open a drawer in the vanity next to the sink. He removed a foil packet and a small tube of lubricant.

"Turn around, sweetheart," he muttered huskily.

Katherine paused for a second before obeying him. She still didn't want him hurting himself from overexertion, but her nipples had peaked and excitement tingled through her body. She craved this wicked man, her partner, and if he felt up to it she longed to feel his cock reaming her arse, penetrating her as deeply as it was physically possible for a man to do.

She wanted him. It all boiled down to the simple fact that she desired him.

"Grab on to the edge of the basin," he ordered.

Katherine complied, but turned her head and shoulders around so she could watch him as he squeezed a large amount of the fluid onto his index and middle fingers. He slicked the lube around with his thumb and rested the tube on the edge of the porcelain near the taps. With his free hand he spread her arse cheeks wide apart, her tiny puckered hole clenching.

"So tiny, so tempting," he murmured.

Without further teasing, he stroked the tip of his index finger over the outside skin of her hidden entrance. The moisture transferred easily and soon he screwed the tip of his finger into her hole. Katherine's breathing turned ragged from the incredible pressure of the intense penetration.

Twisting his finger, he opened her further and slicked the inside of her passage. He corkscrewed left and right, then alternated that with the finger-fucking thrusts of a deepening penetration. Katherine's head bowed as her body trembled. Her back arched, her shoulders dipped down and this stretched her spine and flared her arse to unclench her inner muscles.

"That's it, sweetheart," Garth muttered satisfied. "Open to me. Give yourself over to the blinding passion a good arse-fucking can bring."

"You're not going to fit," she moaned. "I can barely fit your finger, Garth. It's not possible to squeeze your cock in here."

"I'll prove you wrong," he replied, arrogant. Utterly certain. "But I'll tell you a secret, sweet Kate. A man like me, I want you to beg me not to. That just makes it hotter. See, I can read your body, the way you arch into my possession, the way your breath hitches, the trembling along that slender line of your spine. You love this, you crave it. Beg and plead all you want, hell tell me to stop, tell me how small you are and how I stretch you to breaking point. Say I'll split you wide. I want to hear all that and still I'll ram it in harder."

Garth's words were making her hot. Her pussy had grown slick during his little speech, her cream flowing across her lower lips as heat suffused her core. Not only would her pleading make him want her more, but it got her own juices pumping.

His finger fucked her arse hard. Katherine moaned as he slowly pressed his middle finger inside her arse to join his first digit.

Suddenly, she wanted to make him as hot as she felt. Her nipples ached from the need to be caressed, her clit burned with desire and hunger. Katherine could feel her orgasm build inside her and knew she'd not last long once he penetrated her with his cock. Taking his words for truth, Katherine wanted to have Garth lose control as much as she knew she soon would.

Lifting her head, she caught sight of herself in the mirror. Her cheeks were flushed, her blonde hair spilling out of its ponytail and framing her face, strands brushing her shoulder. Better still, with a small turn of her head she could see Garth clearly behind her, his gaze hot and filled with lusty need. She could see his fingers pumping and feel the answering pressure in her full, tight arse.

The scenario took on a whole new dimension as she realised she could watch him fuck her arse without giving herself neck strain. Trembling, she lowered one hand to stroke her clit, the other hand clenching the cool porcelain for support.

"No, Garth," she said in a soft tone, "stop. Don't ream my arse."

His fingers paused and he caught her gaze in the mirror. She gave him her richest, most secret, feminine smile ever. She tried to communicate with her eyes how she wanted to bring his fantasy to life as much as her own. She tried to repeat his words back to him as best she could recall them.

"I'm begging you not to fuck my arse," she repeated. "You have to stop. You'll split me wide with that cock of yours. I'm too small for you, it'll hurt."

His grin widened and, if anything, his fingers pressed harder into her as he caught on. She'd been careful to not make her pleading too fake, and she'd kept her gaze steady, tried to tell him she hadn't forgotten their safe word in the least. He appeared to get the message. The grin that crossed his face thrilled her.

"I'm doing this precisely because you're so tiny. You have no idea how delicious a virgin arse can be, sweetheart," he murmured. "You better hurry up and stroke your clit harder, love. I'm all out of patience."

Having said that, he quickly rolled the thin latex down his hard shaft, grabbed the lubricant again and squirted a generous amount over his cock. Tossing the tube to the floor, he slicked himself up then slowly pulled his fingers out of her hole. Her tiny passage gaped, craving to be filled.

Katherine watched him in the mirror, her eyes riveted on what she could see of his actions.

"I'm going to nail your arse to the wall, sweetheart," Garth insisted, his voice thick with lust. "I've had this image in my head since you questioned me two days ago. Do you know how hard it was not to lift you up, turn you over that table and do this to you, love?"

Panting, she recognised her words from their interview. It felt like a lifetime ago.

Garth seated his enormous head at the entrance of her back channel. The plum-like head appeared almost twice the size of her small hole. Garth kept her cheeks spread wide. With an almost fearful look behind her, Katherine checked the dimensions weren't skewed. Nope. He really was that big.

Returning her gaze to the mirror, she spoke again.

"Garth, are you sure you'll fit? You really do look too big for me. You're going to split me open."

"That's the whole idea, love. A man might love pussy, and heaven knows I adore yours. You're everything I could hope for or dream of in a lover, but a man is flat out lying if he says he doesn't relish fucking his lover up the arse. That tight, clenching hole makes a man feel like he's caught in a slick, virgin vice. And that's what the appeal is, to split you wide and ram myself home inside you."

Katherine knew if he caused her genuine pain he would stop, but that didn't negate the small spurt of fear that mingled with her desire for him. Her fingers twisted around her clit, her pleasure spiking just as the painful pressure filled her arse when Garth pressed his head inside her. Her head fell back, her hair caressing her back, her face scrunching as she felt caught somewhere between agony and bliss.

She panted and moaned.

"Garth, don't. Stop. Oh, damn, keep going, please, move in me. I need it."

Incoherent, her broken words didn't even make sense to her. She pressed back as pleasure rocked through her clit and a large knot grew in her belly.

"Open your eyes, I want to see you watching me as I fuck your arse deep," Garth insisted.

On a shattered breath she obeyed him. Katherine clenched the basin with a hand and lifted her gaze to watch Garth in the mirror. He gripped his hands on either side of her waist, pulling her hips back so she pushed her rear back onto his thick length.

He devoured her with his eyes. Katherine felt possessed and claimed unlike anything she could express. She was his, and he was hers. Forever.

"So fucking good," he moaned. "You're delicious, Kate. Delicate and feminine. Absolutely perfect."

Feeling her core of strength rise up, Katherine opened her heart and soul to Garth in every way. Embracing the pain, she jerked her hips back onto him, thrusting her arse down further onto his cock, swallowing him down more. Surprise flared in his eyes only to be overtaken by lust and pleased pride.

"That's it, beautiful, fuck yourself on me. Take your pleasure."

Katherine could only moan, far beyond actual words. She pressed back on him, her tight channel burning with the pain, but pleasure twisted inside her, mingled with the pain and need. Soon the tight coil of boiling emotions built within her and she cried out, unable to suppress the conglomeration burning in her belly and rear.

"I need, oh fuck, Garth, please, I want... More, please, give me everything," she pleaded.

Without saying a thing Garth reacted. His grip tightened and he rammed himself in and out of her arse. His legs bent and he pushed himself up into her fully, his balls slapping on her thighs as he ravaged her tiny hole. Katherine watched his face and body as he possessed her, like a demon claiming his soulmate.

Over and over, he penetrated her until finally the stimulation of her clit became too much. On the tender edge of her climax, Katherine lifted her hand from the porcelain and twisted her nipple. The coolness of her fingers, coupled with the extra stimulation at her breast, pushed her over the edge.

An orgasm, the likes of which she had never experienced, crashed over her. Instinctively, her body acted of its own will. She closed her eyes, threw her head back as she arched her spine in sheer bliss. She screamed loud and long as pleasure rocked through her, blurring her senses and overriding her body.

Even through this, she felt Garth's thrusts as he roared his release, his hot seed shooting inside her body, filling her anal cavity until his thick cum dripped out of the edges of her deliciously abused hole.

Katherine gripped the edges of the basin with both hands, otherwise she would have fallen to the tile floor as her legs wobbled. Garth leaned over her, his chest resting on her back as he spooned her from behind, his cock still fully lodged in her bum. The aftershocks of his climax rippled through his body and she noted he, too, grabbed a hold of the porcelain.

They panted hard, each winded and struggling for breath.

A minute, then two ticked by as the comfortable silence lengthened between them as they recovered. After a while, Garth pressed a series of kisses to her shoulder and nibbled his way up the length of her neck.

Katherine sighed happily and arched her neck to the side to grant him full access.

"That was magical," she said in a husky, raw voice.

He murmured something unintelligible in return, his lips and tongue busy against her skin. She chuckled and moved her head, lifted his chin with two fingers and kissed his lips.

They drank each other in, the intimacy familiar now. Slowly, she opened her eyes and met her lover's gaze.

"I love you," he said, the words evidently heart-felt.

She beamed back at him. The words were difficult for her to summon. It wasn't because they weren't true—she loved him with everything in her heart, mind, body and soul. It was hard to lay herself so open to a man like this. But she knew she could no longer hide. Not from herself and not from this wonderful man whom she never wanted to be parted from.

"I love you too," she said, the words unusual on her tongue. He seemed to understand what a big admission that was for her and he pressed another kiss to her lips, drinking down their shared confessions.

Katherine wrapped an arm around her man and held him. She knew, in a moment, they'd have to clean up and get dressed — again. There was an awful lot of work ahead of them. But, just for the next few seconds, she wanted to wallow in their shared intimacy and the perfection of this moment when they'd first acknowledged their love for one another.

Reality would come all too quickly.

* * * *

Katherine took the first brief shower and dressed. She remade them a pot of tea while Garth lingered in the bathroom. Ten minutes later, the first trickle of worry entered her mind. She'd been about to call out to him, to assure herself he was okay, when he entered the kitchen.

She noticed his movements were stiff, painful. Katherine frowned, concerned.

"I've made us some tea. You should take a painkiller with it, take the edge off."

He held up his hand, two small pills already enclosed in his palm.

"Way ahead of you there, sweetheart," he replied.

Guilt stirred in her stomach, worry that she'd been the cause of the pain he now suffered. Her thoughts must have reflected clearly on her face.

"Stop that right now. I'd have wanted to share that intimacy even if both my legs had been broken. Trust me, I'd have found a way. A few small twinges now are nothing in payment for the hot vice of your arse, Kate. So put that guilt away and let's get on with the mission."

Garth followed her into the living room and she poured them both steaming hot mugs of tea as he gingerly lowered himself onto the couch. His colour was still good, he didn't sweat from exertion and his breathing was calm. She sighed with relief as she handed him his mug and sat down next to him.

They took their time with the tea. Garth swallowed his pills. Five minutes later Katherine could see some relaxing in the set of his jaw, his posture loosening as he eased back into the couch.

Finishing their tea in silence, Garth sat forward, placed his mug on the scarred coffee table and booted up his laptop. Katherine scooted closer to Garth. He turned the screen so they could both see as he started working.

"I want to start a background search combining Connor and the company that rents out that office space," Garth spoke as he typed.

"Both receptionists knew who Connor was, though he appeared to be a friend—not a collaborator—of James and Robert," Katherine mused as Garth continued working the keyboard. He nodded.

"Agreed. James and Robert frequently came in early, before anyone started for the day, and presumably worked on their websites and posted whatever conspiracy proof they'd unearthed. The receptionist was surprised to see Connor in so early.

"That, coupled with the clear fact he was working on Oscar's hard drive, decrypting it for sure, leads us to believe he must have been an easy contact for Oscar. Someone he knew had skills in computer code and encryption software, but also a tech he had ready, easy access to. It's barely been twenty-four hours since Oscar got his hands on the hard drive, so this was his gut reaction, not a well-organised, structured response."

"So it isn't a leap of logic to conclude Oscar has ties with the corporation itself, or with its owners," Katherine concluded. "He might have used these techs in the past, he might have family ties to it, or possibly it came highly recommended from someone he trusts."

"I hadn't thought of that," Garth confessed as he opened a new tab to start a new search with the extra parameters. "Oscar could have turned to an accomplice, or the Agency mole asked for help and followed their recommendation for whom to turn to. That's a valid point, Katherine."

It didn't take them long to realise MacKenzie Industries — the company that rented the office — was a shell corporation. After copious digging and drinking another full pot of tea they made their first breakthrough.

"There should be a branch of the government to dig into such generic corporations as this," Katherine insisted, exhausted frustration clear in her tone. "Has it struck you that whoever has worked so hard to bury this board behind MacKenzie Industries must have had help?"

"Oh yeah," Garth replied, his eyes locked on the screen. "I can think of two simple answers to how hard we're having to dig. One, Oscar hired a professional to bury all the paperwork and data. That means he's well connected and flush with cash. The other method I can think of is he has a co-conspirator, either the mole or someone else well connected, and they handled this side of their business. Buried everything under so much secrecy and red tape it's creating this nightmare for us."

"If Jennings does have an accomplice it would make sense they'd cover his tracks. By covering Oscar's arse they protect their own. A mole has a lot more to lose than Jennings. Jennings will do hard time, but the mole will be branded a traitor. Lose their standing and privileged lifestyle. We could really be opening a can of worms here."

"You don't sound too worried," Garth shot her a quick smile.

Katherine shook her head. "I'm not. If the toes I step on or the arse I kick is working against the Agency, our government and way of life I'll happily do what I can to bring them down."

"You know what we could really do with?" Garth spoke again minutes later. "Another set of hands."

Katherine tilted her head, a small frown on her face. She wasn't sure who Garth could mean, but then the light dawned.

"You want to call in Victor?" she surmised. Garth nodded and searched her face with his gaze.

"He's paid a steep price for this data, he was prepared to give his life for it. He nearly did by the look of him when we finally helped exchange him. He's Agency, too, has all the clearance needed to run back-traces on all these blocks and red tape being thrown at us."

Katherine grinned, the full depth of Garth's plan becoming clear.

"So we take the heat, act as bait and get both Jennings and the traitor following us, while Victor traces the blocks and flushes out the identity of the mole. We lead the charge. Victor brings up the rear and corners them."

"Exactly, though I'd word it differently to Victor."

Katherine laughed at that comment.

"Victor Adams would chew you up and spit you out if he thought you were putting us out front to protect his arse."

"It's not like I'm coddling him or holding his hand," Garth insisted. "We need the help. Calling him in is logical. I will grant you Victor is savvy enough it will take little thought for him to deduce what we're doing, but he'll be high on drugs. He's pretty battered up. But I do think it only fair to keep him apprised of what's going on."

"He's your mentor." Katherine tried to keep the smug tone from her voice. "You can call him and ask. I'll just back you up with this one. I've heard of Victor's reputation, I don't relish being the one to try to keep him from this when he sees how close we're getting."

Garth shot her a hot glance and Katherine felt her nipples and pussy react. Chemistry sparked in the air around them. They stared at each other a moment, until Garth pulled his cell out of his pocket and dialled the number without looking.

The tone rang a number of times before the line was picked up. Katherine leaned closer so she could hear both sides of the conversation, intrigued as to how Victor was doing and what his reaction would be.

"Yes?" a male voice answered.

"Victor, it's Garth, mate. How are you hanging in there?"

"I'm about ready to get out of this bed, Garth. No one will tell me a damn thing and I'm going crazy. Update me on what's been happening."

In the background Katherine heard a female voice admonishing Victor.

"Dad, you're staying put. You have three broken ribs, a fractured collarbone and the worst series of bruising the doctor has ever personally witnessed. You are not getting out of this bed —"

"Come on, Skye, let the man talk to Garth in peace. We need some tea and sandwiches anyway."

"I'm bringing you back vitamins, Dad. Lots of vitamins."

Both Katherine and Garth snickered as Victor sighed. She had a feeling Victor's daughter's threat was a serious one, based on years of experience and possibly even a mimicking of words her father had said to her in the past.

"I can't wait, sweetheart," he replied, his tone seeming to be caught between amusement and resignation.

Garth explained what had occurred since they had parted.

"Both Katherine and I feel strongly there's more than just luck at play here. We were wondering if you could look into the burying of these documents in more detail from your end? I'm sure Jack can get a laptop to you and it's sure to keep you occupied while you work on getting the doctors to release you."

"That's good work, Garth, I'm impressed," Victor replied. "It sounds like you and Katherine have things well in hand. You're a solid partnership and mesh well together. I presume the two of you will be out there chasing down leads and following Jennings?"

"We plan to compile a list of all other holdings of MacKenzie Industries and anything else this board of directors currently rent under other names. I think Katherine and I will visit them all, sniff around until we uncover Jennings himself, Connor or a new lead to trace."

"Of course," Victor said. There was silence for a moment as the older man thought.

"I think that's a good course of action," Victor spoke again. "I'll do everything possible from this bloody hospital bed. I might even call in a few markers to speed things along."

Katherine relaxed and grinned at Garth. They were on track.

"We'll keep you up to speed with how things go on our end. Keep in touch?" Garth wrapped up once Victor promised to call them if he discovered anything solid.

Exchanging farewells, the men hung up. Katherine threw an arm around Garth and drew his head down for a passionate kiss. Pulling away, she leaned her forehead on his and caught her breath.

"That could have gone a lot worse."

"Only problem we now face is making that list," Garth grumbled good-naturedly. Katherine laughed, kissed his lips a few more times then stood up.

"I'll make us some more tea. You get out pen and paper and we can get cracking."

Chapter Six

Katherine parked the car in front of the fourth block of office buildings they'd tried in the last two hours. She frowned and nibbled her lower lip.

"Do you think we should go back to MacKenzie Industries? If we put the scare on someone there they should be able to give us contact details for Connor," she suggested. The thought had been circling in her head over the last twenty minutes while they had battled against the end-of-day traffic.

"I've been mulling over the same thought," Garth admitted as he unbuckled his seatbelt and turned to face her. "Two things have kept me from mentioning it. The first is Connor's first point of contact almost certainly would have been to Oscar to inform him of the close call he'd sustained. He'd likely have insisted Oscar offer him protection, hide him or give him somewhere else to safely decrypt the programme."

"Since it's been hours and the laptop Scott set up for us hasn't traced any work on that line, Connor would have thoroughly searched the hard drive, found the ring we inserted on to it and destroyed it," Katherine realised.

Garth nodded.

"It's the logical deduction. The data will still have been encrypted — that happened irreversibly as soon as they tried to download the information on the hard drive. But removing the ring and destroying it means they're no longer working on our frequency and we can't trace them like we did earlier."

"Okay, so now Oscar knows we're after him he will have cleaned MacKenzie Industries up or at the very least destroyed anything useful we could find there. Got it. What's your second thought?"

"We have a better chance of finding Connor at one of these offices, not at his home," Garth rationalised. "Connor will know we are after him, and he'll expect Oscar to hide him out. Even if we somehow got his address from MacKenzie or some other means, the odds are in our favour of finding him around here somewhere. Plus, we might get really lucky and find Oscar, too."

Katherine frowned and thought about that.

"You think Oscar will want to keep an eye on Connor, meet him somewhere neutral and safe and watch over his work?"

"Well, think about it. Not only is Oscar desperate to get his hands on all this blackmail material and contact protocols for these people, but also Connor is now a liability. He's come to the attention of the Agency and can tie Oscar with the hard drive, not to mention the possibility Connor knows about the mole, even if he doesn't realise it."

Katherine felt her jaw drop.

"You think Oscar will use Connor then kill him?"

Garth shrugged and opened his door.

"Why not? He's not one of the good guys. Killing a small fry fish like Connor would be nothing to Oscar. Indeed, it probably makes sense to him to tie up the loose end and make his life simpler."

Katherine swallowed hard.

"We better get lucky soon then. I didn't think much of Connor but he certainly is playing out of his league. He doesn't deserve to be sacrificed for trying to make a bit of money on the side."

"We don't know Connor is just being opportunistic, either," Garth reminded her. "But I do agree it would be a waste to lose him. Not to mention we could use the connection he gives us to make a case against Oscar and hopefully someday whoever the mole in the Agency is."

Katherine nodded and opened her door, climbing out of the car.

"Then let's hope we get lucky soon and find him."

They met on the edge of the footpath, keeping well out of the way of the bustling peak-hour foot traffic. Everyone kept their heads down, focused on making it home—or to the local pub—after a hard day's work. Katherine could commiserate, but her day had barely got moving yet. It seemed a long way out of reach for her to be able to go home, put her feet up and soak in the tub, preferably with Garth naked and beside her.

While they were not in the heart of central London, they were not far from it. Tall buildings vied for space with the older stone structures. Gargoyles stared out at them from floors above, looking protective or antagonistic depending on the frame of mind one viewed them in. Katherine dragged her thoughts back on point and glanced at Garth as she gathered herself and checked her weapon under her jacket.

"So this is Lennin's Temp Agency, up on the sixth floor," she recalled. "Owned by one of the board members and claimed on their taxes but with no other visible ties. Another shot in the dark but it's between the computer suppliers we just came from and the next place, Trojan IT Support, which is a few blocks farther down the street."

"Pretty much," Garth agreed. "Most of these are a shot in the dark, but also recon. We need to gather more evidence, or at least a solid connection, before we can get warrants or act with any force."

"Okay," Katherine gathered herself and tried to not get her hopes up again. "Let's go bust some balls. I've got a good feeling about — "

She halted mid-sentence and froze as she caught sight of a lanky man with a scruffy mop of blond hair paused at the entrance to the building they had been about to move towards. Katherine reached out and grabbed Garth's elbow to halt him, but he, too, had seen Connor the exact instant she had.

The young man paced for a moment and checked his watch, looking up and down the street. Garth and Katherine turned their back to him so as to not be seen and possibly recognised.

"Who's he waiting for?" Katherine hissed. They looked up and down the street, not spotting anything out of the ordinary or anyone lurking, looking mysterious or unusual. It was a fluke that Katherine looked on to the street. Her gaze had been moving farther afield, checking over the road to see if anyone lingered there, when she saw the small hatchback with the pizza sign on its roof.

Checking her watch, she figured it was early for the dinner hour. Had Connor's lunch been ruined or missed owing to their interruption of his routine? It was quite possible Connor was starved. The hatchback squeezed into a tight spot, double parked a door down from where Connor stood and a pimpled, teenaged youth stepped out on to the street, two steaming boxes under his arms.

Katherine nudged Garth and nodded towards the delivery boy. Garth wrapped an arm over her shoulder and bent to whisper in her ear.

"It's even money whether Oscar is up there or not," he murmured. "Do you want to call in back-up and possibly have egg on our faces if it's only for that idiot Connor, or do you want to play it safe and make it an official Agency bust?"

She thought fast while Connor eagerly exchanged a handful of bills for the pizzas and disappeared back inside the building.

"We know he's here, for now at least. But I still worry about this mole. I'm not keen to make it official and go through the proper channels until we're certain either paranoia is rabid and there is no leak, or until we've identified who the mole is and have a plan to deal with that issue."

Facing each other, their faces remained close while she debated within herself.

"I suggest we call Walters, Peterson, Jack and Skye in," she put forward. "We know we can trust those four. Jack and Skye aren't, strictly speaking, Agency at all, plus they have an invested interest in the successful outcome of this mission. They've both been involved in the exchange of the hard drive for Victor, Jack is good with a gun and will protect Skye, and Skye is Victor's daughter and likely would enjoy getting her pound of flesh for the damage and pain Oscar has caused."

"And your reasoning behind bringing in Walters and Peterson?" Garth asked, sounding far more curious than upset.

"They're in charge of working out who the mole is and, as a side note, recovering the hard drive. This is technically their mission, though it's far more ours than theirs. They deserve to be in if this turns into a legitimate bust and I think we can trust them. It's worth the risk to me, at least. We're partners, though, equals. What are your thoughts?"

Garth looked thoughtful for a silent moment. He nodded and pressed a light kiss to her lips.

"Make the call to Walters. I'll call Skye," he said. "I like the way you plan. Six of us are enough to contain almost anything we find up there, but not so large we'll look foolish if it's pointless. Plus we get rid of most of the red tape by not making it an official, sanctioned mission. I love your brain."

"Just my brain?" she teased as she pulled out her mobile. Garth winked as he pressed a series of digits.

Katherine scrolled through her phone's address book and selected Walters' number. Hitting the call button, she waited a few seconds as it rang. It was picked up almost immediately.

"Walters," he said.

"It's Katherine. Can you speak freely for a minute?"

"Peterson is here, no one else. Is that all right?"

"Perfect. Garth and I have been following up a few leads on Oscar Jennings. We aren't sure, but we might have found something. We don't want to make this official in case we're jumping the gun, but also... Well we don't want to possibly tip our hand to Jennings again. You with me?"

"Depends on what being with you comprises. What have you found?"

"Scott set us up with a locator for the ring Jack Berick had placed as an encryption device on the portable hard drive. That beacon had us after a skinny blond tech called Connor. No surname as of yet. He's a twitchy bugger, had a gun but no experience with it. Sadly he had two friends there—unknowns and seemingly not related to this job at all—and they covered his escape. Garth was shot and things went to hell, but we've run him down. Confirmed the building he's in, but we don't want to be taken by surprise again."

"So you want us as back-up?" Walters finished.

"Partially," Katherine hedged. "It's pure conjecture at this point, but there's the possibility Connor turned to Oscar for help when he was compromised. The reason we don't want this official, just two mates helping us out, is because it's totally unsubstantiated. If we turned to the Agency with the possibility of our number one current terrorist target, this place would be sealed up tighter than a virgin's arse. We'd be a laughing stock if Connor is hiding out with a tech mate and they're in there with a bunch of pizzas and beer downloading porn."

"So the four of us go in, seal the place up tight and question Connor and find the whereabouts of Oscar or, at the minimum, how to contact him, or the best case scenario is we work the bust of the year ourselves?"

"Six of us. Garth is calling Jack Berick and Skye Adams in too. They were part of the initial exchange for Victor. They might be handy to have present and in part Garth feels we owe them this much to give them some closure. I agree with him on this."

There was a brief silence while Walters appeared to confer with Peterson. A moment later he replied.

"We're in. Where are you?"

Katherine gave him their address, then recommended they park in the side streets.

"The main road here is packed. You've no chance of getting anywhere directly around here, not for at least another few hours."

"We can be there in fifteen. Buzz me if something happens between now and then. Otherwise, we'll see you in a few."

"Thanks. See you soon."

Katherine hung up and turned to Garth to find him replacing his own mobile in his back pocket.

"They'll be here in fifteen minutes. Skye seemed eager, Jack less so on bringing her along but his hands were tied. Soon as she worked out what was going down he'd have had to tie her up to stop her."

"Sounds like it's going to be a party. Maybe we can get that pizza boy to come back and feed us while he's at it. My stomach is starting to growl."

Garth snorted and wrapped an arm around her as she did the same to him. Crossing the street they moved down a few doors where they could loiter. Leaning against a fence, they had a perfect view of the front of the building, but kept out of a direct line of sight.

Time passed. Katherine was pleased the silence between them was easy, there was no strain in the quiet. Instead, it was the waiting stillness of a hunter patiently knowing the prey would come. She enjoyed this moment, the still before the storm.

Katherine caught sight of Skye and Jack strolling down the street first, hand in hand and looking for all the world like any ordinary pair of young lovers. Only an observant eye would catch the fact that Jack carried a weapon under his sweater on the side of his hip in his jeans. He moved with a fluid grace — one that showed confidence, someone well used to stalking and chasing where necessary. It was clear he was no novice.

The couple strolled up to them and greeted them like long-lost friends. Katherine smiled, enjoying the slight glance of surprise Skye cast her. The first time Skye Adams had seen her, Katherine had been attempting to place Garth under an internal review arrest and drag him back to the Agency for questioning. The restaurant they had all gathered in moments later had been a smoking pile of rubble, a rocket launcher having decimated the area.

Katherine was not at all surprised that Skye looked amazed at the about-face their fresh relationship must appear like to her.

"Good to see you again, Skye. I didn't get a chance at the exchange to say how glad I am Victor is doing fine," Katherine said.

Skye nodded, her smile seeming genuine.

"He's stubborn as a goat, but emotionally he seems just fine. Physically he'll heal in a bit of time, but for now he's the same old dad he's always been. You look...good. I'm sorry about Tarek. I know you're partners."

Katherine stiffened. A slight pain ran through her, but she pushed it aside.

"This will hopefully go a long way to giving him peace. It's the least I can do for him considering the circumstances."

Garth tapped his finger on her shoulder, drawing her attention. She looked behind them and saw Walters and Peterson walking towards their small posse. When the two men stood with their group

Garth introduced everyone and gave them a rough catch-up.

"They should be in the offices on the sixth floor," he began in a clear, crisp tone. "Connor is approximately six feet tall, blond shaggy hair and is a twitchy little shit. He had a gun this morning but zero experience. He had made friends with two conspiracy nuts, with similar lack of experience but better aim. I caught one in my lower side so I'd recommend from personal experience not to take them lightly."

"It's always the asshole newbies who get the lucky shots," Peterson commiserated. Garth nodded and continued.

"I figure we should stagger our entry and spread out upon entering. We can confirm Connor, at the least, is inside the building as when we were reconnoitring the area we got lucky for a change and saw him come out here to pick up two boxes of pizza from a delivery guy."

"One man doesn't need two pizzas," Jack interjected, a hard, thoughtful look on his face.

Garth nodded.

"That's my thought, too. I believe it's a safe assumption he's not up there alone, but there could be three of them, or thirty. It's impossible to tell from down here. Considering Katherine and I were taken by surprise last time, however, I want us to be sharp and safe. We enter and spread out in teams of two. Katherine and I enter first and take the main point of attack. Jack, I want you and Skye to enter next and veer left. We don't have communications equipment so we're old school and going to have to shout out commands. Walters, you and Peterson protect our arses. We'll need warning of an ambush from the rear or if they somehow call in reinforcements."

"Do we have a layout?" Walters asked, his gaze steady as he drank in the commands and seemed to take it all in his stride.

"This was just one stop of a dozen on our list," Katherine added with a shake of her head. "We know it's on the sixth floor, a set of office suites for a small IT company. Their tax return information from the public record showed they are a holding with less than twenty people on staff. But how accurate that is could be anyone's guess."

"So we go in assuming the worst and celebrate when we encounter a handful of geeky under-twenty-five-year-olds who all but wet themselves at our attack," Skye said with a grin. "I like it, particularly the part where we put the fear of God into Connor, take back that damn hard drive and destroy it."

Katherine exchanged a glance with Garth. They'd discussed in broad terms what they would end up doing with the data once they'd recovered it. They were certain no good could ever come from such scandalous information, such intimate secrets, vices and personal proclivities coming to the light of day. It was not the sort of business either of them had signed up for.

But neither could they ignore the monumental power such information wielded. The Agency followed the rules where possible, but destroying such power was not necessarily in their best interests. It was a difficult call to make and not one they could take lightly.

"I'd prefer if we returned the portable drive to the Agency," Walters said. Peterson nodded his agreement beside his partner. Katherine and Garth shared another look before Garth spoke.

"Any hypersensitive data like this is under threat while we have a possible traitor," he suggested. "No one person or company should hold such power in their hands — it's too simple a thing to abuse. But we're not sure we should just flat out destroy it, either. When we have the situation — and Connor — contained we can discuss it further and come to a decision then. There's no point arguing about it now.

"One last thing. We should mention the possibility, the remote possibility, Oscar or the traitor or some other highly placed person in this organisation might be present. We gave Connor a good scare this morning, he almost certainly would have turned to his contact and demanded help and protection. The reason we called you in is partly because we trust you, but also because we were caught unaware last time and we didn't want to make that mistake again."

"We're always up for a party," Jack interjected with a wicked grin at Skye. His humour lightened the mood around them. Kate shifted restlessly on her feet, caught somewhere between anticipation and just wanting them to start this. The traffic of people lessened as the sun slowly sank into the horizon. Katherine felt certain that, by the time they had finished, full dark would have fallen.

"Let's go," Garth commanded, his tone firm.

Chapter Seven

The group of them stood huddled behind the door that separated the stairwell from the corridor on the sixth floor. A tiny, slim piece of glass in the middle of the door would give anyone opening it a chance to see if someone stood on the other side to avoid accidents. Garth peered in every direction possible through the small window, checking the layout.

Peterson had handed a handful of cable ties to everyone. None of them knew how many people they were up against, but they had agreed earlier that no one wanted to maim or kill unless they were pressed to. Typical Agency procedure was to restrain—not hurt—others, and Kate had reiterated this in their briefing moments earlier.

As they readied themselves, they drew their handguns. Katherine noticed Skye pulled out a tiny lady's twenty-two. She couldn't hide her grin as Skye surveyed everyone else's gun then looked back to hers. Not one of them held a smaller calibre than a forty-five.

"It might be time for me to get a new weapon, love," she spoke to Jack. "If we're going to keep such rough company, a girl needs some protection."

Jack stroked a finger down the side of her cheek and stared at her, his attention seeming riveted.

"I'm your protection, sweetheart. You don't really think I'd be prepared to face your father to tell him how it's my fault you got shot. I'm all you need, darling. Trust me on that."

Katherine chuckled with the others, the tension thick in the air. No matter how much research and preparation you did, what lay on the other end of the door would be unexplored, unknown territory. Anything could happen. She found the tension built adrenaline, which was definitely one of the most natural drugs that could help keep you alive in situations such as this. "Okay," Garth ground out, clearly as impatient as the rest of them. Katherine felt the fear and excitement of the moment kick in. They were really going to do this. Even if it ended up a complete waste of time, that didn't stop the surge through her body. Her awareness heightened as her body prepared for the coming fight.

"Our target is about two dozen paces in front of us and opposite the elevator. There are clear glass double doors opening out on to an open room, from what little I can see. There is another, far larger corporation at the end of the hall and a small one right beside us here to the right."

"We stay in teams of two," Walters repeated from their earlier conversation. "Subdue and restrain. Only open fire if you have to. Hitchens and I might be able to talk the group of us out of any trouble with the Agency or the police, but we will have the full weight of management behind us if we can get our hands on that hard drive, Connor, or, in the best of all scenarios, Oscar Jennings."

"Exactly," Garth picked up as Walters paused. "Jennings kidnapped and tortured Victor Adams in the failed attempt to get this intelligence. The Agency takes a dim view of this cavalier treatment of their operatives' lives. If we can even get solid evidence to help lock Jennings away it will weigh significantly in the Agency getting rid of any charges or pressure on our actions. But there may be mostly innocents inside, so we roll with the level of threat presented back to us."

"Sounds just like old times," joked Skye.

Katherine found herself impressed by the other woman's bravery. She was not an agent at all, let alone field rated. While Skye had been instrumental in rescuing her father, to Katherine's knowledge this was only the second or third time the woman had seen this type of action. Before she could say anything or commend Skye on her courage, Garth caught her gaze and indicated, with a tilt of his head, they should go first through the door.

Checking her gun one final time, Katherine drew in a deep breath and bounced on the balls of her feet to get her circulation going.

"Ready," she answered Garth's unasked question. He grinned at her, his white teeth flashing as he cupped a hand on her jaw. She moved forward and pressed a hard, fierce kiss to his lips, the soft stubble of his trimmed beard scratching the corners of her mouth.

"Be safe, sweetheart," he cautioned her as she pulled away. Katherine nodded and blew him a silent kiss.

"You too. I've got your back, you go in first and I'll be less than half a step behind you."

"Let's go people," Garth's voice rang out, deep and full of confidence. "We'll start in a logical progression. Clear each room and remember to call out so we keep tabs on one another. Jack, you and Skye head left. Walters, you and Peterson take right. Restrain everyone. Keep an eye out for the black box in case it's just lying around somewhere. If the civilians get rowdy, gag them. Remember we don't have comms. Shout out the instant you need help or if you see Jennings. He's a slick bastard so watch yourself when it comes to him. Any last-minute questions?"

Skye snickered but tried to hide it behind her hand. Garth's eyes roamed over them both, finishing with Katherine. Katherine held his gaze for just a moment. Silently, they communicating their love, then the next instant the door swung open and Garth moved out with a brisk stride.

Katherine followed, not willing to leave his side for an instant. She checked down the corridor behind them to make sure no one stood in a blind spot or paid undue attention to them. Garth threw a look over his shoulder as he stood at the double wide doors. The words 'Lennin's Temporary Solutions Agency — Temp agents of all divisions available here!' were scrawled over the doors in large, elegant gold script.

In far smaller script, the opening hours were etched to one side. Katherine glanced at her watch and found they had twenty minutes until the doors would shut. Jack and Skye lingered to their left, Walters and Peterson to their right. Everyone looked ready to move, waiting for Garth's signal.

Her lover nodded and opened the door, his gun still held in his hand but pressed against the side of his leg so as to not upset anyone too fast. The doors opened into a large room. The setting sun cast an orange-gold glow over the small workstations and terminals. No one seemed present. Two corridors split off with a number of glass-fronted meeting rooms to the far right, down a small passage with a sign for the toilets and tearoom refreshment area. Garth tilted his chin, indicating that Jack and Skye should take one corridor and for Walters and Peterson to take the meeting rooms.

Garth paced down the right-hand corridor. They had entered what looked like a series of smaller office areas for management and the permanent staff, if the plates over the doors were any indication, when the sound of people shouting could be heard from behind them.

"What the fuck do you think you're doing?"

"Hey man, I'm just here for an interview, I don't want any trouble!"

"This is a private meeting. Please, sir, we need you to leave."

"Oh my! Is that a gun?"

"Hey! Now just a minute!"

Garth snapped open the first door, letting it slam back against the wall. He entered with his gun drawn up, held ahead of him. Katherine glanced up and down the corridor and followed right on his heels, her gun raised in readiness, unsure of what they would face.

The office was small, barely large enough for them to both stand in without pressing up against the desk. Garth walked around the wooden table, bending down to check that no one was hiding out of sight — which was standard procedure in a sweep such as this. Nothing was more embarrassing than to not clear a room as safe and be ambushed because of laziness.

"Empty," he grunted. Katherine turned around and walked out, Garth following. She repeated the same procedure with the next door down. Thrusting the door open so no one could hide behind it, she entered with her gun raised. Garth guarded her back. Katherine's gaze roamed around the room, nearly identical to the previous one but with different photos, prints hanging on the wall and personal effects. She checked any hiding places.

"Empty," she sighed and caught Garth's gaze. He shrugged — they hadn't expected it to be easy — and moved out into the corridor.

"Clear!" she heard Peterson shout through the offices. Katherine frowned, concern creeping up on her initial adrenaline rush.

"No one's called out that they've found Connor yet, have they?" she asked. Garth shook his head as they moved down the hall to the second last office. Footsteps sounded at the entrance of the corridor and Katherine and Garth both raised their weapons and focused on their backs.

Walters entered the hall and held his free hand palm up.

"Peterson will be here in a second. We've restrained four people we found in the middle meeting room. Had to gag two of them. Not very happy with us, I can tell you."

Garth returned to face the door and Katherine turned to face him but spoke over her shoulder to Walters.

"Front two offices are empty, no one so far," she informed him, her body coiled tight with tension. Garth slammed open the door and, immediately, this room was different.

"What? Hey, it's you! Help! Help, I'm being mugged."

The voice was high pitched and whiny. Katherine frowned. Garth hadn't even entered the room yet, so the occupant was more than prepared to lie. Walters held out a bandanna and Katherine took it, wound it around her hand, so it would be close to gag the man, and followed Garth inside. Garth had already pulled out a cable tie with one hand, the gun held in the other.

"Help! Help!" Connor continued to scream as he pulled plugs from the hard drive to disconnect it from the laptop he worked on. Connor struggled to push the small black box into his backpack. The scruffy blond looked left and right wildly, a cornered animal seeking escape.

"Let's do this the easy way," Katherine tried to soothe the hysterical youth. "The windows don't open at all, there isn't another way out except past us. Garth here is going to tie your hands together and, if you keep on shouting, I'm going to gag you. That's your choice."

"Somebody! Please help me, they're going to kill me!"

"Oh, for fuck's sake," Katherine swore under her breath as she placed her gun in its holster, grabbed the tie from Garth's hands and came around the desk and punched Connor in the side of his jaw. The young man collapsed over the desk, weeping, though she'd put almost no force behind the movement. She pulled his hands behind his back and snapped the tie tightly around his wrists. She threaded two fingers under the tie to be sure it didn't cut off his circulation.

It was as she unwound the bandanna from her hand that she heard the shouts.

"I've got Jennings!" Peterson called out. Heavy footfalls thumped down the corridor and Katherine swung around to see Garth crossing to the door as both Walters and Peterson sprinted past the office and all but flew towards the area they'd not checked yet.

"Damn, he's really here," Garth swore. Katherine took one glance at Connor, who still sniffled and whined, and dropped the bandanna on the desk. In a few seconds she shoved both the laptop and hard drive into the backpack, zipped it up and pulled it on.

Then she pulled her gun out again and made her way around the desk to follow Garth. As they left the office, they nearly collided with Jack and Skye. Katherine shrugged out of the backpack and hurled it at them.

"The laptop Connor was working on and the hard drive are both there," she snapped out. "Walters and Peterson are chasing Jennings. Garth and I will follow. We need you both to keep tabs on Connor, work out if he's managed to download anything or unencrypted it and then destroy it all."

"But I thought—" Jack said but Garth cut him off.

"There's too much interest in this, it will never go away. Wait until we're all assembled again and we're going to have to destroy it ourselves. The Agency will just have to deal with it, I think."

Not giving Jack or Skye any further chance to argue, Garth and Katherine sprinted off after Peterson and Walters before they lost them completely. The corridor ended in a door. Garth slammed his shoulder into it at almost a full run, opening it and throwing his body through it. They were on the landing of a second series of stairs running the length of the building.

The sound of scuffling could be heard from a floor or two down.

"You son of a bitch," an angry, masculine voice screamed out. A gunshot echoed in the stairwell. Garth and Katherine scrambled down the stairs, Garth in the lead. Katherine's heart hammered in her chest. Who'd been shot? Were Walters and Peterson okay? They wouldn't kill Jennings in their anger or the heat of the moment, surely?

As they turned a corner, Katherine got a view of the floor lower down and saw Peterson and Jennings struggling together. Walters lay on the floor bleeding and trying to get to his feet. His right arm was streaked with red and hung limp at his side. The wound seemed to have made a mess of his shoulder, but otherwise Walters looked fine.

Jennings lifted his head, jerking back as he saw Garth and Katherine almost at him. Oscar cursed, dived for the floor and grabbed his gun again. The gun boomed in the enclosed space, the shot to Peterson's surprised face, at such close quarters, lethal.

Garth snarled like an enraged beast. Casting his body at the man, Garth punched Oscar in the jaw and the two men grappled. One glance told Katherine there was nothing she could do for Peterson. She knelt at Walters and assisted the man to his feet.

"Can't use my gun hand," he panted, his face white and dripping sweat. "He is not going to go down easily — he'll kill or wound us all before he gives in. Katherine, you have to shoot him."

Walters leant back against the wall, sweat from the physical exertion and evident, extreme pain he was in coating his body. Katherine made certain he would not collapse in a heap if she let him go, then circled the twisting mass of the two men. They fought each other, the crunching sound of flesh beating flesh making her stomach roil.

"Give it up, Jennings," she commanded, as she tried to get a clear shot of the man. "There's more of us upstairs likely on their way down now. There's nowhere to run. We have your laptop and the portable drive. It's over."

Oscar snarled something incoherent at her without turning his head, his sole attention focused on Garth. Jennings' fist landed a solid blow to the side of Garth's face and the skin at the corner of his eye split, a small spray of blood splattering his skin. Even though the blow hadn't touched her, Katherine almost felt the pain herself.

Caution flew out the window.

She widened her stance, took a calming breath and narrowed her sights. When Oscar turned to the side, giving her a clear view of his profile, she took the shot, shooting his kneecap out. He screamed in agony and fell hard to the floor, blood pooling under him.

Katherine knelt at his side and removed his belt, tightening it as a makeshift tourniquet to slow the bleeding. Garth staggered and pressed a palm into the wall. When Katherine felt confident Oscar would not die owing to blood loss, she moved to touch Garth's face. He grimaced but let her see to his wounds.

"You aren't supposed to lead with your face, my love," she chided him, caught somewhere between frustration and pride.

"Rather hard to fight fair when your opponent's initial outlay is to knee you in the nuts and then fight dirty. Plus it's not like a stairwell is the ideal place for hand-to-hand combat."

"A learning experience, then," she soothed him. He chuckled then winced, clearly in pain. Jack appeared behind them and whistled as he surveyed the general mess.

"Victor is upstairs. We've called in the Agency and some reinforcements. Looks like I might need to add an ambulance to that mix," he said.

"You don't want to move Jennings until you have at least three or four trustworthy agents present to escort him," Katherine insisted. "Besides, he'll be fine. It's Walters who needs help with his shoulder."

"Peterson will need assistance, too," Walters said, his voice rough and husky. "I know he's gone, but he has a family, a sister he's particularly close to. They need to be called, and someone needs to collect him and make sure he's treated right."

They all nodded. Walters took a deep breath and sank to the floor again, looking on the verge of passing out. Katherine took another look around, then spoke with a hitch of emotion in her voice.

"Well, at least, this time, the building is still standing. We're getting a bad reputation for flame throwers and rocket launchers."

The men chuckled, but their faces showed bafflement as well as humour. Katherine figured they weren't sure how much was genuine humour, and how much was just the let-down as the adrenaline left their bodies.

* * * *

"I'm telling you, we should think about this before we react," Garth insisted as Katherine stormed down the corridor on the top floor of the Agency.

Victor had indeed arrived, somehow magically checking himself out. Garth and Jack had a pool running as to whether Victor had been allowed out of the hospital or whether he had merely escaped. Katherine was tempted to join in and add five pounds to say Victor had talked his way out by convincing the nurses he was someone else. That man had a silver tongue.

"Since when have we swapped over?" Katherine insisted, with an angry glare at Garth. "If you'd asked me a week ago if I would be the one acting all rogue and cowboy-ish, breaking the rules and to hell with the consequences, I'd have laughed. I thought you, of all people, would appreciate the direct response and not beating around the bush."

"Sweetheart, I am all for the direct approach," Garth insisted. "But not when it comes to possibly sacrificing our place in the Agency. Emma Henley is not some small-time agent. She's a team leader. We should lay out a plan, trap her even. Not storm into an upper management meeting and throw around accusations."

Katherine shook her head, her pain and anger bubbling under the surface, pushing her to act, not think or plan. She could hardly believe the difference a few days — and a few deaths — had caused.

"Garth," she hissed, her voice shaking and dangerously low as she halted in the corridor. No one else was around, but they still stood intimately close and whispered to each other.

"Tarek lies in a coma because of information this woman sold out on us. Peterson was shot into an unrecognisable mess as an indirect result of Emma's betrayal. I will not sit on my arse and make some bloody plan, or set a trap with bait. Neither will I go in there guns blazing and get you fired. I'm a mess and emotional, but not suicidal. I genuinely believe the only way to win this is to take her utterly by surprise and hit her with everything we have."

"And what if you're wrong?" Garth growled. "Damn it, Kate, I'm not worried about going rogue or even being fired, though that would totally suck. I'm worried about you being upset when you calm down and take a breath. Since when am I the rational one of the two of us?"

Katherine laughed and wrapped her arms around Garth. Pressing their bodies together she kissed him with every ounce of passion and love in her body. Their lips slid over each other, their bodies flush together as if they both sought to melt into one another. Sparks of electricity arched through her body and her pussy dampened inside her jeans. Katherine wanted him, but she wanted to finish this more.

"If I'm wrong then you can help me plot a real plan when we're sitting next to each other in the jail cell they'll throw us in. And I'll let you do anything you please to me when we get home. If I'm right, then I want full control tonight. I want you to make my every wicked fantasy come true."

Garth licked his lips, his dark eyes blazing into hers.

"Done. Let's go fry the bitch," he ground out. Katherine threw her head back and laughed, delighted.

It had only taken a few questions to find out Emma Henley was in a group task force meeting with the higher managers to discuss the 'possible traitor' and the leaks to Oscar Jennings. Katherine knew this was a risk, but it was one she was more than willing to take. The only way this would end for good would be for all the upper managers to see with their own eyes the fact that Emma was the mole.

Otherwise, they'd never be believed and Emma would be able to do more damage. All the bullshit paperwork and red tape would slow the wheels of justice. Lesser cases had ground to a halt under the pressure. Neither of them wanted that to happen here.

Katherine pushed open the door to the meeting room with a bang. She strode in, covered in sweat, blood and the acrid smell of gunpowder. She recognised most of the men and women seated around an oval table. A few she didn't, but that wasn't her main concern for now.

"And so I really think we ought to — oh, Katherine, what's going on?" one of the other division leaders blinked, clearly caught unawares.

Garth took the folder from her hands, the folder of evidence that Victor had managed to accumulate in his hours of research. Katherine activated the screen to enlarge the phone records and other documents to present them before those gathered.

"Ladies and gents, I apologise for the interruption, but this simply can't wait. We have uncovered the identity of the mole," Katherine began. An excited murmur rose, but Katherine locked gazes with Emma.

The slender woman's dark brown eyes caught hers, her long, honey brown curls twisted into a top knot. Katherine let her stare bore into the other woman's, and it only took her a moment to understand what was coming. Emma stood and smiled.

"Miss Hitchens, while I value your input as always, I really think it should be Mr Walters and Mr Peterson who should present such astonishing findings to us. They are the agents in charge of this hunt."

Katherine smiled, though it wasn't a pleasant or humorous gesture.

"I'm afraid, Ms Henley, that won't be possible," Katherine paused before continuing. "My partner Tarek was very nearly murdered just a few days ago. Now Peterson is dead as well. He was slain not an hour ago in a large bust we made. Peterson was shot point blank in the face. By Oscar Jennings."

Only because Katherine had kept her eyes locked on the other woman did she see the small start of surprise jolt through the team leader. Katherine crowed internally, certain the hit had made its mark.

"Jennings," the men murmured to one another. A division supervisor stood up, drawing the attention to himself.

"Did you capture Jennings?" he asked. Katherine returned her attention to Emma and nodded.

"Oh yes, we captured him," she replied.

Emma's eyes narrowed, anger seething in the brown orbs.

"Better still, we're questioning him now. Victor Adams is out of hospital and has him in interview room B. They have quite a bit to catch up on since the last time the two gentlemen were together."

"But why are you here? What are these records you're sharing with us?" another man asked. "Surely if we have Jennings he can tell us who his contact is."

"Garth Spenser and I merely thought you'd appreciate seeing some evidence. You see, as we feared, the traitor is quite highly placed."

An uncomfortable tension filled the air as the inhabitants around the table glanced at one another. Katherine decided she'd milked the moment all she needed now.

"It's Emma Henley. She's been feeding data to Jennings for months now. She started slow, but in recent weeks nearly every confidential briefing has been compromised. Practically —"

"Oh, please! It's all lies," Emma hissed and stepped back from the table. Garth moved protectively and Katherine stepped forward to face the woman.

"Do you really think Jennings won't want to make a deal? To keep himself alive and in the best position possible?" Katherine asked, scorn dripping from her tone. "Agency workers are dead, Emma. Not protecting Queen and country, but because of actions you performed, of information you leaked. Victor Adams almost died and you were the one who gave Jennings his flight itinerary and the taxi service he preferred. Do you honestly think Victor won't get that information out of Jennings in minutes? Hell, he's probably singing his confession arias already."

"This is the last thing you'll ever do for this Agency," Emma swore.

"Now just a moment here!" one elderly man huffed out, his cheeks red. Pandemonium ensued. A man picked up the phone and called down to the interview room but Emma launched herself at Katherine and the two women began to fight. Shouts rang out and security was called.

Katherine fought the arms that tried to snare her, until she heard Garth's voice in her ear.

"Easy, sweetheart. It's me. Don't gouge my eyes out, please."

Katherine stopped struggling and relaxed. The man on the phone seemed to be having an intense discussion and was nodding at the guards who restrained Emma. Despite their inherent amazement, the managers appeared to be reacting to the truth of the matter.

Emma Henley had been the mole and now was in custody to be questioned.

Adrenaline left as quickly as it had appeared. Katherine sagged against Garth's side.

"It's really over," she whispered, for his ears alone. Garth took her hand in his and threaded their fingers together. Pressing a kiss to her knuckles he licked his tongue over her sensitive flesh.

"You were right," he said after a moment. Katherine turned to capture his gaze. Heat pooled in her body as she understood what he was telling her without expressing the words exactly. She grinned.

"Anything I want, hey?" she teased him. He nodded and the sensual promise in his dark eyes and in the wicked tilt of his mouth had her body tingling in excitement.

"Not to mention you've avenged Tarek and Peterson. Neither man worked in vain. That's a wonderful thing you've done there."

"And to think," she kidded, "I only had to join the dark side to do it."

Garth tilted his head, confusion on his features. Katherine nudged him with her shoulder.

"Throw the rule book out, dance on the side of you cowboys for a change. You realise every mission won't be as easy for you. Usually I am very law-abiding."

Garth laughed heartily.

"Sweetheart, with you as my partner I'm sure I can corrupt you properly. Slowly and over a long period of time."

"How long?" she teased, but also found herself curious.

"I think we should start with the rest of our lives, but we can negotiate for any time after that."

Katherine smirked, pleased with his response.

"I think that sounds wonderful."

Reluctantly they returned their attention to the mayhem in front of them. Katherine had no doubt the next few hours would be filled with questions, reports, statements and a plethora of explanations. She couldn't find it within herself to mind, though. Her evening tonight would be full of Garth, laughter and wickedly hot sex.

Tonight and every night from here on in. The thought warmed her and caused a tingle to arch from her clit through her stomach and to peak at her nipples. Tonight she'd be able to do anything her heart desired to her man. Maybe tomorrow night she'd allow him the same privilege.

The thought of him reaming her arse again, penetrating her in that most intimate of ways as she toyed with her clit and tweaked her nipples had a flush reaching her cheeks. Garth shot her a wicked, hungry look, his own thoughts clearly mimicking her own.

Yes, she could withstand hours of mind-numbing reports if her nights and future were filled with Garth, passion and electric hot sex. That was a no-brainer. She not only had him for her hours after work, but if their chemistry was any indication they would make an amazing partnership at the Agency as well.

She could hardly wait.

About the Author

Elizabeth Lapthorne has been writing professionally since 2002. She has a number of books released and is continually surprised by how much fun she has starting a new book and discovering new characters and situations that they put themselves in. She enjoys going to the gym (usually to chew over her latest problem scene), is rarely without a partially read book and has a weakness for chocolate.

Elizabeth loves to hear from her fans and checks her email religiously.

Elizabeth Lapthorne loves to hear from readers. You can find her contact information, website details and author profile page at http://www.total-e-bound.com

Total-E-Bound Publishing

www.total-e-bound.com

Take a look at our exciting range of literagasmic™
erotic romance titles and discover pure quality
at Total-E-Bound.

www.ingramcontent.com/pod-product-compliance
Lightning Source LLC
Chambersburg PA
CBHW032027240626
47154CB00003B/819